DUSTY DEATH

DUSTY DEATH

J. M. Gregson

This first world edition published in Great Britain 2005 by
SEVERN HOUSE PUBLISHERS LTD of
9–15 High Street, Sutton, Surrey SM1 1DF.
This first world edition published in the USA 2005 by
SEVERN HOUSE PUBLISHERS INC of
595 Madison Avenue, New York, N.Y. 10022.

British Library Cataloguing in Publication Data

Gregson,   J.   M.
   Dusty death
   1.   Peach, Percy, Detective Inspector (Fictitious character) - Fiction
   2.   Police - England - Lancashire - Fiction
   3.   Squatters - Fiction
   4.   Detective and mystery stories
   I.   Title
   823.9'14 [F]

   ISBN 0-7278-6179-4

Typeset by Palimpsest Book Production Ltd.,
Polmont, Stirlingshire, Scotland.
Printed and bound in Great Britain by
MPG Books Ltd., Bodmin, Cornwall.

To James, a two-year-old distraction,
who may one day read this

' . . . And all our yesterdays have lighted fools
The way to dusty death.'

Shakespeare, *Macbeth*

One

No one was anticipating tragedy.

The high brick wall stood firm at the first blow. It had stood here for a hundred and thirty years, and it was not going to go down without a fight. For a moment, it seemed as if it had a stubborn resistance of its own, gritting its teeth against this sudden and brutal assault.

That was a fleeting illusion. The huge steel ball on its thick chain swung slowly away, like a heavyweight boxer setting himself for the killer blow against an opponent punched beyond any defence. The arm of the crane moved slowly to the right, allowing the great steel sphere to swing out beyond it. Then, as if in slow motion, the ball swung back, hitting the filthy old bricks with an impact which could not be resisted. The wall faltered for a moment, like the drunks which had for a century struggled for balance in the cobbled street beneath it, then fell with a dull, reverberating roar on to the piles of rubble below it.

Peter Jennings's lips spread into a thin, involuntary smile as he watched the fall of this, the biggest building of his morning session. He had been operating cranes like this for eight years, had grown used to the power he controlled, was now adept at applying it where it would be most telling. Yet when he saw walls which had stood for so long falling so quickly and easily, terraces which had once housed people descending so inevitably into anonymous industrial detritus, he still felt the same feeling of power which had surged through him all that time ago, when he had moved the big ball so much more tentatively to demolish his first building.

1

Yet this was also the point at which an odd and disconcerting sadness hit him, a feeling of chilly dejection at the obliteration of those many and infinitely varied lives which had been lived out for so many generations in these houses. So many lives, so much tragedy and hardship and joy, should not disappear so quickly, with so little ceremony.

Yet disappear they did. There were glimpses of the lives that had been led here, but no more than glimpses, as the walls fell. The porcelain of a lavatory bowl rose bizarrely against the sky, then crashed into many pieces, before the dust and broken bricks obliterated it. A kitchen unit, looking for a moment strangely modern amongst so much that was old, reared itself like a cry for help, then splintered and disappeared.

Peter Jennings told himself that it was foolish for a man in his job to be nostalgic. These had never been good houses, even at their best. They had been built in the nineteenth-century heyday of King Cotton, when terraces of mean dwellings were thrown up quickly in the Lancashire towns which spun and weaved fortunes for those fortunate few who owned the mills and their chimneys. For the most part, it was the mill-owners who built the dwellings which would house their workers, developing a secondary source of profit as men and women flocked eagerly into the towns in the high noon of the Industrial Revolution.

When they were built, these houses had been a cut above the worst. They had not had shared yards and privies. Each dwelling had had its own tight, narrow yard at the rear, its low brick privy with its wooden aperture giving on to the 'back' at the rear, where the night-soil men would come once a week to cart away the waste.

In later years, after Hitler's war and the death throes of cotton which followed it, some of these places had been much improved, had become what admiring visitors with pardonable hyperbole called 'little palaces'. Bathrooms had been built into their cramped first floors, kitchens had been extended into the little alcoves beneath the stairs, where coal had once been stored behind a curtain. Central-heating pipes had even been run through into those icy front parlours, which had until then been reserved for Sunday teas and pre-funeral corpses lying in open coffins.

And all this history, all these lives, with their triumphs and disasters, their reminders of the petty aspirations and passing achievements of the men and women who had lived and died here, were swept away with the savage, inhuman blows of Peter Jennings's wall-crusher. Dwellings which had existed for centuries, which had housed sinners and saints and the vast variety of humanity between the two, were gone in a few seconds of noisy mayhem, a few minutes when clouds of noxious dust shut out the sun, and a variety of sour scents rolled over broken bricks and across the bleak industrial site.

Progress, they called it. And progress indeed it was, Peter Jennings told himself firmly. These places had had their day. New and better buildings would arise phoenix-like from the tired old site. No one would have wanted to live in these narrow, rotting houses now. They were buildings, that was all: bricks and mortar, and not very good bricks and mortar at that.

Peter swung the crane round again, measured the next blow with his eye, and swung the ball a long way through the dank February air.

You were never without a crowd when you were perpetrating this spectacular destruction. People were fascinated to see what had taken years to build disappear in minutes. You could see that from the crowds which invariably assembled to see nineteen-sixties tower blocks brought down. Explosives made such demolitions into more spectacular sights than anything Jennings could achieve with his crane. But people were roped off half a mile and more away from these city spectacles; they could get much nearer to his destruction, feel much more involved in the sudden and violent alterations to their local landscape.

At the end of February, most of his audience was juvenile.

3

It was the school half term, and the crowd of children had grown as the morning proceeded. The sounds of his destruction carried through the still air, over the house tops and the office blocks to the new estates and the private housing beyond them. There was a ragged cheer with each major collapse of walls, a round of applause each time a long swing of the steel ball achieved something particularly dramatic.

Peter Jennings kept his eye upon this enthusiastic but undisciplined audience, but he knew that there were people on the ground below him who would ensure that the children did not sneak too dangerously near to the falling buildings, as excitement got the better of them. The ground was uneven and unstable, because a few of these houses had had cellars beneath them.

But most had been the quickly built, shallow-foundationed houses, thrown up as cheaply as possible by mill-owners anxious to house their workers as near to their work as possible. It was important then that the clogged feet did not have far to shuffle to work before the factory whistle sounded.

Those days, like the mills themselves for the most part, were long gone. A Labour council had long ago recognized that these tight terraces of old houses were below the accepted standards for modern living, and made them part of a slum-clearance programme. It is one of the axioms of modern town planning that such clearances inevitably take much longer than the periods originally mooted for them. This area had been unoccupied for ten years and more. The rats had enjoyed themselves, but once the windows had all been broken and the area sealed off as dangerous, there had been no other life here.

The pest-control people had been here last week, on the last of their periodic visits. But rats are resourceful creatures, and the broken remnants of ancient sewers are difficult to penetrate. Colonies of survivors raced clear of the falling walls, seeming to know from the vibrations when Jennings's crane was moving crucially near to them. The scurrying vermin appeared and disappeared within the smoke and dust of the demolition, bringing yells and hastily thrown stones and bricks from the bolder boys, and screams from the girls.

But it was something else which stopped Peter Jennings, which made him twist the levers in his crane and desist abruptly from the work he had planned to complete by the end of the morning. He thought at first that it must be an illusion, that his eyes were playing tricks upon him as the clouds of dust swirled and eddied among the smashed masonry below him.

For minutes which seemed to stretch like hours, he waited for the dust to settle. An acrid smell rose to his nostrils. He felt dry dirt upon his lips, but he made no move to reach for the mask beside him as he leaned out of the window of his cab to get a better view.

It must surely have been an illusion. This was the thing which happened to other demolition men, one in a thousand of them. But never to Peter Jennings.

By the time the scene below him became clear, he found he could not be sure exactly where he had seen that gruesome thing. Or imagined he had seen it. He thought he had kept his eyes fixed on the place, even as the dust of centuries swirled between him and the spot.

Then, just as he was exhaling a sigh of relief that he had been mistaken, he saw it again.

An arm, vertical. It seemed to be groping towards the heavens he had suddenly exposed above it when he struck down the houses. An image sprang into his mind from the schooldays he had thought for ever dismissed. A poem that woman teacher with the grey hair and the thick glasses had tried to make them learn. An arm had appeared above a lake, 'Clothed in white samite, mystic, wonderful'. Holding a glittering sword. He couldn't remember who'd written the damned poem, nor anything else about it, except the arm and the sword.

But this arm held no sword. And it was not white. And it certainly was not wonderful. Yet it was surely an arm: that became more certain with each passing second. Peter Jennings climbed stiffly down from his crane and went unwillingly towards it, shouting hoarsely to the children to keep their distance.

It was a human arm all right, putrid and decaying. What flesh remained on it hung in grey strands. He knew that it was merely an accident of its unearthing that it pointed so vertically at the sky, with a single one of its poor broken fingers rising towards heaven.

But it seemed to the stricken Peter Jennings to be a limb demanding justice.

Two

Detective Chief Inspector Denis Charles Scott Peach, universally known as 'Percy' to his associates, was looking out of the CID section at a grey February afternoon.

The clouds seemed to sink a little lower with each passing minute. Thin drizzle drifted past the glass on a raw East Lancashire afternoon, and twilight was dropping early over the stark industrial silhouettes of the town. It was difficult to feel happy when you beheld a landscape like that.

And when you were contemplating a session with Chief Superintendent Tucker, Head of Brunton CID, you had every reason to feel deeply dispirited.

Percy breathed the deep sigh of the perennially abused, put the big folder under his arm, and climbed the two flights of stairs to the penthouse office of Thomas Bulstrode Tucker. This world, he told himself, was never meant to be perfect. Life on earth, he recalled from his starkly religious childhood, was but a vale of tears, an ordeal designed to prepare our souls for a much better existence in the next world. That had seemed logical as a child, when he had more faith in that eternal continuance in bliss.

He wondered if the person they had turned up on the building site this morning had found that eternal reward. It was difficult to handle that notion, when you saw what was left behind in this world.

'I haven't much time, Peach, so I'll have your briefing as quickly as you can give it!'

Chief Superintendent Tucker was in one of his brusque

moods. He waved his hand vaguely over a broad expanse of empty desk, as if to indicate how busy he was, how good it was of him to take these few minutes from a busy day to listen to the concerns of a lesser brain.

Tucker was an impressive figure, a man who might have been designed for public relations. He had regular features, good teeth, and just enough lines in his early fifties to give the appropriate gravitas to the statements he gave to press, local radio, and occasionally to television. His crowning glory was his hair. He still had a good head of that, and it was silvering attractively around the temples. Who could fail to trust a man like this?

Percy Peach could, for one. He had little but contempt for the man he called Tommy Bloody Tucker. Peach was a copper's copper, a man who was on the side of right and had a mission to be the unrelenting enemy of villains. He might cut the occasional corner in his pursuit of justice, but there was never the faintest hint of corruption about his determination to lock away all who operated outside the law, all those unscrupulous and vicious strong men (DCI Peach never thought of the criminal fraternity as anything other than male) who preyed upon the weak and the helpless to make their fortunes.

Peach was almost as unprepossessing as his chief was impressive. Bald at thirty-eight, he looked if anything a little older than his years. Short for a policeman, but stocky and powerful, with a black moustache and a black fringe of hair which seemed only to emphasize the whiteness of the bald pate above it, he had carried Tommy Bloody Tucker on his broad shoulders for the last nine years. Peach got results, and Tucker rode cheerfully and shamelessly upon those results.

Peach's results had taken Tucker up the ranks to Chief Superintendent, and because he could not reach such dizzy heights without taking his benefactor with him, Percy Peach had been promoted to the supposedly obsolete police rank of Chief Inspector. Tucker detested the younger man, but he was sensible enough to recognize how completely his reputation depended upon him. He had to tolerate Peach's insubordination, because the alternative would have been much worse. It would have involved running the Brunton CID section efficiently and keeping in direct touch with the business of crime detection, both of which Tucker had demonstrated to himself as well as to others that he could not do.

Peach began the Monday briefing he had to give to a Tucker who could not read or could not remember the content of his memos and e-mails. 'There's the usual Saturday and Sunday night domestics, sir.'

'Don't bother me with small crime. I have to take a broader view.' The back of Tucker's right hand waved away the concerns of lesser men.

'Yes, sir. Your overview is the most valuable thing we get from you. I often stress that to the men and women at the crime-face.'

Tucker peered at him suspiciously, but Peach's dark eyes were directed to the wall above his head. 'Well, if you're telling me nothing of note has happened over the weekend, I'll—'

'Racial punch-ups in the town centre on Friday night, sir. Usual ritual insults on both sides. There are more injuries among the British National Party boys this time. The Asians are beginning to look after themselves. Inevitable, if we can't protect them, I suppose.' This was a reference to Tucker's ignoring of the escalation of racial incidents in the town, in the mistaken hope that the trouble would go away. The truth was that for a long time Tucker and the Brunton hierarchy had not cared to admit that a serious problem existed.

'I'm sure there's nothing there that you and your team can't handle, Peach. Routine violence, I expect. Male hormones running riot on drink.' Tommy Bloody Tucker might not be very bright, but he had a certain low cunning, a well-developed instinct for self-preservation. There was no kudos and only brickbats from the public on both sides if you got yourself involved in trying to sort out racial disturbances. Let your underlings get on with it.

'The Muslim element doesn't drink, of course, sir. But you're right, it's dealt with. The ringleaders appeared in court this morning. The matter is taking its course without your involvement.'

'Good. Well, if that's all you have to tell me, I think you might now be better employed in—'

'There is this, sir.' Percy Peach took his time as he carefully drew the big photograph from its folder, building up his moment of drama, enjoying the older man's impatience.

'What on earth is this, Peach? I must warn you that unless it's something of real importance, I have much more . . .' Tucker stopped: even his considerable resources of verbiage were arrested by this dramatic black and white photograph. He said stupidly, 'It's a body.'

Peach resisted the urge to congratulate his chief on his percipience. Instead, he nodded and said, 'Certified as such at 12.47 hours today by the police surgeon, sir.' It was one of the more bizarre features of police procedure that even if a skeleton which was centuries old was discovered, it had to be certified as officially dead by a qualified doctor, as the first step in any investigation.

'How old is this?' Tucker stared at what was scarcely more than the outline of something human, still encased in the dust and soil of the clearance site. He was reminded of those pictures of corpses which had been miraculously preserved for two thousand years in the ashes of Pompeii.

'Can't say yet, sir. We'll need a post-mortem report and anything else the forensic team can give us before we know where to start.' In the presence of this bleak and distant death, Peach found all inclination to score points off this high-ranking buffoon had left him. The stark monochrome reminder of the mystery of mortality which lay across Tucker's desk overshadowed more petty concerns.

Tucker studied the picture for a moment longer before he said quietly, 'Where was this found?'

'In the last terrace of houses being demolished for industrial redevelopment, sir. The area out beyond Montague Street.'

Tucker nodded slowly. He seemed unable to take his eyes off the picture. 'Not that old, then. Not as old as it looks here.'

'Probably not, sir. Those houses haven't been occupied for at least ten years. Except by mice and rats.'

'But this could have been put there after that. Or could have been killed somewhere else and dumped in there.'

Just for a few minutes, they were coppers united in the face of a puzzle. Peach could not remember when he had last had that feeling. 'Yes. We'll need to wait and see about the circumstances. For what it's worth, it's pretty certain the body had been hidden somewhere in there. The clearance company's staff inspect all property carefully before demolition. It's standard practice, apparently. No one saw any sign of a corpse anywhere in that terrace of houses before the breakers and bulldozers moved in; even the cellars were carefully checked.'

'Or should have been. No one's going to admit he didn't do his job, in these circumstances.'

Police cynicism, born of hard observation. Peach felt the pleasure of shared experience again with this man who normally seemed so far away from crime. 'Exactly, sir. But it does seem probable that this body had been hidden away somewhere. The police surgeon couldn't tell us much, and of course he couldn't strip anything away from the body for fear of destroying evidence. But he did say that it seemed to be partly mummified.'

Tucker had still not taken his eyes away from the photograph. He said slowly, 'Yes. These look like scraps of flesh, here. And skin, perhaps.' He picked up a ball pen from his immaculate desk and pointed at two different points on the big photograph.

'Yes, sir.' It had been difficult to be certain of anything beneath the mud and dust and mortar which had clothed that mysterious figure, amidst the bricks and the plaster and the broken tiles. Percy Peach felt he could still smell the stink of death and decay upon himself from his visit to the site, though he had showered in the station since his return.

11

J. M. Gregson

'Ten years or more ago, you say. I don't suppose you recall any local missing person from that time.'

'I wasn't around here then, sir.' Peach was less scathing than he would normally have been in the face of Tucker's fumbling after the truth. He did not point out how many thousands of people went missing in Great Britain every week. Chief Superintendent Tucker knew that well enough. He was simply groping after somewhere to start. Percy Peach said, 'I was just a DS then, sir. Not even working in Brunton.'

'No. But it was on my patch. I was a Detective Inspector here at that time. All those clearance areas were environments for crime. All kinds of people on the fringes of society operated there, once the last official residents were cleared out.'

Everyone knew that. The flotsam and jetsam of society moved in; the down-market prostitutes, looking for somewhere to offer a quick knee-trembler; the druggies on the way down; the squatters who had missed out on legal accommodation. But for once Peach wasn't irritated by Tucker's stating of the obvious. He felt the man floundering, wondering where to start on this. He had experienced similar sentiments himself an hour earlier, when he had stood and looked at what had once been human, and watched the Scenes of Crime team commencing its work on that squalid, foetid site. He said quietly, 'I've begun to set up a team, sir. We aren't certain it's murder yet, but we certainly have to treat this as a suspicious death. Hopefully we'll get some accurate estimate of how long ago it occurred within the next twenty-four hours. The National Forensic Laboratory at Chorley has agreed to give this one priority.'

'We had a lot of trouble with those slum clearance areas.' Tucker repeated himself, casting his mind back to those harsh days when he still involved himself directly in the investigation of serious crime.

'I'll get on with it, then. I'll report back as soon as we know a little more.' Peach picked up the big photograph and put it carefully back into its folder. 'By the way, sir, one of the only

12

things we are certain about at the moment is that the body is that of a female.'

It was the first stage in giving an identity to this thing. The first move towards the translation of the shape in that picture into something which had been vital and human, with emotions and opinions and a personality.

Three

It was still scarcely half past three, but the arc lamps were on to enable the Scenes of Crime team to go about their work.

The lamps gave a sense of theatre to the scene, with the brightly lit square of uneven ground cordoned off by the plastic ribbons as the stage. The audience consisted of a motley group of children, housewives and pensioners, standing outside those tapes and cast into early darkness by the brightness at their centre. A thin drizzle was beginning to descend upon the place as Detective Sergeant Lucy Blake arrived there.

The scene, with its acrid smells of decay, its thousands of fragments of cheap, shattered bricks, its soot and its crumbling mortar, could scarcely have been more drab or depressing. Lucy wondered as always at the random and dejected-looking crowd which always assembled on the periphery of a Scenes of Crime search. Most of them, she supposed, had never seen anything as dramatic as what had occurred at the centre of this brilliantly illuminated stage.

Yet what *had* actually happened here? DS Blake put on the plastic coverings offered by the constable at the entrance to the site and trudged forward to the man in charge of the operation. Sergeant Jack Chadwick gave her a nod of greeting. 'Percy tied up?' he enquired laconically.

She nodded. 'He's making phone calls to speed things up. Getting everyone to make this a priority. Last time I saw him he was preparing himself to brief Tommy Bloody Tucker about it.'

Chadwick nodded. When he had been injured in a shooting years ago, it had been Percy Peach who secured him this job as Scenes of Crime Officer, when others higher up the ranks would have retired him as a young man on sick pension. It was something both of them knew very well, but neither of them ever mentioned. Jack Chadwick was probably the only member of the Brunton force who would rather have had Percy Peach visit him here than this pretty, shapely girl with the striking chestnut hair, who was still in her twenties. 'There's not a lot for him here, anyway. Probably scarcely worth his time.'

Lucy bit back her reaction. She wasn't going to say that it seemed all right for a woman to waste her time, whilst the men got on with more important things. It was a question of rank, she told herself firmly: Chadwick thought that a DS was all that was required here, that it wouldn't have been worth the considerably more expensive time of a Detective Chief Inspector. She watched the men and the single woman on their knees amidst the debris and told herself how lucky she was. Sergeant Chadwick had returned to the notes on his clipboard. She said, 'So what have you found, Jack?'

'Not much. You wouldn't expect much, on a site like this. For one thing, this woman died a long time ago, so most things which might have been useful have long gone. We're not likely to find fingerprints or hairs from a guilty party's head here, are we?'

She wondered if he'd have bothered stating the obvious to Percy Peach. But she was used to the fact that, if you didn't look like the traditional copper, people, even policemen who should know better, didn't take you seriously. And most of the people working at a Scenes of Crime investigation weren't coppers, nowadays. She said tersely, 'That sounds like you've already assumed this is a suspicious death. Have you any reason for thinking that?'

Chadwick grinned ruefully at her. He had been looking forward to a ritual moan with his old friend Percy Peach about the hierarchy, and the weird ways of Chief Superintendent Tommy Bloody Tucker in particular. Instead, he had this fresh-faced, eager girl to talk to; it scarcely seemed fair to visit his old sweat's cynicism upon her.

But she wouldn't be Percy Peach's sidekick unless she was a bright lass: he'd give her whatever help he could. And beneath his surface scepticism, Jack Chadwick was an enthusiast for his work, the best Scenes of Crime Officer around: experienced, intelligent and meticulous. When he decided to close down his work at a scene, you could be satisfied that there was nothing more to be learned there.

Now he led Lucy Blake across the site to where a splintered piece of wood lay inside a transparent polythene cover. Lucy saw a panel in it, realized that it was probably part of what had originally been a door. It was covered with grime on one side, but this was the side that interested Chadwick. He pointed to a point near the end of the wood, where the black of the grime shaded to a dark brown. He said simply, 'I'd be surprised if that isn't blood.'

Lucy thought that she would not even have noticed the slightly lighter patch on the blackened surface. But if Jack Chadwick thought it was blood, it was odds on it was. He voiced the immediate query which came into her mind. 'Nothing to say it's the blood of your corpse, of course: forensic will tell us if it's the same group.'

'Anything else?'

Chadwick shrugged. 'We've found various fibres, which have been bagged up for the attention of the boys and girls in forensic. Whether they've any connection with the corpse or the way she died is another matter. We may never know that, unless you can pin down when this death occurred and who was around at the time.'

Lucy stared at the neat plastic bags, watched the rain falling more steadily now through the fierce beams of the arc lamps, smelt the decay as the men in oilskins carefully turned over another pile of mortar and brick. It seemed at that moment, in that desolate place, that it was most unlikely they would ever pin down the detail of this woman's death.

Half a mile away from the place where the corpse had appeared so unexpectedly, there were terraces of nineteenth-century

16

houses still standing and still occupied. At seven o'clock on that Monday evening, DI Percy Peach rang the bell of one of them and stepped over the worn stone doorstep to the interior.

The old woman's face clouded with concern when she saw him. '''E 'asn't done nothing, Mr Peach. 'E's never in trouble again, is 'e?'

Lizzy Bedford was well into her eighties now, the only woman Peach knew who still wore the woollen shawl about her shoulders which had once been the standard garb for women clattering in their clogs to the mills. She had lived a hard life, and her face was worn and lined with the wear of it. Percy saw her only at irregular intervals, and each time she looked even smaller. But she had the bright, alert look of a street sparrow.

'He's not in trouble, Mrs Bedford. I'd just like a few words with him, that's all. I think he might be able to help me.' He took a bottle of Guinness out of his briefcase and put it beside the battered radio on the small table at her elbow.

Her head did not move, but bright eyes glanced sideways and glittered. 'There's an opener in the top drawer of the kitchen cabinet.' She watched him find the opener in the fifties kitchenette, take a thick glass tankard from the shelf above, and pour the dark fluid carefully into it, tilting the glass sideways so as to avoid excessive foam. It was not until he delivered the brimming tankard into her bony hands that the old lady said, ' "Helping the police with their enquiries" you call it, don't you? That means 'e's in trouble, doesn't it? What's 'e been up to this time?'

'Nothing, that I know of, Mrs Bedford. I just want to ask him a few questions about what happened years ago.'

She looked at him suspiciously, then nodded her relief and took her first appreciative pull at the Guinness. 'Billy's done 'is time for that. You're never going to bring all that stuff up again.'

'No, we're not. I just think he might be able to help me with some information. You as well, perhaps. You've lived round here for a long time.'

'Aye. Since my man were alive and I worked at Bank Top

17

Mill and Billy were nobbut a lad.' The bright eyes stared past him, seeing through the long, sad decades to a time he had never known.

'Aye.' Peach dropped automatically into the Lancashire response. 'You'll remember more than most, then.' He caught the sound of a movement behind the door and called, 'You'd best come in here now, Billy.'

Billy Bedford shuffled sheepishly into the room. He was a man made for shuffling: a slight, stooping figure who carried guilt like a cloak upon his narrow shoulders. He was sixty-two now, and looked older. He said, as automatically as if Peach had touched a nerve, 'I ain't done nothing, Mr Peach. 'Onest I ain't.'

Percy eyed the shifty face beneath the greasy grey hair with distaste. 'I doubt that, Billy Bedford. You've usually been up to something, haven't you? But I'm not here to take you in. Surprising as it may seem to you, you may actually be able to help us.'

'Ain't no grass. Billy Bedford don't grass on anyone.' The thin lips set into a line as automatic as the words.

'This isn't grassing, Billy.' Peach tried to keep the contempt out of his voice. 'This is straight information about the district. You and your mum might be the only people still around to help us on this one.'

Bedford lifted his hollow eyes for the first time, checking that this was genuine. It wasn't often that he was asked to be of help to anyone: it was quite a pleasant feeling, which took him by surprise. 'If you're not asking me to shop no one, I don't mind 'elping you.'

Peach gestured with his arm towards the darkness outside. 'That area over there. The houses that have been cleared for slum clearance and new industrial developments – '

Old Mrs Bedford followed the direction of his gesture as if she could see the long, low terraces which had once stood proudly on each side of the cobbled streets. And indeed she could, in her mind's eye. She could see them sixty-five years ago, at the beginning of Hitler's war, when house-proud women had covered their doorsteps with yellow sandstone and young Lizzy Bedford had clattered free and lighthearted in her clogs to the mill with hundreds of other girls. She said, 'You mean Alma Street, Sebastopol Terrace, Balaclava Street, that area. It's all gone now.'

The names meant nothing to Percy Peach, but he said, 'That's it. When were the people cleared out of them, do you know?'

'Ten years ago and more,' said Billy Bedford, surprisingly promptly.

His mother was slower, but even more accurate. 'More than that. Betty Dickinson's husband died a week before they were due to move out to the new estate. She had the funeral the day she should have been flitting.'

'But you don't know exactly when this was.'

The old lady allowed herself a thin smile and a surprisingly large swallow of Guinness. 'Yes I do, young man. 1989. I saw his stone in the cemetery when I was up there last week.'

'You're sure of that?'

'Course I'm sure. I can even tell you when it was in the year. It was the week of that Bloody Emperor Hirohito's funeral. Him what tortured my Albert in his camps during the war. He was never the same, when he came back. And that bloody Duke of Edinburgh went and attended the bugger's funeral, didn't he?'

'I expect he was told to go, Mrs Bedford.'

'Then he should have bloody refused, soft bugger. He's old enough to know what went on, 'e is!' She snorted, then took another long, consoling draft from her tankard.

This was more than Peach had expected. They could check the date of Hirohito's funeral and get a pretty exact date for the vacation of the houses. He said, 'That's very helpful, Mrs Bedford. I knew you'd come up trumps for us!' He took the second bottle of Guinness from his briefcase and put it beside the empty one on the little round table beside her.

A hand as hot and rough as a sun-warmed lizard's foot dropped on to his wrist. 'Don't open it yet, Mr Peach. I don't like it flat. It'll last me all night, if I go easy at it.'

Billy Bedford felt a vague resentment that his old mother

could be so useful. He said as scathingly as he could, 'There were people in those streets after they'd been emptied, though. After old Betty Dickinson and the like moved off to the new council estates, there were still people in those houses. In some of them, anyway.'

'Squatters?'

'Aye. I suppose that's what you'd call them.' He suddenly wished that he hadn't spoken after all.

Peach could read his too revealing features as easily as a book. A large-print book. 'Got up to your old tricks round there, didn't you, Billy?'

Billy Bedford was an incorrigible peeping Tom and an occasional flasher, one who was brought in as part of the investigation into most local sex crimes, though he had never proceeded beyond flashing to indecent assault or rape. He was part of the detritus of modern society, universally despised, but in Percy Peach's informed opinion, relatively harmless.

Billy said sullenly, 'I don't know what on earth you're talking about, Mr Peach. I gave that sort of thing up a long time ago, well before the time the Dickinsons were moved out of them 'ouses.' He drew himself ridiculously up to his full but diminutive height. 'And I resent—'

'Bollocks, Billy Bedford!' Peach found the alliteration beguiling, and the old lady had surely heard much worse. 'Indecent exposure beside the Corporation Park, 1993. Peering through curtains at women undressing in Queen Mary Street, 1996.' He had looked up Billy's record on the computer before he left the station. 'Which means you were no doubt in your randy heyday at the time we're talking about. Prowling the streets and flashing your pathetic equipment at anyone you thought you could impress.'

'I had a dog then.' His mouth twisted into a crooked smile of lecherous remembrance.

'Spot,' his mother said unexpectedly. 'He were only a mongrel, but very affectionate, Spot. I still miss 'im.'

Peach remembered now. Bedford had used the well-behaved little dog as an excuse to prowl the streets at all hours of the night, spying on women undressing whenever he got the chance, getting close enough to the town's prostitutes to savour their provocative dress and no doubt watch them in action when the occasion offered itself, and just occasionally leaping out of hedges to shock the matrons of the town by waving his penis at them. He said, 'You must have enjoyed it when the squatters moved in.'

'They didn't bother with curtains. The curtains went when the proper residents moved out.' Billy Bedford's eyes shone for a moment with reminiscent excitement.

'So you and Spot spent a lot of time round there.'

Billy fell back into his familiar whine. 'What if I did? Wasn't doing no 'arm to no one, I wasn't.'

Peach looked at the 62-year-old wreck of a man and tried not to show his revulsion. 'I'm not interested in what you were doing there, Billy. Not now. I'm interested in who was occupying those houses and when.'

'There was people there for two or three years after the Dickinsons and their like 'ad moved out. It was a bad time in the town, that, Mr Peach. Thatcher and the bloody Tories. Lot of poverty about. That were when that cardboard city started in London.' For a moment, there was a glimpse of the sharp, well-informed being that might have emerged, if things had been different for this man in his youth. If he had not lost his father in 1950, perhaps.

Peach said, 'Can you recall those streets, Billy? Even individual houses, perhaps? It's a long time ago.'

'Fifteen years. Well, somewhere about that. But I can remember a lot. I've a good memory, Mr Peach. And Spot and I used to go up there most nights.' He was pathetically anxious to be helpful, to show that he was more useful than the society which had discarded him thought he was.

It was in the days before Peach came here, when Tommy Bloody Tucker would have been the Inspector in charge. Percy couldn't see Tucker being anxious to protect squatters from peeping Toms or flashers; he would have been more than content to pretend that the squatter problem didn't exist. And people living like that were never going to report the likes of Billy Bedford. He must have felt that the squatters had fallen from heaven into his squalid world. Peach said, 'You must have known the area like the back of your hand, Billy! I bet there's no one knows more than you about what went on there at that time.'

Bedford enjoyed flattery: indeed, he had met so little of it that he found it irresistible. 'That's right, Mr Peach. You'd win your bet, all right. I was up there 'most every night, like I said.'

'I'll tell you what, Billy. When I can pinpoint the actual house I'm talking about, I'll come back and see you. Find out if you can tell me anything about what went on in there.'

He didn't really think he would get much more from the man. But with what they got from forensic added to Billy Bedford's recollections, they could begin to get a picture of the time and the place where this death had occurred. He said, 'I'll be back, when I can pinpoint the time we're interested in. Don't do anything I wouldn't do, Billy!'

Bedford laughed as if this was the most original joke in the world. 'I won't, Mr Peach!' He glanced down at the full and the empty bottles of stout beside his mother. 'I'm not a Guinness-drinker myself.'

Peach took the hint. 'I dare say there might be half a bottle of whisky in this for you, Billy Bedford, if you can provide something really useful for us.'

The wretchedly thin man saw him off at the door of the old terraced house. His face was grey and fleshless. Peach had a sudden apprehension that he might die before the frail but feisty mother within the house. In a life that had offered little but hardship, that would be the worst thing of all for old Lizzy Bedford.

Four

The post-mortem report yielded more than it might have done. Percy Peach announced that firmly to his team. It was important for morale that they felt progress was being made. Whether consciously or unconsciously, it was all too easy for an old crime like this to be written off as insoluble.

There were multiple fractures in the bones of this female corpse, but they were probably all recent. In other words, the body had been considerably damaged by the heavy machinery brought in for the demolition of the houses. Had it not been for the crane-driver's keen eyesight and his glimpse of that gaunt forearm rearing itself so dramatically from the rubble, the body might never have been discovered, might have been anonymously interred for ever beneath the concrete foundations of the new office block which was to rise on the site.

The blood group was confirmed as the same as that of the patch discovered by the observant Jack Chadwick at the scene of the crime. That made it likely but not certain that the corpse had lain for years against that wood, which was confirmed as the lower part of what had originally been a substantial door, belonging either to a large cupboard or perhaps even to a room. A cluster of fibres found in the grime of that wood, six inches from the dark brown smear of blood, matched those from the sweater, parts of which still clung to the torso of the body even after its years of entombment.

That was the next detail in the emerging picture. The partially mummified state of the body suggested that it had been enclosed after death in some relatively airless place.

DC Brendan Murphy looked up from his notes. 'Hidden away, you mean, sir?'

Peach nodded. 'Almost certainly yes. Possibly beneath floorboards. But the presence of blood and fibres on what's left of that door suggests that the body rested tight against it for quite some time. The probability is that she was locked away in a cupboard. Or that the wood from a door was used to hide her somewhere else, like a chimney breast where fires were no longer lit. The body is too damaged for us to be certain, but we're not talking evidence in court here. We're simply trying to build up for ourselves a picture of how this woman might have died.'

Lucy Blake said, 'Jack Chadwick had found a lot of other fibres at the site. Has anything useful come of them?'

'Not as yet. They come from a dozen different garments and furnishings, but some of them may have predated this death by several years. Forensic will retain them, in case we can match them up with anything we discover on a suspect at a later stage in the investigation. The probability is that we won't get anything very useful from them.'

DC Gordon Pickering was the latest addition to Peach's CID team. He was lanky, fresh-faced, twenty-two and very keen. He said, 'Are we any nearer to an identification of this woman?'

'Nearer, perhaps, but we're not nearly there yet, lad. We don't know who she is but we know a little more than we did yesterday. She's young, for a start. Probably between eighteen and twenty-five when she died, as far as they can tell from what's left of her.'

'Dental records?'

'It's in hand, but it takes time. She hadn't had a lot of dental work, but hopefully there's one filling, and a distinctive enough jaw pattern to get an identification. Eventually. None of our Brunton dentists has found a match, so she's probably not local.'

'How long before we know?'

Peach allowed himself a rueful smile; he was as anxious

as young Pickering to pin down this victim, so he was not going to squash his enthusiasm. 'Impossible to say, because it's out of our hands. They got a bit of DNA from a nerve still there at the base of a tooth, but that will only be useful at a later stage, when we've got a possible match. We've asked dentists nationally to check their records, but we're dependent on them for the degree of urgency they give it. We really need a name. However, we've got something already. One of the people in the forensic lab at Chorley is apparently an expert in what he calls "Tooth Morphology". He reckons teeth are fascinating little things – takes all sorts, I suppose. Apparently this lady had "shovel-shaped incisors". This means that she was more likely to come from an Asian group than a Caucasian one.'

Lucy Blake said, 'So she was probably Indian or Pakistani.'

'Not necessarily. There's a strong incidence of this type of teeth in the Chinese, for example. And don't forget she's probably not from our Brunton Asian group.'

DC Murphy said, 'I suppose we're quite sure this is a suspicious death?'

Peach smiled grimly. 'I thought you'd never ask. In fact, we're quite sure this was murder. There isn't much flesh left on the skeleton, and what there is is severely damaged by the fractures and abrasions caused by the clearance machines. But the PM shows quite clearly that this girl was strangled.'

The discovery of a body beneath the rubble of Brunton received muted coverage in the national newspapers and television.

It would have been different if they had been able to carry a picture of that skeletal arm, rising from the ground as if beseeching justice from the heavens, but that image was denied to them. And as yet there was no hint of the sexual dimension to this crime which would guarantee their full attention. They had to be content with the bald police announcement that the unidentified body of a woman had been discovered on an industrial site, that it had been there for some time, and that until more facts could be established the death was being treated as suspicious.

Local radio was rather more excited about it. The News Editor at Radio Lancashire made as much of a sensation as he could of an event which could enliven a drab time at the end of February. He sent a young woman reporter to the place, who described the landscape as if it were a bomb site in Iraq, teeming with unseen terrorists, rather than a levelling of the ground for a five-storey office block, near the centre of a run-down East Lancashire town. She then focused in to provide a graphic word-picture of the floodlit arena at the scene of this crime, emphasizing the diligent work of Jack Chadwick's team, dwelling on the number of pictures the official photographer was taking and the number of possible clues being bagged from the debris. She made excellent bricks from very little straw, her mind on a more national job with BBC or ITV and greater things ahead.

There was much local interest in her report, of course. An old corpse and thoughts of mischief long buried were bound to arouse curiosity in Brunton itself, especially when many of the older listeners could play the game of pinpointing the exact place where this body had been discovered.

One man, especially, listened to every word of the young reporter's coverage with rapt attention. He caught the first news of the discovery on the Tuesday lunch-time bulletin, then listened again to the evening coverage, eager to see if anything had yet been added to the bald facts.

He stared at the radio for a few moments after the announcer had switched to the sports news, willing the uncaring box to give him further facts, to tell him exactly how much those policemen and civilians at the site had discovered; what the police were thinking at this moment; how many resources they proposed to devote to this old crime with the scents gone cold.

He learned none of this, of course, and he found that his feverish speculation disturbed him far more than the known facts. He could not settle in the house. Normally he liked being alone, enjoyed his privacy and having to answer to no one, but tonight he wished he had company. It would have distracted him, forced him to think of other things and deal with other issues.

He was surprised when he looked at his watch and found that it was still only ten past eight. He went out into the cool night. The clouds were lifting and he could see the stars. There would be a frost tonight. He felt as if the elements were conspiring against him, that he would much rather have had it cloudy. He could not quite say why that was.

He drove into the town, stopped to buy a copy of the *Evening Telegraph* at the brightly lit Pakistani one-stop shop on the main road. He put the light on in his car and read the front-page coverage of the body found in the area of what had once been Balaclava Street. They had pinned the name down for locals, as the radio reporter had not been able to do. It wasn't the street he had expected, but it was the next one to it, one he had walked along many times.

The very sight of that once-familiar name in print made the hairs rise on the back of his neck.

But other than that, the paper had nothing to add to what he had already learned from the radio. He should have expected that, of course: they must have gone to press well before the evening radio report was compiled. But he felt he had to explore every source, to rake together whatever scraps he could to feed his hunger for facts about what they had actually found at the place.

He read the newsprint painstakingly again, looking carefully at the pictures of the piles of rubble. They were given perspective only by the single factory chimney in the background, included in each shot by a photographer anxious for anything to give depth and interest to this drab and featureless scene. The man turned as he was bidden to page four for the conclusion of the material, and found only an official statement from a Superintendent Tucker that enquiries were proceeding and that this death was being treated as suspicious until it could be proved otherwise.

The car was getting cold and the windows had misted up.

He must have been sitting there longer than he thought, reading and re-reading the evening paper. He felt suddenly that he must not draw attention to himself. He switched off the internal light, directed the fan on to the windscreen, waited impatiently as it cleared agonizingly slowly. None of the pedestrians who passed seemed to be taking any interest in the parked car or its occupant. Why should they? the driver told himself irritably. And why should he be getting himself so wound up over what had happened a long time ago?

He drove slowly into the town, conscious that he wanted to keep a low profile but telling himself that he was uncertain which road to take. It was only as he was picking his way through the one-way system, quiet at this time of night, that he acknowledged where he was going. Instead of hastening his progress, the knowledge made him drive even more slowly.

He kept glancing at his rear-view mirror, though he knew perfectly well that nothing could be following him, that no one could challenge his right to drive here. It was years since he had ventured into this district, and he could not believe how much the landscape had changed, how many landmarks which had once seemed permanent had been removed. He lost himself twice, had to go back to the main road to get his bearings and start again from there.

He was glad now he had got rid of the old sports car. The Vauxhall Vectra would be much less noticeable. He shook himself physically, trying to get rid of the tightness which had suddenly made his shoulders rigid, telling himself that there was no reason at all why he should not be here, that the worst thing he could do was to give anyone the impression that he felt guilty. He eased the car round a sharp bend and over the first set of cobbles it had ever encountered.

He was in the area now. The street lights had ceased abruptly, and all he could see was the corridor of bright white light thrown up by his headlamps. He put them on full and crawled forward. He could see the damp cobbles glistening ahead of him, but he was not sure how far he could drive before what remained of the old street petered out into rubble.

He crawled forward for a hundred, two hundred yards like this and then came up against a red sign which said blankly: 'NO THROUGH WAY. IT IS DANGEROUS TO PROCEED BEYOND THIS POINT'. There was nothing but darkness behind him, nor in front of him when he switched off the car's lights. He took the torch from the glovebox, snatched his anorak from the seat beside him, and eased himself slowly, reluctantly, out into the night.

In this derelict place, it seemed even colder than elsewhere. He found that there were rough tracks flattened through the debris, presumably made by the machines of the development company. He picked his way through the undulating mass of broken bricks and stone, using the small circle of pale light cast by his torch to make sure that he trod always upon crushed bricks rather than mud, so that the soles of his trainers would leave no trace behind him. He realized that he was behaving like a guilty being, but the knowledge did not alter the tactic.

He came eventually to strands of new barbed wire. He lifted the torch, casting its pale beam away into the darkness, wishing he had thought to renew the batteries before he came here. At the very fringe of his vision, the light of the stars caught the gleam of a wide, shallow pool of standing water. The scene in the darkness and the silence reminded him irresistibly of a First World War battlefield.

Except that only one body had been buried here, he thought, as he turned out his torch. He wanted to turn away, but he was held for a moment like one at a graveside, paying a last homage to the departed one. It was then, in the darkness, that he saw the covering tarpaulin sheets and the single light, a hundred yards and more away across this no man's land of detritus.

That must be where she had been found. The police had finished their work there now, had taken away anything which interested them. He wondered exactly what they had found amid this bleak and desolate industrial wasteland. He was going no nearer than this, that was for certain. He wondered belatedly why he had come here at all.

He moved more quickly on the way back to his car, picking his way still on hard ground, resisting the urge to break into a trot as the shape of the car loomed up through the gloom. He threw himself quite hard into the driver's seat, feeling the shape of it like a protection around him, shutting his door hard to cocoon himself in his cave of warmth against a hostile world outside.

He had always known that she would be found eventually, he told himself. The discovery of her body meant nothing, without evidence.

He had moved away too quickly for the solitary constable who now guarded the site to ask him why he had come there at this hour of the night. The PC had to content himself with noting the illuminated registration number of the Vectra, as it lurched swiftly away.

Five

'You'd better put me in the picture about this clearance site murder of yours,' said Thomas Bulstrode Tucker.

Typical of him, thought Peach. All the murders which look like being insoluble are mine, all the straightforward domestics where we have a confession with hours and a killer pleading guilty are his.

But at least the sun was shining brilliantly into the Chief Superintendent's office on this last Wednesday morning in February. Peach gave his chief his most brilliant smile and said, 'I think you'll find this is one of yours, sir.'

Tommy Bloody Tucker responded with the look of apprehension which always cheered his Chief Inspector. 'It's no use trying to shrug these things off, you know, just because you think they might be difficult. I didn't secure your promotion to DCI just so that you could—'

'Wasn't even around, sir, when this one died, I'm afraid. Right in the middle of your patch it seems to have been, when you were still a humble DI yourself, slaving away at the crime-face. If you can still remember those days, sir.'

'Of course I can, Peach. But before you shuffle off the responsibility, you should be very sure that—'

'I'm very sure I wasn't around when this woman died, sir.'

'I don't see how at this stage you can be so certain exactly when that—'

'Hirohito, sir.'

'Pardon?'

'Hirohito. Japanese Emperor, sir. In power at the time of the 1939–45 War, sir. Said the Japanese had to fight on to the

31

last man, sir. Americans dropped the atom bomb and changed his mind, sir. Apparently. I wasn't around at the time myself. Don't suppose you recall the—'

'Of course I don't, Peach! And what on earth has this Haryhoto in 1945 got to do with—'

'Hirohito, sir. And he hasn't got anything to do with it, sir, not in 1945.' Peach took pity on the blank-faced man on the other side of the big desk. 'His funeral was on the twenty-fourth of February, 1989, sir. And that's the week when those terraced houses where the body was found were vacated by their last official tenants, sir. So I am reliably informed.' He didn't think it politic to inform Tucker that his reliable inform-ant was the 86-year-old mother of a petty criminal.

'And you think this woman was killed at around that time?'

'Not clear on that yet, sir. Could have been before or after that date. We have a house-to-house going on at the new estate to which most of the inhabitants were transferred. But as yet no one has come up with an identification of the victim, or given us any reason to think they may be concealing signifi-cant information.'

'But you think that this death dates from around that time?'

Peach repeated himself patiently. 'Probably a little before or a little afterwards, sir. When you were the CID Inspector dealing with that particular patch.' That thought seemed to give Percy Peach considerable satisfaction. He nodded thoughtfully two or three times at the wall above Tucker's head and then said brightly, 'You don't recall anyone report-ing a particularly puzzling MISPA in the area at around that time I suppose, sir?'

Tucker shifted uncomfortably. 'Thousands of people go missing in this country every week, you know.'

'Actually I do know that, yes, sir.'

'You really can't expect me to remember a particular MISPA at this distance in time?'

'No, sir. I didn't really expect that. Especially as there's nothing on the files.' He didn't think there was much chance of Tommy Bloody Tucker remembering the Abominable

Bleeding Snowman, fifteen years on, but he might as well make as much as he could of a murder on Tucker's patch that had passed him by. 'Files seem pretty sparse for those years.'

'In those days, we didn't have the abundant clerical help and the computers which you have, Peach. Now, if you've quite finished taking up my few spare minutes, it's time for me to get on with a busy day.' He waved his arm expansively over his empty desk, as if the gesture could produce the paper evidence of a hectic schedule.

'You don't recall any reports of a young Asian woman going missing, sir?'

'Asian?' It seemed a new concept to Tucker, though the town had one of the highest intensities of Pakistani immigrants in the country. He made a pretence of giving the matter some thought, then said, 'I can't say I remember any Asian girl being reported missing at the time. They tend to be close-knit families, you know, the Asians.' He sounded as if he were announcing some mystical religious rite, the result of intensive research on his part.

'Really, sir? I'll bear that in mind.' Alongside all the other blindin' bleedin' obvious clichés you visit upon me. 'There's a strong possibility this woman isn't a native of Brunton, sir. The local dentists haven't turned up anything for us. And we're not likely to have any success with dental records nationally without a name.'

'Then I suggest you set about the business of finding a name, Peach. It's already nearly two days since this corpse was found, and you haven't even got an identification yet.'

Peach thought as he went back down the stairs how hard he had worked the system to have got what little they had by this stage from forensic and the post-mortem. For a few delicious minutes, he toyed with the beguiling thought of burying the body of Tommy Bloody Tucker beneath tons of concrete and a five-storey office block.

But his first piece of luck in the case was waiting on his desk.

* * *

'I suppose you're involved in this latest murder case, our Lucy. This woman who was murdered years ago in a slum house.' Agnes Blake found herself falling into a ritual of anxiety about the well-being of her only daughter.

DS Blake said stiffly, 'We're not allowed to talk about cases at home. I've told you that before, Mum.'

'Glad to hear you still think of this place as home.' Agnes ticked off a small point scored in the mother–daughter phoney war.

Lucy looked round the familiar low-ceilinged living room in the cottage where she had grown up. It held many dear memories for her, but at this moment it seemed a long way from her own neat modern flat. And even further from that bleak and cheerless spot where the anonymous woman had been unearthed by the bulldozers and cranes. 'This will always be home to me, Mum.' She looked automatically at the mantelpiece, where the silver-framed photograph of her dead father in his cricket gear held pride of place, with the more surprising image of Percy Peach, dapper in his white sweater and red cap, now beside it.

Agnes Blake was nearly seventy now, but her brain was as acute as ever. She caught her daughter's glance and exploited the situation immediately. 'It's true I don't feel quite as worried about you now that I know that Percy is around to look after you.' She smiled at her daughter and added, complacently and unnecessarily, 'He's a good lad, your Percy.'

'Some lad! He's thirty-eight and bald as a coot! And I'm not sure he'd like to be described as *my* Percy.'

'Oh, but he would, you know! He's smitten, is your Percy. Men are a daft lot – without the sense they were born with, most of them, when it comes to women. But your Percy's got his head screwed on the right way. He's got all his chairs at home, has Percy.'

'It's a long time since I heard anyone use that expression, Mum.' DS Blake played for time, trying to think of a way of diverting this conversation from where she knew it was heading. It was a source of lasting surprise to Lucy that her mother and Percy, whom she had thought would have so little in common, had got on like a house on fire since their first meeting.

Agnes went and picked up the picture of Peach from the mantelpiece, looked at it fondly for a moment, and set it down even nearer to the black and white photograph of her dead husband. 'Percy will be wanting to settle down, I don't doubt, now he's given up cricket.'

Lucy decided to ignore this glorious non sequitur. 'He's very wrapped up in his career, Percy. He's a Detective Chief Inspector now, don't forget.'

'He's not so wrapped up that he doesn't recognize a pretty girl when he sees one. And he's bright enough to see that this girl has more than good looks and a few curves, too. And don't give me this Chief Inspector stuff. He's not interested in rank, your Percy. He's interested in villains, and locking villains away.'

Agnes gazed out of the stone-framed window at the long slope of Longridge Fell, and her daughter was left wondering how the old lady who rarely journeyed even as far as Brunton could know so much about her man. 'You're probably right, Mum. About putting villains away, I mean. He was even refusing the promotion at first, because he knew an inefficient superintendent was riding upwards on his back. I had to badger him into taking it.'

'Listened to you though, didn't he, our Lucy? When he wouldn't have listened to others, no doubt. I shouldn't think our Percy listens to many people. It's time you let him make an honest woman of you. He'd listen to you about that as well, I've no doubt.'

Lucy found herself blushing in spite of herself. 'We wouldn't be allowed to work together if the police authorities realized we had a serious relationship, Mum.' It was one of the few good things about Tommy Bloody Tucker's inefficiency, that he still didn't recognize that she and Percy Peach had become an item.

'There's ways and means, I'm sure, our Lucy,' said Agnes

Blake gnomically. 'It's high time you two were thinking about giving me some grandchildren. I shan't be here for ever, you know!' But by the set of her chin, she intended to survive for a considerable period yet.

'I've a career to think of, you know. I enjoy my work.' The familiar argument sounded a little desperate even in Lucy's own ears.

Agnes sniffed. 'Modern women!' The phrase carried a contempt for the whole of contemporary mores. 'You can't stop the march of time with your talk of careers, you know, our Lucy. You might pretend not to hear it, but your biological clock is ticking, all the time.' She nodded home the phrase; she had been storing it up all week, since she had heard it bandied about in the supermarket where she still worked part-time.

It was uncomfortably near the thoughts Lucy had been indulging herself, but she could never admit that here. 'I've worked hard to get where I am, and I don't want to give it up now.'

Agnes smiled unexpectedly. They had this conversation about three times a year, and it was time for her to switch her ground if she was to keep it going. 'I'm not against women having a career. I'm glad you've had opportunities I never had. But you needn't give up your career when you have a family. Not nowadays. Not in the police force.'

'It's good to have such a well-informed mother,' said Lucy acidly.

'Perhaps I'd better ask Percy, if I can't get any more sense out of you,' said that mother darkly. If persuasion and sound arguments didn't work, you might as well try threats.

'Don't you dare!' said Lucy, a little too hastily, her mother thought. She added earnestly, 'I really do like the work, Mum. This latest death you mentioned, for instance. That body found under the bricks and mortar is a real puzzle.'

Agnes knew when she was being diverted, but she'd said her piece. She contented herself with a derisive sniff. 'So long as they don't find the skeleton of my daughter in a place like that, in twenty years' time.'

'There's no danger of that, Mum, and you know it. But we don't even know who that poor woman is yet. And when we do, we'll have a devil of a job discovering who it was that killed her all those years ago.'

Agnes was silent, thinking for a moment of the hidden sufferings, of the life that the world might never know about which lay behind this obscure tragedy. 'It's not the sort of thing that I ever thought a daughter of mine would get involved in.'

But she could not keep the disapproval in her voice as she spoke. She would enjoy telling them when she got to work that her daughter was involved in this case, the latest local sensation.

As if responding to a cue, Lucy Blake's mobile phone shrilled in her bag. She picked it up and looked at the call indicator. Percy. She went into the kitchen and put the instrument carefully to her ear.

'Where the bloody 'ell are you?' said Peach, characteristically benign.

'I'm on my day off, as you very well know, DCI Peach,' she said firmly.

'Not in the bath are you?' he said hopefully.

'No. Not likely to be at just past midday, am I?'

'I were always an optimist.' He dropped into the broad Lancashire accent he adopted on occasions just for her. 'I'd be prepared to scrub thee back for thee, lass. Get the coal dust out. And then I'd—'

'I'm having a conversation with my Mum, actually.' She pushed the kitchen door to with her foot and lowered her voice. 'The one about babies. She's on about biological clocks.'

'Bright lass, your mum. And a woman who knows about cricket. There's not many of them about.' He changed back to his normal voice. 'Something's come in about the Sebastopol Terrace body. I'm planning to do an interview tonight. Thought you might want to be involved.'

'I'll be there.'

Before my biological clock sounds off its damned alarm.

Six

There were not many empty seats in the Bridgewater Hall in Manchester. The Hallé had its main conductor, and the programme was a popular one. You could always pull them in for Beethoven. He was the surest of all the great composers when it came to putting bums on seats.

And of all the piano concertos, the Emperor was the most sure-fire hit. The old sweats among the orchestra players, the second violins and the back-row brass who had seen everything, said cynically that you could even get away with rubbish fingering in the Emperor. Great music could always triumph over crap playing. And concertos didn't come any better than the Emperor.

Yet even the most sceptical among the Hallé players realized that they were in the presence of something special here. Those who had heard the young John Ogdon thirty years earlier felt a stirring of remembrance when they witnessed the extraordinary virtuosity of this young man. It was undemonstrative, but it was undeniably brilliant, that word musicians are always reluctant to allow because it is so overworked.

There was a rapt silence among the audience during the limpid account of the slow movement. Silence is always significant in a concert hall at the end of February, that peak time for coughs and snuffles. The coughing which had preceded this, in the pause at the end of the first movement, had been a release of tension after the excitement of the soloist's electrifying performance and the way the playing of the whole of the Hallé Orchestra had risen to support it. It was as much an acknowledgement of greatness in its own way as the roars would be at the end of the performance.

Now the piano delicately, diffidently, picked out the notes of the great final theme and then, having found it, sounded it out triumphantly, with the full orchestra thundering behind it. A pleasurable tension swept through the listeners, as the hands of the slight young man at the centre of it raced up and down the keyboard. There were ten minutes of this yet, as Beethoven teased and delighted his listeners with what he had never been able to hear perfectly himself, and his accomplice at the Bechstein grand detonated the fireworks he had set up for them.

The fingers sped faster and faster, the crescendo built and rebuilt; the notes glittered clear and individual as icicles, even as the speed seemed impossible. There was no flourish from the slight shoulders or those lightning hands until the very last, triumphant chord. And then there was that tiny, absolute pause which always seems to happen on the greatest musical occasions as a prelude to the audience's salute.

The applause when it came cascaded like a cataract down the tiers of the hall. It flooded round orchestra and pianist, whilst the sweating conductor smiled, mopped his brow, beamed his own delight at his role in the occasion, turned, and motioned to his players. The orchestra rose as one, their instruments set aside or held awkwardly to allow their hands to applaud.

Musicians are a cynical lot, especially where conductors and soloists are involved. They are sometimes asked to rise in acknowledgements of soloists which are more theatrical than genuine, and they usually resent that. But they identify greatness more readily than any other artists, and when they recognize it, they are delighted to be involved in it.

The players were genuine in their applause for the young virtuoso. Most of them had begun their lives by playing the piano as children before they progressed to other instruments, and many of them had attained a fair degree of expertise at the keyboard. That was what enabled them to estimate the prowess of this man. And they had no doubt that they were in the presence of a huge talent.

Once he had left his instrument, the pianist looked ill at ease in the tailed evening suit which he had worn so little; he was embarrassed now as the applause built to a tumult, and he was called back for repeated bows. His career was still in bud; it took time to establish an international reputation. But his fellow musicians had no doubt that this slight, gauche young man would be a household name within the next generation.

Outside the main concert hall, in the deserted corridors leading to the dressing rooms, two figures were challenged, for the third time since they had entered the building. It was over a decade now since the IRA had devastated the centre of Manchester, but new terrorist threats had appeared since then, and security in public places remained very tight. The man here had his orders, and even policemen could not be allowed to penetrate the inner sanctum he patrolled.

When the Chief Inspector produced his warrant card, the official examined it carefully and shook his head sadly. 'It's in order, but you can't come past here. Not during the concert.'

DCI Peach surveyed the man, who was fiftyish, overweight, swelling pompously with the burden of his authority. DS Lucy Blake felt suddenly quite sorry for him.

Peach said with ominous clarity, 'We can, sir. You'll find that you've done the right thing, letting us through. Dressing rooms down here, are they?' He peered past the formidable figure, who seemed to be trying to enlarge himself like an animated drawing to block the width of the ten-foot-wide corridor.

'This area is reserved for the major artistes.'

'Good. That's why we're here.'

'You don't understand.' The self-appointed security man listened to the applause in the distance, bursting towards a fortissimo as a door opened from the auditorium, and felt the beginnings of panic. The great men would be here soon, with these obstinate policemen still waiting to upset them. He said as patiently as he could, 'These are the rooms where the major performers relax after a performance. Wind down, you see. Receive their privileged visitors.'

Peach smiled the smile which any Brunton copper could have told the man was very dangerous. 'That's us, sunshine. Privileged visitors. We have things to discuss with Matty Hayward.'

'Matthew.' The portly man could not keep the outrage at this lese-majesty out of his voice. 'It's Matthew Hayward. It's usual to afford the major soloists their full titles, you know.'

'I'll afford you a boot up the backside if you don't get out of the way,' said Peach calmly.

There was no malice in his delivery, but that made it some-how more frightening to a man who had not been threatened like that in thirty years. It sounded like a simple statement of fact. He eyed Percy Peach's brightly polished shoe apprehen-sively. 'This is most irregular.'

It was a sign of weakness, and Peach was past him like an eager whippet, with his Sergeant slipping easily into his considerable wake. 'Just what it is, sunshine. Most irregular. I wouldn't be working at this time, wouldn't be swanning around Manchester like this, if it wasn't irregular. Just show us young Matty's dressing room, and then you can be on your way. It's private this, as you might imagine. So don't you go telling other people that young Matty is involved with the fuzz, will you?' He passed rapidly down the corridor, inspect-ing the doors as he went.

Three yards behind him, the man's voice became a wail of protest. 'This is the dressing room reserved for this evening's soloist, but I really must protest in the strongest terms—'

'That's the idea, sir. Protest away. And in the strongest terms, as you suggest. I'll give you the full names and titles of my senior officers, if you require them. On the way out, that will be. When DS Blake and I have finished with young Matty Hayward. In the meantime, if you have his interests at heart, you'll make sure we're not disturbed.'

Peach had somehow managed to secure the position of

41

advantage with his back to the door, which he now opened behind him. He surveyed the empty room with the chair in front of the mirror and the other seats around the wall, and apparently found it satisfactory. He ushered Lucy Blake into the room and said, 'I should get back to your post now, sir. There might be unauthorized persons trying to get into these rooms. And we wouldn't want that, would we?'

The man said through the door which was slowly closing upon him, 'It's my job, you see. I have to—'

'For the next twenty minutes or so, your job is to see that we're not disturbed with Matty, see?'

This formidable guardian could hardly believe it. He found himself saying to the closed door, 'I'll make sure you aren't disturbed, Chief Inspector.'

The man knew he was dying.

In a hospice, most people knew. They went there to spend their last days with people who were experts in death, and they went tranquilly into that long good night. It was a triumph of the hospice movement that the humble, industrious experts who worked in places like this had restored the dignity to death. They had also taken a lot of the fear away from it for most of the people who spent their final days and nights in hospices.

A lot of the fear, but not all. This man, despite the drugs which had dulled the pain, was not going quietly into the great unknown. He held hard to the hand of the woman who sat at his bedside and said in a voice which had declined now to a croak, 'Why me?'

'None of us knows why, Gerry. There's no rhyme or reason in it, and it's no use us even asking why.' She stroked the brown skin on the back of the hand which was little more than bones now, whilst the seconds stretched out in the silent room. There was never any hurry here, even when most of the people in the beds and the chairs had so little time left. 'Perhaps it will make more sense to us in the next life. Perhaps we shall see things more clearly then.'

The lips twisted briefly in scorn; she was glad to see that tiny burst of energy in what might otherwise have been a cadaver. 'It's always "perhaps", with you people. You call it faith, but I call it stupidity.' She carried on holding his hand, feeling the fingers tighten a little in response. At least a minute later, when she thought he had drifted off again, he said, 'It's all right for you, sister. You have beliefs. Some of us know there's nothing after this.'

She was surprised that he had remembered she was a nun. They didn't wear uniforms in here, and religious trappings least of all. It was one of the rules that no one preached at these people in their last days. If they wanted a clergyman or last religious rites, they would ask for them, and it would be arranged.

She was amazed once again at the odd things which stuck in minds that were mortally sick, when more obvious things disappeared. But perhaps he thought she was a hospital sister, a nurse in charge of his treatment, not a religious one. It mattered little, so long as she could ease his suffering. She eased the sheets gently away from the emaciated body. He was lying on his back, and she took the opportunity to smooth a little cream on to the bedsores she was trying to control on each of the hips. The skin felt as thin and smooth as cling-film; it seemed impossible that it did not split and peel away from the bone beneath it.

She reached over and eased off the earphones from ears delicate as paper, catching the applause from the Hallé broadcast at the end of the concerto. He'd asked to listen to the concert earlier; but she wondered how much of it he had heard through the haze of drugs and pain. As if he registered her thought, he said without opening his eyes, 'Tremendous performance. He's going to be one of the greats, that chap. Pity I won't be around to see it.'

She smiled, smoothing down the sparse white hair, wondering if she could get him to take a drink. 'It was the Hallé, wasn't it? I haven't heard them for a long time. Not since they used to play in the Free Trade Hall.'

43

'Barbirolli.' The dry, thin lips beneath her enunciated the syllables as clearly as if they had been fulfilling an elocution exercise. 'Sir John Barbirolli was the conductor of the Hallé when I used to go. Those were the great days. His wife was Evelyn Rothwell. Played the oboe in the orchestra. I used to live near them in those days. In Fallowfield, in Manchester.' It had been a long speech for a dying man. The bloodless lips managed a thin, exhausted smile, and she hoped his mind was back reliving those blissful days.

She wasn't at all surprised by the detail. Fifty years ago was often much more vivid than yesterday, as you approached the end. She said, 'Everyone says the Barbirolli days were the best for the Hallé. "Glorious John" they called him, didn't they?'

But he had gone from her now, drifting off into some peaceful oblivion. She felt suddenly weary, realized for the first time that she had been working for over twelve hours, with minimal breaks for food and drink. When people needed you, you gave, and you scarcely noticed fatigue creeping up on you, because you were needed. It was at moments like this, when the work was suddenly switched off, that you found that the weariness seemed to have crept into your very bones.

She would spend a few minutes in the chapel before she went to the sparsely furnished room she loved so much. Probably she'd say her night prayers there, letting that warm, dark silence envelop her like an insulating cocoon. Then she'd be able to hop straight between the cool, welcoming sheets, without kneeling with her elbows on the sides of the bed. She'd take a hot drink to her bed, and try to read a few pages of her book before she fell asleep and let it crash to the floor.

Sometimes she missed the communal worship the nuns had conducted together in the priory, with the thin, high singing rising to the vaulted stone ceiling, the ritual of the service, the togetherness of the sisterhood, and God looking down upon them from the altar.

But not often. She liked the work here. She knew she was needed, and she knew that she was good at the work, at the combination of nursing and listening and sheer hard, grinding toil, which was so necessary if people were to have dignity and consolation in death. She would sleep deep and easy tonight.

Sister Josephine looked down at the still, wasted face which would be dead by the weekend. He might even die tonight; the doctor had increased his morphine again today. She placed both of her hands on top of his single, pitifully bony one for an instant and said a prayer for him. Then she put the headphones back on their hook above the unconscious man, holding one of them to her ear for a moment to hear the announcer wrapping up the live broadcast.

It was then that she caught the name of the soloist. Matthew Hayward. She told herself that it needn't necessarily be *her* Matthew Hayward, that it was a common enough name, that her Matt surely wouldn't have been good enough to scale pianistic heights like this.

But even as she told herself these things, she knew that she was wrong. And with that knowledge, she was back in a world she thought she had put behind her for ever. An alien, dangerous world, where evil had lurked and she had been a very different person. A world where Sister Josephine, servant of God and comforter of the sick, had not even existed.

And suddenly she knew that she would not sleep soundly after all through this night.

Seven

Matthew Hayward took his final bow, held out his arms towards the audience in genuine, astonished appreciation of their reception, and left the platform.

His own part in the evening was finished, but the orchestra had still got Beethoven's seventh symphony to play to conclude the concert. It would take the audience a little while to settle again, after the excitement of his performance in the Emperor concerto. He felt a selfish pleasure in the thought of the whole of the Hallé orchestra having to wait because of the excitement he had caused.

Matthew was beginning to settle into the role of virtuoso.

Whilst he was performing and receiving his applause, he had been borne along effortlessly on wings of adrenalin. He could have played on for hours, could have risen from the stool and beamed and bowed and held out his arms appreciatively towards his listeners indefinitely. Now he was alone in the corridor, with the sounds of an audience settling and the orchestra retuning beyond the double doors through which he had made his final exit. He felt suddenly very tired.

He had been tense all day as he waited for this concert, his first concerto with the Hallé. The Emperor: that was starting at the top all right! And he'd brought it off, there was no use dousing what he had done with false modesty. The reactions of the audience and the musicians had been there to prove it. But he realized now how much his performance had taken out of him. He was still on a high, would need to sit and wind down slowly in his dressing room. He certainly needed a rest. It would be only prudent to take it easy for a while before he drove the forty miles back to his house on the edge of the Ribble Valley.

He was startled to discover two people in his dressing room. He found himself fumbling for the words which would dismiss them. 'You shouldn't be here, you know. It's not your fault, I'm sure, but you shouldn't have been allowed to get into the dressing rooms. There's a strict—'

'It's all right, sir. Our presence here is quite in order.' Peach held out his warrant card, saw that the man was still too excited to focus upon it, and said, 'We're not journalists. I'm Detective Chief Inspector Peach and this is Detective Sergeant Blake. We're here to speak to you about a non-musical matter.'

Matthew's brain reeled. He was in no condition to deal with this. Not now. He needed to savour his triumph, to shut his eyes and think of what he had done, to come back to this dull earth slowly, like a man descending from a light aeroplane after a flight in the clear skies over Everest.

He couldn't direct his mind back to the mundane concerns of a stocky, bald-headed policeman now. Not in this precious hour of his triumph. Matthew Hayward said, 'Can't this wait until tomorrow? I'm really in no state now to give you accurate information.'

'I'm afraid it won't wait, no, sir. That's why we've made the journey over here from Brunton at this hour. Had it not been urgent, we would have seen you at your own house in the morning.'

Matthew registered dimly that they were from his own area, that they knew where he lived. The first shiver of apprehension troubled his elation. 'I – I can't think what you can want with me. I think you must have the wrong person.' He looked round the bare, rectangular room as if seeing it for the first time, trying to convey what he was still too modest to put into words, the idea that the dressing room of a virtuoso was not the context for police activity.

Lucy Blake said patiently, 'You mentioned information, Mr Hayward. That is why we are here. We think you are very probably in a position to give us certain information.

Information that we think might be quite vital to an important investigation.'

Matthew looked wonderingly into the young, attractive face with its frame of rich chestnut hair. She didn't look like a policewoman to him, with that open, unlined face, and the crisp white blouse and straight maroon skirt emphasizing her curves. He realized that he had hoped when he saw her in his dressing room that she was a fan. He said, 'I think this must be a case of mistaken identity. I can't think that I have any information that can be of any possible use to the police.'

Peach said, 'Do you drive a silver Vauxhall Vectra saloon, registration number MZ51 CBV?'

'Yes. I've had it for several months. Look, if this is a motoring offence, there was scarcely any need to come—'

'No offence, sir. No motoring offence, at any rate.' Peach let the suggestion of something ominous hang in the air, watching the face above the winged collar and the evening suit as if it was of absorbing interest to him.

'If it isn't motoring, I can't think what on earth it could be. I've been preparing for this concert pretty intensively for the last week or two, as you can perhaps imagine. I can't think that—'

'It isn't recent, sir, this information we need from you.' Peach managed to make that news sound very sinister indeed.

Matthew Hayward could hear the rhythms of Beethoven beginning to thunder, majestic but muffled, from the concert hall, which seemed suddenly very far away. He said, 'How – how long ago are we talking about? The period of this information which you keep mentioning, I mean.'

Peach nodded, as if confirming something to himself, choosing a more oblique angle of attack now that he had the man's attention. It was in his nature to conduct most interviews as attacks, even those with perfectly innocent people. And this man might be very guilty indeed, if they were lucky. 'This silver Vauxhall Vectra, registration number MZ51 CBV. You've now admitted to ownership of the vehicle. Were you driving it last night, sir?'

'I really can't remember.' Matthew realized as soon as he'd said it that it was a mistake.

'I see. We'll wait until the recollection returns to you, then, shall we?' Peach looked at his watch. 'We're talking about twenty-four hours ago. It shouldn't take very long.'

Matthew Hayward fought hard to gather his wits. He had moved from relative unknown to eminent soloist to police suspect in such rapid succession that his emotions were reeling. And his brain seemed to be a victim of those emotions. It wouldn't work as he wanted it to. As he needed it to, indeed: he didn't like the watchful observation of this contrasting pair.

He said. 'I'm sorry. This has been a stressful evening for me, and for a moment I couldn't cast my mind back, even for a day. But yes, I did go out in the car last night. for an hour or so. I recall it now. Bought an evening paper, I seem to remember.'

He was talking too much in the effort to recover his ground. Percy Peach liked that: people gave away more of themselves than they wished to when they talked too much. He said, making it a statement rather than a question, 'You drove into the centre of Brunton. Took a very odd route indeed, for a musician going innocently about his business.'

'I don't know what you mean.'

'I think you do, Mr Hayward. But I'll refresh your memory for you, since it seems to be working so patchily at the moment. You drove round a redevelopment site. An unlit area. A no-go area for drivers, actually, because of the heaps of rubble and God knows what else which are left after the demolition of buildings. A dangerous area, indeed, in the darkness. Dangerous even for those who were familiar with it in the days when rows of houses stood there.'

It was a random arrow, but it struck home. Matthew Hayward looked at him with racing senses, then stupidly said the only thing he could think of. 'I'm free to drive where I want. This isn't a police state.'

Peach smiled at him; Lucy Blake was reminded of a cat relishing the splayed limbs of a mouse beneath its paw. 'No.

49

The police are merely pursuing their enquiries. And you're merely helping the police with those enquiries, Mr Hayward. The duty of every good citizen. No one has cautioned you, as yet. No one has placed you under arrest.' He spoke as though that was only a matter of time. 'But it does excite our interest, when we find someone prowling around in a place like that at dead of night.' It had been just before nine o'clock in the evening, according to the uniformed PC's report, but a DCI was surely allowed a little artistic licence. 'We have acquired certain experience over the years, you see. And experience teaches us that people who drive into areas like that are usually up to no good.'

An experienced lawbreaker would have told him to piss off, or worse. But this was not an experienced lawbreaker, and Peach knew his man. Hayward was thoroughly discomforted by now. With the conviction draining out of his voice, he said, 'I didn't do anything wrong last night. There was no reason for you to be following me.'

'You weren't followed, Mr Hayward. You were observed. By a man patrolling the scene of a serious crime. You would have been questioned on the spot about your presence there, if you hadn't made off so hastily. Suspicious, that, the speed at which you departed.' He looked at DS Blake and they nodded their agreement on that, like stage policemen confirming their suspicions.

Matthew Hayward was in no condition to decide whether their gesture was theatrical or not. He said, 'I didn't do anything wrong. I didn't intend to do anything wrong. I was – well, I was curious, that's all.'

Suddenly and without any warning, Peach beamed at him, his round face splitting almost from ear to ear beneath the black moustache, revealing teeth that were disconcertingly white. It was much more unnerving to Matthew than his previous frowns. 'Curious, Mr Hayward? Now what was there to be curious about in a dark, dreary and deserted place like that?' Peach nodded his relish at the alliteration, as if he had discovered hidden depths within his resources, and was pleased by them.

Matthew couldn't recall how he had been brought to this point. At the outset, he had never intended to reveal what he was now going to say. After fifteen minutes with this man, there seemed no alternative. 'I read about the body which was found there on Monday. It gave the details of the place in the evening paper. I was – was sort of drawn to the place.'

'And why was that, sir?'

Matthew wanted to say it was just curiosity, to brazen it out, whether they believed it or not. They couldn't do much about it if he did, whatever they thought. But somehow he didn't think he was up to brazening it out. Not here. And not with this man. He turned away from those penetrating dark eyes, but when he looked into the mirror, he could see the two of them behind him, observing him as if he was some specimen under a microscope. It was almost worse than facing them directly. He said very quietly, 'I thought I might have known that girl. A long time ago.'

The seconds seemed to drag like minutes as he watched for a reaction from those faces in the mirror in front of him. When Peach spoke, he was as quiet as the flustered man in evening dress had been. 'There was nothing in the press release to say this was a girl, Mr Hayward.'

'I'm sure there was. I'm sure I heard on the radio that the body of a girl had been found when—'

'There were no details given, beyond the fact that the body was female. They were deliberately withheld. I did the release for the media myself with the press officer. But the interesting thing for us is that you are quite right, Mr Hayward; this was a young woman. So now you must tell us how you knew that.'

'I didn't know.' This was worse than he had expected. He couldn't see a way out of it.

Lucy Blake leaned forward on her chair and said gently, 'You'll have to do better than that, Mr Hayward. You must see that.'

He looked directly at her. She seemed to be trying to help him. It was a relief in any case to look away from those gimlet black eyes beneath the bald dome and into this softer, less aggressive face. 'I – I thought I might have known her once. A long time ago.' His voice seemed even to him to come from far away, as if someone else were speaking.

'Around 1990, that would be.' Blake's voice was as soft as Peach's had been harsh a few minutes earlier.

'Around that time, yes. Perhaps a little later. How do you know that?' His reeling brain was wondering now quite how much they did know. Perhaps it was everything.

'We don't reveal our sources, Mr Hayward.' Lucy Blake was quietly insistent, the voice of quiet reason. Peach was suddenly taken with the thought of how delighted Billy Bedford would be to be described as something as lofty as 'a source', to know that for the first time in his life his confidences were to be respected and protected.

'No. No, I suppose you wouldn't. I thought this might be a girl I lived with. Early in 1991, that would be.'

'You were partners?'

'No.' He shook his head vigorously, as if trying to clear it. 'There were several of us lived there. Five or six of us. After those streets had been cleared. When the real residents were gone.' He was suddenly impatient, anxious to have this over with and these two out of his life.

'You were squatters.' This was Peach again, switching back from questions to assertions.

Matthew nodded his head as if a string had been pulled in his neck. 'I suppose you'd call it that. Sebastopol Terrace, it was.'

'Number?'

'Twenty-six.' The number came up from his subconscious as promptly as if it had been yesterday, surprising him as much as his hearers. He would have said before tonight that he no longer knew it.

Peach nodded, pursing his lips, wanting to encourage a man who was now being honest. It tallied. He'd spent an hour with an old street plan at the site today, trying to decide exactly which street and which house had been the ones where the body was found. It was on the right hand side of the street, somewhere in the three houses 26, 28 and 30.

Until now, there had been the possibility that the body had been killed somewhere else and merely dumped there by someone who knew it was a good hiding place. Now, it seemed likely that this girl had actually lived there, been killed on site, by a fellow squatter or a visitor to the place.

That made it more likely that they would catch the killer. His spirits rose as his hunter's instinct kicked in. He said, 'How old would you say this young woman was at the time of her death?'

Matthew was suddenly cautious. He thought he had given up attempts at concealment, but now he could suddenly see the danger of admitting too much. He said, 'I don't know when she died, do I? I don't know anything about her death. When I knew her, she was about twenty.'

Peach nodded. 'This girl was about that age, when she died. Did you kill her, Mr Hayward?'

Even Lucy Blake was startled by the brutal abruptness of the question. Matthew Hayward's brain reeled for a moment. Then he mustered all the outrage he could put into the words as he said, 'No! Of course I didn't kill her!'

Peach grinned over his shoulder into the mirror, totally unabashed. 'Just thought it would save us a lot of time, if you were prepared to admit it now. Difficult case wrapped up with a confession, inside two days, you see: lovely, that would be, if you look at it from our point of view. Doesn't work like that very often, more's the pity. So tell us about this squat.'

Matthew noticed that the man hadn't accepted his assurance that he wasn't a killer. 'There were five or six of us, as I said. Including Sunita.'

They had a name. It was far more than he could have expected at this stage, two days after she had been found, with the scents long gone cold. 'Tell us about these people in the squat.'

'I can't. Genuinely I can't.' It was suddenly very important to Matthew to convince them of that. 'People came and went, disappeared as suddenly as they'd arrived. We didn't tell each other much about ourselves. I suppose most of us had something to hide.' He looked down wonderingly at the black trousers of his evening dress, as if he could not comprehend how different his life was now from those almost forgotten days. 'It seems like another world, now. It seems more than thirteen years ago. Another world entirely.'

As he repeated himself, they saw just how exhausted he was. They were going to have to come back to him, to press him hard for every detail they could get. They weren't going to get much more from him tonight. Peach said softly, 'Sunita, you said. What was the girl's second name?'

Matthew shook his head wearily. 'I don't know. I don't think I ever knew. We didn't give away much about ourselves. I was just Matt. She was just Sunita.'

'That doesn't sound English.'

'She was Asian-English. Brought up here from birth, I think, but her parents were immigrants. Pakistanis, I think. Well, I'm sure they were.'

'From Brunton?'

'No. Not far away, though. Lancashire, somewhere, I'm sure. I think it might have been around Bolton.'

It tallied. They were getting nearer to an identification. Peach gave no hint of his excitement as he asked calmly, 'You're sure you don't recall a second name?'

Matthew shook his head exhaustedly. 'No, and I won't get one, however long you give me to think. I don't think I ever knew her second name. I told you, we kept our own secrets. And what people didn't tell you, you didn't ask too much about. It's one of the rules, in a squat.'

He could hear the final movement of the seventh symphony thundering out triumphantly now, even through the walls and the closed doors. That showed how silent it was in here. 'The apotheosis of the dance', Wagner had called this symphony; a fanciful idea which seemed a long way from his examination by these two watchful adversaries in this private cell of interrogation.

Peach looked at his man, wondering how much more he could take, deciding that he had probably got beyond the stage where he was capable of any elaborate deceit. But there was still one highly important area to be explored. 'Mr Hayward, you've admitted you were driving around the area because you thought the corpse which had been discovered might have been this girl Sunita. Why did you think that? Why, when you heard that the body of a woman had been found during excavations, did you immediately think that it might be this particular girl?'

They'd come back to that, when Matthew thought they'd left it and moved on. He wanted to construct some elaborate and convincing reason for his journey to the site, but he was beyond it now and he knew it. He said dully, 'She disappeared. One day she was with us, the next day she was gone. No one knew where.'

'You asked the others about it, at the time?'

'Yes, I asked. No one knew.'

'Do you think that someone did know, but was concealing the information from you?'

'No.' He shook his head hopelessly in his fatigue. 'I don't know, do I? It's a long time ago. I think I decided eventually that Sunita had just gone away. People did that, all the time.'

'But in all probability she didn't, did she? If we assume for a moment that this body is that of Sunita, she died at twenty-six Sebastopol Terrace or very near to it. That is where the corpse was unearthed on Monday.'

Matthew stared unseeingly at his casual clothes on the hanger on the wall. 'How did she die?'

'How long were you there after she disappeared, Mr Hayward?'

'I don't know. A month, maybe two months. I can't be accurate about the detail, all these years later.'

'We'll need the fullest possible details of the people who were in that house with you.'

'I can't recall much about them. People came and went, and it's a long time ago. Is it important?'

55

It was Lucy Blake who answered him, her lighter voice perfectly clear as the symphony in the concert hall reached its climax. 'I think you know it is, Matthew. Have a good night's sleep, and then give the matter your fullest possible attention, please. Anything you can recall about the people who shared that house with you may be quite vital.'

He looked at her, trying to follow her thoughts, but weighed down now by a great fatigue. He repeated doggedly, 'How did she die?'

'It seems that she was murdered, Matthew. By person or persons as yet unknown.'

They watched his face closely as it crumpled into silent, wracking tears.

Each of them had the feeling that Matthew Hayward had known all along that the woman would have died like this.

Eight

'Still no identification of this demolition site corpse? I hope you aren't slacking on this one, Peach.' Superintendent Tucker jutted his jaw aggressively towards the industrial world outside the long window of his penthouse office. To his mind, a bright Thursday morning at the end of February was the ideal time to be letting his staff know who was in charge.

The silly old sod's trying to bollock me. Must have another day on his hands with not enough to do, thought Percy Peach. He tried not to sound aggrieved as he said, 'We were over in Manchester until ten o'clock last night, sir, DS Blake and I. Didn't get to bed until nearly midnight.' We made up for it then, though, didn't we, Lucy and I? Percy tried hard to control the smile which forced its way on to his lips with the recollection.

Tommy Bloody Tucker did not consider the notion that his bête noir and the delectable Lucy Blake might have been in the sack together; it was yet another feature of Brunton police life with which he was out of touch. He said grumpily, 'No doubt the overtime budget is taking a bashing again.' He sighed. 'I don't know how my DCI expects me to keep the finances in balance, when he goes racing off to Manchester at the drop of a hat.'

'It's not bloody Barbados, sir.' Peach lapsed into a rare moment of open resentment at the injustice of life with Tucker.

'Indeed it isn't, Peach! And I'll thank you not to swear at your superior officers!'

'Sorry, sir. It must be the fatigue, sir.' But he knew irony would never work with Tucker. That was what had betrayed him for a moment into something much more blunt.

57

'What on earth were you doing in Manchester, anyway?'

'Attempting to determine the identity of the corpse on the demolition site, sir. The one you were asking about. Trying to establish the framework for a murder investigation.'

Tucker recognized dimly that he might have been a little unjust. It only made him more tetchy. 'Pity you couldn't do that in Brunton. Pity you had to do it at that hour of the night.'

'Yes, sir. Exactly what DS Blake and I said, when we were driving back over the moors beyond Darwen in freezing fog.'

Tucker peered at him suspiciously. 'What were you doing in Manchester anyway?'

'Interviewing a pianist, sir. Matthew Hayward. At the Bridgewater Hall. He was a soloist with the Hallé. Going to be as good as Alfred Brendel, some people reckon.'

Music was not one of Tucker's enthusiasms; he even wondered if the great Alfred Brendel might be an invention of Peach's. 'What on earth were you doing swanning off to Manchester to interview a pianist?'

'Possible murder suspect, sir.'

'A soloist with the Hallé orchestra?'

'That's right, sir. Evening dress and all that. Matthew Hayward. Very good, he seemed, from what little we managed to hear.'

Tucker didn't like the sound of this at all. A high-profile suspect, and Peach wandering round like a loose cannon. It sounded like a recipe for disaster to him. There could be bad publicity from this, and bad publicity was Tommy Bloody Tucker's worst nightmare. 'You'll need to proceed very carefully here, Peach. What possible connection can an eminent musician like this have with a murder in the back streets of Brunton in 1990?'

'Remains to be seen, that, sir. I'm keeping an open mind on it, as you've advised me to do so often. By the way, it now appears we may be looking a little later than 1990, sir.'

'I thought you said—'

'Residents moved out to the new council estate in 1989, sir. Place apparently became a squat after that.'

'I don't like the sound of that. I don't like squats.' Tucker looked from his sullen visage as if he hoped to change the facts by the force of his personal preference.

'No, sir. Fact of life, though. Don't suppose you remember any squats in that area, around late 1990 or 1991?' No harm in reminding the bugger that he was in charge of things then.

'Of course I don't. We were busying ourselves with more important things than squats, I can tell you, when I was in charge!'

'More important than murder, sir?'

Tucker glared at him, but, as was usual on occasions like this, he found his DCI was staring at the wall above his head. 'I note your insolence, Peach. And I remind you that I am your senior officer.'

'Quite, sir.' Peach allowed himself a long sigh at this unhappy state of affairs. 'Well, it seems that our eminent pianist was at this time a member of a squat in Sebastopol Terrace.'

'An eminent soloist living in a squat?' Tucker smiled his most patronising smile. 'I really think this must be a case of mistaken identity, you know. You'd better check your—'

'Admitted it to us last night, sir. Living in a squat thirteen years ago. Times change, sir.'

Tucker shook his head reluctantly. He liked his VIPs to come from the right background, but you couldn't be certain of anything, in the modern world. And this Bohemian world of music was a closed book to him; he'd heard that artists were strange people. He said vaguely, 'But a pianist, Peach. He'd need to practise, you know.'

'Don't think he had a grand piano in the squat, sir. They'd likely have broken it up for fuel, wouldn't they? But he says he was there, sir. And he's been able to give us a clue about the victim. It seems she was probably a young woman who was in the squat with him at that time.'

'You have an identification?'

'Not yet, sir.' I'd have told you if we had, wouldn't I, you silly sod? 'It seems she might have been Asian, sir.'

'Asian?' Peach might as well have said Martian, to judge by Tucker's goldfish look of incomprehension.

'I think I mentioned that possibility to you before, sir. Quite possibly Pakistani, Hayward thinks. And probably from Lancashire. Possibly the Bolton area. We're following it up, sir. We're pressing the dentists in that area for an urgent examination of their records. Let's hope it produces a match with the dental chart from forensic.'

'You could e-mail them, you know.' In 2004, Tucker was floundering desperately into the new century.

'Been done, sir.'

Tucker was disappointed. Then his face brightened. 'Do you think it might be worth my arranging a media conference? If you think we might have an announcement which would show them how much we're on the ball, I'd be delighted to—'

'Much too early for that, sir. We'll need to contact the next of kin, if we think we have an identification. And I'll need to get back to Matthew Hayward today, to see what else we can screw out of him about his dubious past.'

It was a danger signal for Tucker. 'This man seems to be a person of some importance, Peach. The media are always ready to listen to people like him, you know. Go carefully with him, please: we certainly don't want any bad publicity at present.'

'No, sir. I wasn't planning any threats or violence: rather the reverse. I thought I'd take DS Blake along with me and try to distract him. Get her to flash a bit of gusset at him, get him off his guard and see what it produces.' He moved his glance up the wall and licked his lips lasciviously, lost in a fantasy about the lubricious assets of his Detective Sergeant.

Tucker blanched most pleasingly. 'You'll do no such thing, Peach!'

'Maximizing the use of our assets, sir.' Peach pronounced the word as 'aaarsets' and rolled his eyes at his chief in a manner suggesting a horrid complicity between them.

'You will conduct this interview strictly by the book, Peach.

There will be no miniskirts or flashing of thighs involved. Is that understood?'

Peach looked deeply disappointed. 'Not even the odd glimpse of blue lace knickers, sir? I'm told there are some very beguiling bra and pants sets available now, which have been known to make strong men surrender all control. But of course as a married man you'd be much more privy than me to that sort of knowledge.' He surrendered himself to the image of Tucker's formidable thirteen-stone wife, popularly known around the station as 'Brünnhilde Barbara', disporting herself around the Tucker bedroom in lace lingerie.

Tucker was almost certain that he was being taken for a ride here. But not quite: he was never quite sure of his ground with this infuriating, inscrutable man. 'If this is the way you go about acquiring information, I'm not sure that you should even be allowed to—'

'You wouldn't care to do the interview yourself, sir? I'm sure your grasp of protocol and vast experience would be much appreciated. Especially as you no doubt were familiar with this squat at the time.'

'I don't interfere with my staff, as you well know, Peach,' said Tucker stiffly. The thought of being thrust back into real policing quelled his opposition immediately, as always.

'I'll try to control the display of our aarsets, sir. I'll report back in due course.'

As he descended the stairs, Percy Peach reflected that it was a good thing Lucy Blake would never know the part she had played in his exchanges with his Superintendent.

Billy Bedford, 62-year-old flasher and society reject, looked even more disreputable by day than by night.

Percy Peach set down the two pints on the small, scratched table and slid on to the uncomfortable bench seat opposite him. At half past two in the afternoon, the seedy pub was almost empty. The barman viewed his few remaining customers with distaste, hoping they would not hang around much longer. He would be closing the doors in ten minutes:

this was not one of those successful hostelries that found it worthwhile to stay open all day.

Bedford took a cautious sip of his bitter; he looked as though he suspected it might be poisoned. Then, apparently finding it acceptable, despite the fact that it came from a policeman, he took a longer pull at it and said, 'I shouldn't be seen in 'ere talking to the police. I've a reputation to think of.' But he put both of his bony hands round the pint mug and pulled it towards him, as if he feared it might be removed after this show of resistance.

Peach found the idea of Billy Bedford having a reputation to preserve a richly entertaining one. But all he said was, 'We'd better get on with this, then. I haven't got time to waste. Want to be out catching murderers, you see, Billy. And the odd flasher, of course, if there's nothing better available.'

Bedford dropped into his habitual whine of complaint. 'I ain't done any of that for years, Mr Peach. I don't know why you keep bringing it up.'

Peach gave him a grin which would have withered a stronger man than Billy. 'Don't believe it, Billy. Still, I'm not interested in your present activities, at the moment. I'm interested in the dim and distant past, when you were watching every window at night and flashing your limited manly equipment at the startled matrons of Brunton.'

'You're unfair to me, Mr Peach, really you are. I've never 'ad a decent crack of the whip from—'

'Fourteen or fifteen years ago, Billy. Sebastopol Terrace.'

'It's that body you've found, innit? I can be useful to you, if I—'

'You're going to be useful to me, Billy Bedford. Here and now. This is a murder investigation we're talking about. I wouldn't like to think there was any question of your obstructing the police in the course of their enquiries.' Another, different grin appeared beneath the jet-black moustache; there was the look in Peach's eye of a pike which has spied a juicy minnow.

'I'm only too anxious to 'elp, you know that, Mr Peach.' Bedford took another, this time nervous, pull at his beer.

'I want to know all about the squat you used to spy on, after those roads were cleared of the original tenants.'

'There was more than one squat in those streets, in the years after the people was moved out to the new council estate.' Despite his companion, Billy could not prevent a grin of lascivious recollection, his broken yellow teeth appearing like a horrid caricature in the leering mouth.

'Twenty-six Sebastopol Terrace. That's the one that interests us, Billy. Concentrate all the power of your filthy mind upon number twenty-six.'

'I remember that. Remember it well. It was the only squat in Sebastopol Terrace, see? The other squats were further away from our 'ouse, in the other streets that 'ad been cleared earlier.'

'You used to be up there every night, then. Passed it on your way out and on your way back, I expect.'

'I 'ad to walk the dog, Mr Peach. He were a good dog, were Spot!'

'And very useful, I'm sure, to a flasher/wanker/waster like you, Billy Bedford. Stood around patiently whilst his master got an eyeful and a handful, did he?'

'Mr Peach, you're not fair to me, really you're not. I don't know why I put up with you going on about—'

'Because I protect you, don't I, Billy? Because I save your miserable skin from worse things.' Peach took a long pull of his own beer, then looked into the glass, as if the thought of protecting this pathetic misfit had turned its contents sour. 'I want to know exactly who was living in that house around the end of 1990 and the beginning of 1991. I'm not interested in the details of what you were doing in the shadows outside.'

Bedford could not keep relief off his thin-featured face. 'They didn't change as much in that squat as in the others. I can remember some of them quite well. They 'ad bare light bulbs, in all the rooms. And they never 'ad curtains up at the windows, downstairs or upstairs.' His watery eyes opened wide with that detail, which had been so important to him.

Peach leaned forward, sensing that if he could make this piteous man feel important, he might get more from him. 'So tell me about them, Billy. Tell me anything at all that you can bring back. This one's out of your league, so don't try to hide anything. One of the people you saw in there could be a murderer.'

'I know, Mr Peach. I've worked that out. I'm not stupid, you know.' His puny frame seemed to swell a little with that assertion. The stench of his breath swept over the man on the other side of the two glasses as he said, 'I've been thinking about it, since you came to the house the other night. There were six of them in there, as far as I can remember. Three men and three women.'

This was much more definite than Peach had hoped for. He wondered how much he could rely on it, how much Bedford might be trying to inflate his own unaccustomed importance. 'How certain are you of that, Billy? You're not stupid, as you said. In which case, you'll realize we're going to be looking for these people.'

'Passed that place twice every night for months, didn't I? Walking Spot, you see.'

'And you no doubt lingered outside for long periods around bed-time. No curtains, you said.'

'There were three women.' He took another good drink from his almost empty glass, but the lubricious remembrance brought a smile to his thin lips nonetheless when he had put the glass down.

And thus three men, if his original figure of six in the squat was correct. Peach would have put money on the fact that Bedford's memories of the women were going to be far more vivid than those he retained of the men. 'You said you'd been thinking about this, Billy. So give me what you have.'

'One was a Paki.'

'An Asian woman. Not Indian?'

Bedford's face clouded. 'I thought they were all Pakis, round here.'

'How old was she?'

'Young. I'd say the youngest of the three. Nice tits she had, small but shapely. I'm not prejudiced, you see, Mr Peach.'

Percy wondered if this proof would be accepted by the Race Relations industry. 'And the other women were older, you think?'

'Not old, though. A bit older than the Paki, but still quite young.'

Peach went and got them two more pints, quelling the reluctant barman with a single devastating look. Bedford looked at the beer as if he hoped to see the image of the woman he was recalling reflected in its surface. Then he took a quick drink and said, 'One of them was tall and blonde, moved about well.'

'Junoesque,' said Percy appreciatively.

A baffled Billy Bedford looked at him with his head on one side and his eyes glistening, like a bemused geriatric sparrow. 'She were a looker all right. Nice face. Smashing tits and arse, when you saw her stripping.' He realized he had admitted to being a peeping Tom, thrust his face momentarily in his beer, made a great play of wiping the froth from his mouth with the back of his hand. 'You couldn't help seeing, Mr Peach. They 'ad no curtains, you see.'

'I bet you couldn't,' said Peach dryly. 'Natural blonde, was she?'

'I couldn't say, I'm sure. I didn't ever see her in the buff, you know. I was just walking Spot. You mustn't think—'

'How old?'

'Couldn't say, not for sure. I'm not as good as you policemen at guessing ages.'

'And it wasn't her face that had your attention, was it? Was she over thirty?'

'No. Definitely under. I told you, they were all quite young. I'd say about twenty-five, but I can't be sure. It's a long time ago now.'

But the image is still sharply etched into your grubby little mind. Fortunately for us. 'Anything else?'

'No. Well, yes. She had a mark on the back of her leg, the blonde one did.'

'Birthmark? Tattoo? Scar?'

'Never got close enough to be sure, did I?' Bedford sounded quite indignant about the injustice of life. 'Not a scar, I don't think.'

'Back of her leg, you said. Whereabouts? On her calf?'

'No.'

'Where, then?'

Bedford was suddenly coy. It sat very ill upon his lamentable presence. 'Higher up. Back of her leg, at the top. About where the stocking-top used to come, in the days when they wore suspenders.' His small eyes misted with the memory of that golden age.

They were the only two left in the pub now. Peach wondered whether this tall blonde was still slim, fifteen years on. Or still blonde, for that matter. He said, 'All right, Billy, you're doing well. Let's have your erotic reprint of the third of these women.'

Bedford was so rarely praised for anything that it threw him for a moment. 'Thank you, Mr Peach. I'm doing all right, aren't I, for all these years on? She was dark-haired, the third woman. Not as tall as the blonde, but . . .' He fumbled for the word, and produced only a low, involuntary growl of desire.

'Buxom?' suggested Peach. It was a word which came readily to mind, after his night of bliss with Lucy Blake.

'That's it, Mr Peach! Buxom!' Bedford ran the two syllables around his mouth and savoured them. 'Buxom! I like that. Not short, not tall, but well built. And buxom, very buxom!' He seemed to be committing the word to his memory, as if it could conjure up the images he required at some later, more private time.

'Do you recall anything else, beyond her curves?'

Billy dragged himself reluctantly back from a contemplation of that bouncing bust and that ample, irresistibly desirable bottom. 'She had a different kind of face from the blonde woman. More like the Paki, in a way.'

66

'Strong-featured, you mean?'

'That would be it, I suppose, yes. Strong-featured.' Bedford nodded, pleased with the adjective he had never used before. 'She had a bigger nose than the blonde woman. More – more definite.' He raised his hand to his own thin, insignificant proboscis, as if that could confirm to him the features of the woman he had not seen for nigh on thirteen years.

'Anything else?'

'No. Nothing I can remember.' He waved his hands vaguely in the air, indicating voluptuous curves, then clapped them hard upon his beer mug, as if they might betray him if he allowed them free rein. 'She was about the same age as the blonde bint, I think. I couldn't say which of them was older.'

Peach drank his beer and gave his man a grim smile. 'You must have been in your grubby little element, Billy Bedford. Your own little harem to spy on. What do you remember about the men?'

Predictably, it was much less. They were all young, all under thirty, but Bedford couldn't say what age within that band. He thought they were all fairly tall, but every policeman knows that people of diminutive stature tend to think that everyone is tall. Billy couldn't even recall what colour of hair they had, though he thought two of them had worn it long. That wouldn't mean much, fifteen years later.

Peach pressed him as hard as he could for any detail he might recall, and Bedford said suddenly, 'One of them had a beard. And 'e were a big bugger. And 'e had a tooth missing.'

Peach knew suddenly why he was getting this unexpected series of personal details. 'He came out and caught you, didn't he, Billy? Came out and caught the dirty little sod who was spying on the women!'

Bedford's voice rose into its familiar, apprehensive whine. 'They'd no curtains, had they? It wasn't my fault, Mr Peach! And I told him, I 'ad to walk Spot, didn't I?'

'Local bloke, was he?'

'Don't know, Mr Peach. He had me by the throat. Threatened

to tear my 'ead off, 'e did. He had fierce eyes, nearly black I think, like yours. And a beard, like I said.'

They finished their beers, whilst Peach probed earnestly but unsuccessfully for any more detail about these men, who were so much less vividly imprinted on Bedford's memory than the women. The barman banged the double doors of the pub noisily shut behind them as they left.

Percy Peach walked the short distance back to the Brunton police station ruminatively. It was still possible, of course, that someone had dumped this body in the empty house, that they might have to look for an outsider. But it seemed likely that the Asian girl Bedford had seen there was their victim.

And it was possible, even probable, that one of the other five who had occupied the squat with her had been her killer.

It was a detached nineteen-thirties house, one of a row of almost identical properties in a quiet suburban road.

Expectations are conditioned by experience. DC Gordon Pickering met hundreds of Asians in the course of his work, but it was still a surprise to him to find them living in a house like this in a prosperous suburb of Bolton. The man who stood on the doorstep above him was dark-skinned and austere. Pickering said quickly, 'Mr Akhtar? I'm Detective Constable Pickering and this is Police Constable Pat Rogers. I think someone rang you about this visit.'

'Yes. Otherwise I shouldn't be here but at work.'

They were off on the wrong foot already then. 'It's really rather important, sir, or you wouldn't have been troubled.'

He nodded, looking them up and down as if he might divine their purpose by a close examination. He did not disguise his distaste for the young woman in uniform who stood slightly behind Pickering. Nor did he trouble to disguise his reluctance as he said, 'I suppose you had better come inside.'

The sitting room into which he led them was very British in its furnishings, with a heavy three-piece lounge suite dominating it. Only a heavily patterned carpet and an abundance of ornaments suggested a different taste. An olive-skinned woman in a headscarf acknowledged their introduction but did not speak; she assessed her visitors for a few seconds, then cast her eyes back to the carpet.

Gordon Pickering hadn't been looking forward to this meeting to start with, and the fifty-minute drive from Brunton had only added to his tension. He wished the man would sit down, but sensed that it wouldn't be well received if he asked him to do so in his own home.

Pickering said nervously, 'I understand you have a daughter?'

He had addressed his question automatically to both of them, but it was the man who responded. His face set like stone as he said, 'We had a daughter once. We no longer have a daughter.'

For a moment, Pickering thought they knew already what he had come to tell them. But then Akhtar went on, 'She chose to disobey her parents. She chose to reject us and the way we live. So we no longer have a daughter.'

It was his wife, sitting in an armchair so huge that it made her look slight and vulnerable, who said, 'Sunita left home in 1990. We have not heard of her since. Do you have news of her?'

'We think we might have news, Mrs Akhtar. Not good news, I'm afraid.'

Akhtar glanced at his wife as if she should never have spoken. 'She rejected our guidance. She chose to disobey the wishes of her parents.'

His wife shot a look of smouldering resentment at his rigid back, but he was totally unconscious of her disgust. She said, 'Our daughter rejected our choice of a marriage partner. It is traditional, in our culture, for the parents to choose the partner. But Sunita had lived all her life here, had all her schooling here. She was never going to find it easy to accept our choice of partner.'

Akhtar said without looking round at her, articulating each syllable like a man only just in control of himself, 'She should not have had this difficulty. She knew from birth what our system was. But she said she had the right to make her own

69

choice. She defied us. From that moment, she was no longer our daughter.' He seemed to grow taller with the force of his iron conviction on the last sentence.

The young female uniformed constable had the sense to realize that it would not be taken kindly if she tried to take the initiative here. She sat down at the end of the settee nearest to Mrs Akhtar, reached out a hand and put it gently on top of the older woman's hand, which lay on the broad arm of her chair. The Asian woman looked at her first with surprise and then with gratitude, and left her hand where it lay.

DC Pickering said rather desperately. 'As I said, I'm afraid we do not bring good news. Three days ago, when a site was being cleared of old buildings in preparation for redevelopment, a body was found. It was the body of a young woman of about twenty, of Asian extraction.'

Pat Rogers felt the thin hand under hers tighten with tension. Then Mrs Akhtar said in a voice hollow with grief, 'This girl was murdered, wasn't she? I heard that on the radio this morning.'

'I'm afraid she was, yes.'

Akhtar's face might have been carved from marble. He said in an even tone, 'This was not my daughter. She ceased to be that as soon as she defied us and walked out of this house.'

'Defied *you*.' The words came so quietly that it took them a moment to realize that they had come from the very still woman in the armchair. '*You* drove Sunita from this house. And now she is dead. Murdered. Murdered!' Her voice rose towards a scream on the repetition of the word.

'It was her own choice.'

The rift was deepening between them, whilst they spoke absurdly into space, refusing to look into each other's faces. Pickering sensed that he was in the presence of something he had never witnessed before. Deaths usually brought parents closer to each other, but this was a rift which would never be bridged in whatever lives this pair had left. He said desperately, 'We're not even absolutely sure yet that this is your daughter.'

'Do you need an identification?' Mrs Akhtar was as still and composed as her husband, as if she wished to show that she could control her different emotions as well as he.

'That isn't possible, I'm afraid. The body had been buried for a long time, you see. It is – well, damaged.'

'Rotting. Decomposed. Unrecognizable.' Mrs Akhtar uttered each word as if she was driving a dagger into herself. 'Our daughter. Sunita!' The scream lurking at the back of her throat almost escaped on the name.

Pat Rogers fastened her young hand more strongly on the older one underneath it, feeling the bones beneath the skin, as Gordon Pickering said, 'But I have to tell you that the body discovered on Monday was almost certainly that of your daughter Sunita. A Bolton dentist, Mr Ensten, has come up with a match for the dental chart our forensic laboratory took from the remains unearthed by the site equipment. I'm very sorry.'

Akhtar said like one speaking in a trance, 'There can be no doubt that this is Sunita?' It was the first time he had used his daughter's name. He pronounced the syllables as if they had grown difficult for him with disuse.

Pickering wanted to offer some consoling words, but he sensed that they would not be welcome. 'I'm afraid there can now be no reasonable doubt that this is Sunita. We'd like you to give us a DNA sample, for comparison with samples taken from the body, but I'm afraid that I can't offer you any realistic hope that this will not be your daughter.'

The two police officers left as quickly as they could, letting themselves out of the silent house. The bereaved parents had still not looked at each other. They stared unseeingly across the comfortable lounge, contemplating this awful thing which would lie between them for the rest of their lives.

71

Nine

The village of Waddington is one of the prettiest in the Ribble Valley. And the modest stone cottage in which Matthew Hayward lived was one of the most attractive residences in this pleasant setting. The stream which ran through the centre of the village passed in front of the cottage, several feet below its garden. On the morning of Friday, the twenty-fifth of February, the fells rose steeply behind it towards a blue sky and the invisible Trough of Bowland beyond them. The air was crisp and clear, the sky a brilliant blue, there was warmth in the sun, and it seemed that spring could surely not be far away.

It could hardly have been a bigger contrast with the squalid, sparsely furnished squat from thirteen years earlier which was now the focus of a murder inquiry.

The cottage was at the top of the village. Matthew Hayward was standing in its low doorway as Lucy Blake drove the police Mondeo over the little bridge which spanned the stream. He had been looking anxiously out of the window for the last twenty minutes. 'Thank you for coming out here to see me.'

'No problem, sir. You're merely helping the police with their enquiries, as yet.' Peach threw the final phrase in beneath a breezy smile. He had a nose like a sniffer dog's for nervousness, and he smelt it here. His research showed that this man was thirty-three: only five years younger than Percy was himself. But he looked callow by comparison.

Hayward took them into a long, low-ceilinged sitting room, which was dominated by a single piece of furniture, the

72

magnificent rosewood grand piano at the far end, beside the long, low window which looked up the hillside. 'I've been thinking back to those days when we lived in the house in Brunton, as you asked me to on Wednesday night.'

'The squat in Sebastopol Terrace. That's good,' nodded Peach. No harm in reminding the man that he'd been breaking the law at that time.

'We were a collection of misfits really. All down on our luck in various ways.' Matthew laughed nervously, looking instinctively towards Lucy Blake, where he sensed he might get a more sympathetic hearing.

'Most squats are occupied by people like that. And worse,' said Peach ominously.

'Yes, I suppose they are. Well, people came and went. That's also typical of squats, I believe.'

'But this one was rather more stable than most.' Peach spoke with authority, and Matthew divined with an unwelcome shock that he was not the only source of information about that derelict house.

'Yes, I think it was. I was there for quite a few months myself. And there were several of us who—'

'Six, our information says. Correct?'

This wasn't going the way Matthew had expected at all. He had thought they would be grateful for whatever information he chose to give them, that he would be able to reminisce and present the picture of himself and others that he had chosen to reveal. Now it seemed that they already knew things, that whatever he said would be set against some other account. Perhaps they had more than one witness already; perhaps what he had to say would be weighed and found wanting, if he chose to be selective in his recall. He said uncertainly, 'Six is the figure I had in mind, yes.'

'Including the girl who was killed. The girl who is now officially a murder victim.'

'Yes. Have you found someone else as well as me who was there at that time? I'd like to—'

'We never reveal our sources of information, sir. Not until

they become official witnesses in a court case. We won't tell other people about what you have to tell us today. Not initially.'

Matthew wondered why he felt that he was being warned rather than thanked for his co-operation. He said defensively, 'We didn't get to know a lot about each other, you know. When you're living like that, most people have things to hide. They don't welcome questions. You learned to respect their privacy.'

'And to preserve your own skin by doing so, no doubt. Some dangerous people live in squats.'

'Not in that one, I'm sure.'

'Oh yes there were, Mr Hayward. Very dangerous, in one case at least. One of you was a murderer.' They weren't actually sure of that yet, but Percy wasn't going to weaken his position with this nervous man by making that qualification to his statement.

Matthew licked his lips. 'I think the victim was the girl called Sunita.'

'Correct.'

His replies were being checked off against a list, when he had expected them to be welcome information. He had better be very careful; this bouncy, broad-shouldered man had in effect just told him that he was a murder suspect. Matthew wished he was not sitting so close to that shining bald head, with its fringe of jet-black hair and matching moustache, to the very white teeth and very dark eyes, which seemed about to pierce his very skin.

He swallowed and said, 'You'll want me to tell you all I can about Sunita. I don't know exactly where she came from; probably she never told us. She'd fallen out with her family and she didn't want them to find her. That wasn't unusual: most of us had had blazing rows, or worse, with one or other of our parents. But Sunita was almost paranoid about it. She wouldn't register for social security, because she was so afraid they'd find where she was.'

'How long was she there?'

'She was there when I got there.'

74

'Which was when?'

'I've been trying to pin it down exactly. I think it was about November, 1990. You might as well know why.' He had nerved himself to this, feeling sure they would ask about it, and it came out in a rush, like water bursting past an obstruction. 'My father died when I was eleven. My mother had a succession of boyfriends after that. Some of them weren't too bad, but the one who eventually moved in was the worst of all. He knocked me about a lot, even when I was in the sixth form at school. He was big and strong and delighted in showing me that I wasn't, especially when my mother wasn't around. Eventually, after I'd played the piano at a school concert and got a bit of publicity, he tried to hit the back of my left hand with a coal hammer. Fortunately, it was only a glancing blow, but I realized that he would cripple me if I stayed around, so I got out.' He turned his hand over and looked at the back of it now, as if even after all these years he could scarcely believe that it was intact.

Peach watched Lucy Blake making swift notes with the small gold ball pen she always carried. 'And you say Sunita Akhtar was there when you arrived?'

They knew her full name. Knew more than he had realized. 'Yes, but she'd only just arrived. Not more than a day before me, I think. They're suspicious of you, the people already in a squat, when you move in. I remember that both of us felt we were being watched, for a few days.'

'Drew you together, that, I expect.'

He knew far too much, this man. 'Yes. We got on together, Sunita and I. We'd arrived together, and we were both fugitives from home.'

'Lovers, were you?'

'Who told you that?'

You did. No one else. But thank you for the information! Peach gave him a wide, appreciative beam. 'Couldn't tell you who it was, even if I wanted to, Mr Hayward. Fall out with each other, eventually, did you?'

'No!' Matthew was aware that he was losing it, that his

denial was too emphatic. 'It's too simplistic to say that we were lovers. We were thrown together by circumstances, as I've said, and eventually we slept together. But we never became an item.'

'And did you regret that?'

'No. We weren't in a position to form lasting sexual relationships, either of us.' He wondered how convincing his denial sounded.

'Put it about a bit, did she, this Sunita?'

Matthew almost shouted at him again. Instead, he controlled himself and said with venom, 'The poor girl's dead. Do you have to be so offensive?'

'Probably do, yes, Mr Hayward. Just trying to get the fullest possible picture of what went on at twenty-six Sebastopol Terrace all those years ago, you see. So I'm asking you again, were you the only person who enjoyed the girl's sexual favours?'

'No. I don't think I was. Sunita went off the rails a bit, I think. She'd had a very strict upbringing, and it seemed to be a kind of rebellion against that.'

This wasn't what a CID team wanted to hear. Sex meant passion, and passion meant possible violence. If the girl had offered sex around, it increased the possible number of suspects. 'You think she slept with other people in the squat?'

The slim shoulders shrugged hopelessly. 'I think she might have done. I think she probably did. I'm not certain of it.'

'And others as well?'

'I – I think she might have. It's a long time ago and I can't be certain.'

'She didn't have a job?'

'No. She did bits of work where she could pick them up. I remember she stacked supermarket shelves for a while, but it didn't last. She didn't like working with Asians, because she was worried it might get back to her parents and they'd come after her. I told you, she was almost paranoid about that.'

'So she needed money, didn't she? If she was refusing to take Unemployment Benefit.'

'Yes. She was a proud girl, Sunita. We didn't need much, in the squat, but she didn't want anyone to think she was sponging off them.'

'So she might have sold sexual favours to raise money.'

'I suppose she might. I don't have any knowledge that she did.'

'When did you leave that squat, Mr Hayward?'

'April, 1991.'

And why did you go?'

'No one really wants to live in a squat for ever, do they? By definition, it's an insecure and impermanent existence. I'd got myself together again. Before things blew up at home, I'd already secured a scholarship and a place at the Northern College of Music, in Manchester, to begin in September. I'd thought that was all off when I left home, but I realized that it could be my salvation. I got a job for the summer playing the piano in a pub in Blackpool. Even got the odd booking in theatre orchestras for the summer shows, when the regular players were ill; I can play the violin well enough to get by. I had cheap digs and I got myself back on my feet.'

It had come out in a rush again, like a prepared statement. But there was nothing wrong with that: they had asked him to spend twenty-four hours thinking back to that vanished time in his life, hadn't they?

'And Sunita was still there when you left?'

Matthew wondered if he could get away with saying she was. It would be a large step to putting him in the clear for her killing. But they had another source of information: he couldn't be certain how much they already knew about this. 'No. She'd disappeared a little while before I went. About two weeks earlier, I'd say. I can't be precise, at this distance from it.'

'You must have been curious to know what had happened to her.'

'No. Well, not very curious, anyway. We weren't very close to each other by that time. And people come and go in squats. Sometimes they tell you what's happening, what's turned up for them, sometimes they don't. You're never very curious when someone leaves.'

'No, I realize that. But you used the word "disappeared", for Sunita. Wouldn't it have been more natural to say she left, as you did?'

How sharp he was, this man! And he was right; Matthew had implied there was a mystery, that he was worried about her going, when he had not meant to. He said carefully, 'It's just a question of semantics. I suppose it seemed to me like a disappearance, because it was so abrupt. She hadn't said anything about going, as I said.'

'I think you're right. Because it now looks to me as if she vanished so abruptly because she was killed, Mr Hayward. Especially as she'd said nothing to you, or to anyone else as far as you know, about leaving.'

He nodded, wary now of words.

'It's interesting that you thought of it as a disappearance at the time, rather than a simple exit from the group, like yours. Perhaps you had an inkling at the time that something had happened to Sunita.'

This man, whose dark eyes watched him so intently, who had been so quick to pick him up on a word, hadn't said 'knowledge', but only 'inkling'. He hadn't accused him of murder, but he hadn't let him off the hook either. Matthew said, 'Perhaps it was hindsight which made me speak of her disappearing rather than leaving. Perhaps it was a result of what I have learned over the last few days.'

'Perhaps. But you must see that this sudden, unexplained, apparently unpremeditated disappearance increases the likelihood that one of the people in that squat killed her. I'd put money on it, if I were a betting man.' Peach gave the man opposite him a contented smile on that thought.

'I suppose so.'

'And of course, experienced coppers, older and wiser men than me, would say that the man who left so soon after the dispatching of this poor girl would be the most likely killer. The prime suspect, they'd call a chap like that.'

78

'I didn't kill her!'

It was a reaction so childishly prompt and instinctive that in a few seconds they were all smiling at it, though Matthew, after the surprise of his smile, felt hysteria welling briefly at the back of his throat. This meeting was not going as he had envisaged it at all.

Peach said, 'No one has accused you, yet. You're helping us with our enquiries, as a good citizen should. If it's any consolation, what you have told us so far has been most helpful, Mr Hayward. So let's be generous to you, and disregard your unfortunate departure so soon after what we now think is a murder. There were five of you as well as the murder victim in that squat at number twenty-six Sebastopol Terrace. So on the simple statistics, you're four to one against as our killer. The best way to become an outsider rather than the favourite is to tell us all you can about the other four unlawful occupants of that house.'

It was a crude logic he was using, but Matthew in his now fevered state couldn't argue with this Chief Inquisitor. He said feebly, 'I can't remember much about the others. It's a long time ago now.'

'Nevertheless, you've had a day to think about it. You've done quite well with yourself and Sunita. Let's see what you can tell us about the others. It's very much in your own interest to give us all you can.'

'There were four others. That's correct.'

'Two other men, apart from you, and two women.'

He felt another chill of apprehension at Peach's simple statement. How much more did he know? Was he playing cat and mouse games, trying to catch Matthew out in lies? Did he know even now far more than Matthew could recollect about that house and its occupants?

Lucy Blake on the other side of the fence was amazed once again by what skilful use Peach was making of the minimal recollections of that pathetic creature Billy Bedford. She said, ball pen poised over her notes, 'Can you confirm the names of these people for us, Mr Hayward?'

79

Her eyes were dark green in the clear light filtering into the room, as if they caught the green of the hills outside. He found it a relief to turn to this softer presence beneath the lustrous red-brown hair after Peach's remorseless stare, though he was aware that he must be just as careful in his replies. 'I've been thinking about that. The girls were called Jo and Emmy.'

She made a careful note, taking her time, using Peach's technique of allowing silence to build into tension. 'And the men?'

'One was Wally. He called himself that, but I never felt it was his real name – I don't think any of us did. It was a kind of joke in the place, because he said it in that way himself, but not a joke that we laughed at very much.'

'Frightening bloke was he?'

'He was, yes, as I remember it.' It seemed easier to admit things like that, to this pretty, understanding girl. 'Of course, I was very young at the time. He was probably only four or five years older than me, but that seems a lot when you're that age.'

'Indeed. But there must have been more than his age between you.'

'We didn't fall out, never had any serious disagreements.' He wondered if he had been too quick to say that. 'It was just that he seemed – well, formidable, in that context. He was a powerfully built man. Not particularly tall, as I remember it, but heavily built. Like a prop forward.' He grinned despite himself at this sudden image from his past. 'And he came and went as he pleased, without reference to any of us. I may be wrong, but I don't think any of us ever knew what he did outside the place. And he always had stubble round his chin, before it became a fashion to have it a few years later. I think he grew a beard in the later stages of my time there. Dark-haired, he was, and swarthy.'

'Did he have a tooth missing?'

Again evidence that they had other sources than him, that what he had to say was being weighed against other accounts, that if he got this wrong he would be in trouble for deceiving this contrasting but equally observant pair. 'I think he did, yes. I'd forgotten about it, but now that you—'

'Upper or lower jaw?'

He made himself pause, as if giving thought to the matter. 'Upper jaw, I think. Not quite in the middle, but near to it.'

Lucy made a careful note of that, trying not to imagine what the photofit compilers might make of the detail at some later date. 'And you don't think he will be going by the name of Wally now?'

'No. I think it very unlikely that it was his real name at the time. But I've no idea what has happened to any of them, since then. And I've no idea how long they were there after I left.'

'I see. What about the other man?'

'He was coloured. Very black.' Matthew grinned unexpectedly at himself. 'Well, I suppose he seemed even darker, in that place, in winter. We hadn't a lot of light, in most of the rooms. He was West Indian, I think. Extraction, I mean – I'm sure he'd lived all his life in this country. I can't recall a name for him. Wally used to call him Sambo sometimes, to try to wind him up, but I never saw him react to it.'

DS Blake had a sudden picture of the grim life in this squat, but she knew it was only a snapshot, that they would probably know a lot more about the place before this one was solved. 'Any idea what he did to support himself?'

'No. I think he had work, for at least part of the time, but I'm not sure what.'

'Age?'

'He was young. Younger than me, I think, but much more streetwise.'

She could believe that. Matthew Hayward, successful concert pianist with the musical world at his feet, looked younger than his thirty-three years even now, with his unlined face and his attractively tousled dark hair. It was difficult to think of him as a potential murderer. She said, 'What about the other two girls?'

'I can't remember a lot, apart from the names. Jo was a

couple of years older than me, I think. So about twenty at that time. Dark-haired. Rather a striking sort of face. Strong nose.'

'Build?'

'Quite sturdily built, as far as I remember.'

'Buxom.' Peach threw the word in when Matthew was concentrating on his replies to the girl. It was not the word he would have used in this context, but it was uncomfortably accurate. He wondered how many of the other occupants of that squat they had already interviewed before him.

'Yes. That wouldn't be a bad description of her.'

'Anything else?'

'No. I didn't think I could remember as much as that.'

Lucy nodded slowly. 'And the other girl?'

'Emmy. I don't know whether she was Emma or Emily, but she called herself Emmy. She was taller than Jo and Sunita. Almost my height, I think; probably an inch or so less than me; so about five feet nine, say.'

'Age?'

He paused for a moment, his brow wrinkling into a frown. 'I was going to say older than Jo. But she may not have been much different. She was more worldly-wise than any of us, except for Wally, and that made her seem older, I expect. Now, I think she was probably only twenty or twenty-one.'

'Dark-haired?'

He wondered again if they were trying to trap him. 'No. Definitely blonde.'

'Figure?'

'Quite shapely.' Absurdly, he felt himself blushing.

'Pretty face?'

'Matter of opinion, that, isn't it?' He gave a weak smile, but it brought no response from these two. 'I think she had blue eyes, but I honestly can't remember much of the detail of her features, at this distance.'

'Natural blonde?'

'I don't know. I was even less of an expert in such things then than I am now.' Again he grinned weakly; again his smile dropped from his face like a stricken bird. 'I think she may well have been natural. It wasn't easy to be anything else in that place. We'd no hot water, and I suspect none of us was as clean or washed as often as we'd have liked to.'

'What else?'

'Nothing, I'm afraid. It's all a long time ago.' He looked from one to the other for a response, found Peach nodding thoughtfully, as if he accepted this.

The DCI said, 'Do you remember a mark on the back of her thigh?'

'No.'

'Not sure which leg. Just below the buttock, it would be.'

'They wore trousers, the girls. It was damn cold in there, most of the time. I wouldn't have seen a mark like that, would I?'

The DCI gave him a smile which developed from small beginnings into something much grosser. 'Sleep with either of these two, did you?' Peach shot the question across the six feet between them with relish.

Matthew felt a moment of panic, told himself firmly that it was completely irrational. 'No.'

'Reasonable question. Lot of it goes on in squats, doesn't it? And you've already admitted to sleeping with a murder victim. And you make the other two sound very beddable. Wouldn't be surprising if a young, virile lad like you, freed from home restrictions for the first time, was putting it about a bit.'

'Well, I wasn't!' Matthew felt a desperate need to stem the flow of Peach speculation.

Peach studied him with his head on one side for a moment, then grinned conspiratorially. 'OK. What about the others?'

'I don't know. Really I don't. We kept ourselves to ourselves, didn't enquire too much about what the others were up to. It was one of the rules of the squat, and you soon learned to stick by it.'

'I understand that. But when there's been a murder there, it alters all the rules. And brings some new ones of its own into play. Relationships, whether temporary or more lasting,

83

might well be important. As might jealousy, sexual or other-wise.'

Matthew said stubbornly, 'I can't remember anything of that sort.'

'No tantrums?'

'I can't remember any. We were all under various kinds of stress, but I can't think of anything which might be significant to you.'

Peach regarded him steadily for a moment with those dark eyes which seemed to be seeing far more than they should. Then he said, 'Thank you for your time, Mr Hayward.' He looked at the music on the piano as he stood up. 'Good luck with the concerts! Keep on thinking about this matter, please; other things may come back to you, over the next few days. No doubt we shall need to speak again.'

Matthew wondered why that sounded so much like a threat.

Lucy Blake had driven three miles before she said, with reluctant admiration, 'You're a clever devil, Percy Peach. Matthew Hayward thinks we know a lot more about that squat than we actually do.'

He was silent, and for a while she thought he was revelling in this praise. Then Peach said, 'The next interesting research is to discover exactly what it was that he was holding back from us.'

Ten

Tommy Bloody Tucker on television was a thing of wonder. It was over a year since his last such appearance, and Percy Peach, watching him on the monitor in the privacy of his own room, admitted to himself that he could not have done anything like as well.

Percy could never have inspired such confidence in the public by his very appearance, for a start. Tucker was in his best uniform, spruce as a matinee idol, earnest as a bishop, with his still plentiful and lightly waved hair specially trimmed for the occasion. The silvering at his temples gave just the appropriate gravitas to his message. The Chief Superintendent's regular features had been skilfully treated by the make-up girl; he contrived to look healthy, vigorous, and yet weighed down by an appropriate concern.

The police needed the public's help, he said, in the matter of the woman's body unearthed during the demolition work near the centre of Brunton four days earlier. A moment's thought would make it obvious to every citizen how difficult an investigation of this kind, into a death which had happened many years earlier, must be.

He had taken personal charge of this investigation from the moment the corpse was discovered, and he was gratified to report now that substantial, some would say surprising, progress had already been made. For a start, there was not a shadow of doubt that this was murder. Chief Superintendent Tucker faced the camera head-on and made a suitably melo-dramatic use of that word, which always chilled and excited the public.

The victim was a young woman named Sunita Akhtar, nineteen at the time of her death. Diligent enquiries had revealed that this seemed to have taken place early in 1991, probably in March. To pinpoint the time of death so accurately thirteen years later was no mean feat of detection, as Tucker reminded his questioner with a modest smile.

It seemed the young lady had been living unlawfully in a house which had been condemned for slum clearance and cleared of its legitimate occupants – what was commonly known as a 'squat'. The immaculate Tucker pronounced the word with distaste and took the opportunity to emphasize the dangers to young people in choosing to inhabit such places. His interviewer enquired gently whether the police should not have been checking on such unlawful occupation back in 1991, and perhaps even preventing it.

Tucker was ready for her: as Percy Peach noted with reluctant admiration in his private viewing, he hadn't risen to the dizzying rank he held without honours in bullshit. His interviewer was obviously far too young and pretty to remember it, Tucker implied, but back in 1990 things were very different. Cardboard cities were springing up throughout the kingdom. Perhaps the authorities had been happy to see young people with a solid roof over their heads, even in a condemned property. And no doubt the policemen then in charge had had other and more serious crimes on their hands at the time, he added tolerantly. He contrived to imply that this was long before he was on the scene, and his interviewer was too far away to pick up the sound of Percy Peach's fiercely grinding teeth.

The modern police force was a formidably efficient unit. Tucker produced a visual aid, in the form of a street map centred on Sebastopol Terrace, the scene of the crime. The cameras had shown the desolate waste on the building site in the introduction to this item. Tucker pointed to his map and explained that he had now been able to establish exactly where this partly mummified body had lain for all these years. It had been hidden not in the squat in which Sunita Akhtar had lived out the last months of her short life, but in the unoccupied house next door.

Paint samples from fragments of wood and the clothing of the deceased revealed that a broken door had been used to immure the corpse in the chimney breast of this derelict house, where it had lain undiscovered until the development firm moved in with its heavy machinery.

Peach was fascinated despite himself as he watched the latest forensic findings, which he had delivered to his Chief Superintendent that morning, now made to seem a product of the individual diligence of Tucker himself. The man made a passing reference to his team, but he contrived to imply that they were dull plodders, who would have been lost without the forceful direction and insights of their chief.

The girl interviewing this modern Colossus of detection, newly arrived at Granada Television from local radio, now offered an observation so much to Tucker's taste that Peach wondered if she had been primed with it before the exchange began. She said that she supposed the police team could know very little as yet of the people who had occupied this long-departed squat, who it now seemed had contained a murderer within their number.

Tucker raised a benign, controlling hand. 'We must not jump to any such conclusion. The layman might do that, but the experienced senior policeman in charge of a case like this knows that he must keep an open mind. It is still possible that Sunita was killed by some other person entirely, who merely hid her body in that bleak place.' He allowed himself an enigmatic smile. 'Nor is it true to say that I know nothing of the people who occupied that squat.'

Tucker made the dramatic pause of the experienced ham and looked straight into the camera, his grey eyes filling with a steely threat. 'I already know that there were three males and three females in that squat at the time of this death. One of the females was the deceased. We are anxious to make contact with the other five people who were living unlawfully at number twenty-six Sebastopol Terrace in the early months of 1991. One of them has already been found and interviewed. It is only a matter of time before the others are discovered. I urge them now to come forward and declare themselves. This is a serious crime, and that is their duty. No one who is innocent has anything to fear.'

'You sound very determined, Chief Superintendent Tucker. Is this case something of a personal crusade?'

His smile as he regarded her was modest, understanding and confident at the same time: a masterpiece of public relations art. 'I cannot say that, Jenny. The modern senior policeman has to keep an overview of crime, to have an eye for the broader picture. But you are right: I take a crime of this sort on my patch very seriously indeed. I shall not be counting the hours I work in the days ahead.' He took a deep breath whilst he turned the full force of Tucker sincerity on the camera in front of him. 'It is fair to say that I am confident of a successful outcome, and determined to bring to justice the person responsible for this dreadful murder.'

The Chief Superintendent jutted his chin at the camera with a grim smile. Percy Peach, a man not given to spitting, was at that moment sorely tempted.

Not all of Superintendent Tucker's interview was shown on television's evening news. But one man in particular gave intense attention to the Chief Superintendent's update on the Sunita Akhtar case.

David Edmonds, partner in and unofficial Chief Executive of Brunton's oldest estate agents ('dealing in Lancashire property for over a hundred years'), watched the news item with mounting apprehension. Even his wife noted his interest. 'Sold the site for that office development, didn't you?' she said, as she passed him with her youngest child on her arm.

'Yes, I think we did. A few years ago, though. I didn't have anything to do with the sale myself.' He wondered if that sounded as casual and offhand as he wished it to.

David Edmonds was left on his own in front of the television set as the newsreader went on with the rest of the news of the north-west. He did not register any of it. He sat for a moment with his head in his hands, willing his brain to come up with a solution to this. But that brain told him logically enough that there were some situations to which there were no solutions.

He went into his study and shut the door of the small room carefully behind him. He could hear the sounds of his wife and his children over his head. He picked up the phone and dialled his father-in-law's number. 'Good evening, Stanley.' He made himself use the forename of the older man, a habit which still came hard to him even after ten years. 'Sorry to bother you at home. I have a small favour to ask of you.'

It sounded oddly formal, when he wanted to minimize the impact of what he had to say. But apparently Stanley Ormerod didn't notice that. He said affably enough, 'Pleasure to hear from you, David, as always. Baby-sitting, is it? I'll get Mary for you if—'

'No, it's not that. It's connected with the children, though.'

That sounded desperate in his own ears, but all the older man said on the other end of the phone was: 'Fire away, then!'

'You remember that I was thinking of taking them away for a little break?'

'Down to Devon for a day or two at half term, didn't you say? I thought you'd given up the idea.'

'Well, I had, yes. But they're looking pretty pale and feeble at the end of the winter, I think. And so is Michelle. I'd like to give them a dose of sun. Spain or Portugal, I thought. For a fortnight.' He tacked the important bit awkwardly on to the end, trying to slip it by under a welter of other facts.

'A fortnight?'

'I know we hadn't planned it. But it's a quiet time at work, as you know. It seems like a good opportunity. Things will pick up from Easter onwards as usual, I expect.'

'But I thought you didn't want to take the children out of school.'

David could hear the puzzlement in the older man's voice.

He forced himself to laugh. 'I decided I was being an old fuddy-duddy about that! Amy's only two, so it doesn't affect her – she'll be better off abroad at this time, before the sun gets too strong – and the others are only five and seven. They aren't going to miss anything vital, I'm sure, at this stage of their schooling. And with the Ormerod genes, they're bright enough to make up any lost ground in no time! Mens sane in corpore sanum, and all that!'

'Mens sana in corpore sano,' Stanley Ormerod corrected him automatically.

'There you are, then! There's the Ormerod genes, you see. Latin had more or less gone out, by my day.'

'When are you proposing to go?'

Stanley Ormerod wasn't going to make difficulties! David's heart leapt absurdly with the thought. 'End of next week, I thought. Give me time to clear up everything outstanding at the office. Leave everything shipshape. And there are some terrific bargains available, after the school half term is over!' He was pleased with himself for that afterthought. Economy always appealed to the older generation, even to someone as well-heeled as Stanley Ormerod.

'All right, if you're set on it. I'm sure we can handle the work side of it. And as you say, it will do Michelle and the children good to get some sun and sea air, at the end of the winter.'

David Edmonds tried to prevent the relief from creeping into his voice. 'That's great, Stanley! Thank you for being so understanding. The family will really appreciate it. And I shall return to the office bronzed and fit, a giant refreshed, ready to do great things when the new selling season gets under way!'

He put down the phone and prepared to break the news of the wonderful surprise to his wife and family. Better to do it with the children there, he thought. Michelle wouldn't be able to question this sudden change of plans, in the face of their juvenile excitement. He'd better get one or two convincing reasons ready to put to her later; she was sure to question him about it, once the kids were safely in bed and asleep.

David was elated by this release from his immediate problems. Then he realized that he hadn't really solved them. He might merely have postponed a crisis, rather than averted it. He had better put his mind to what he should do to cover his tracks in the longer term, rather than think how clever he was in removing himself from the scene.

But nothing could disguise the fact that this was a good time for him to be out of the country. He'd get something booked for the end of next week, and keep a low profile in the interim.

Eleven

'I tell you, this is just what I need!'

After watching Tommy Bloody Tucker on television, Percy Peach felt entitled to a diversion. He needed to forget it all, to convince himself that there were other and better things in life.

Suiting the action to his words, he buried his face dramatically and expertly into the very centre of Lucy Blake's scantily covered bosom.

Lucy said practically, 'It's too cold in your bedroom in February to cavort about like this in a semi-naked state.' She shivered.

It was a mistake. The shiver agitated her uncontained breasts, and Percy took it for an erotic response to his gesture. He uttered a low, prolonged moan of sexual satisfaction. It was muffled, but exquisitely expressive.

Lucy knew from experience that the man wouldn't be easily dislodged. It would take some remarkable force of nature or some unrefusable offer to do it. She decided on the latter. 'Never mind these half measures! Let's get into bed and get on with it. At least I'll be warm there and—'

It was an unrefusable offer all right. The face buried between her soft breasts uttered another, more urgent moan of pleasure and agreement, came up briefly for air, and moved his powerful legs purposefully forward. The two of them fell in disarray upon the bed. Percy, so dapper in dress, so orderly in his normal daily life, thought this sensual confusion was a very heaven.

'I like a woman capable of sexual experiment,' he said

appreciatively. 'I hadn't thought of the effect a moustache might have in tickling up nipples myself, but I must say the effect is quite impressive. Let me just—'

'Don't just anything!' said Lucy Blake hastily. 'And I can assure you that any effect you think your moustache might have had is purely accidental.' She tried to examine her nipples surreptitiously in the mirror, but the light was too dim in Percy Peach's bedroom for her to be certain whether his moustache had secured the effect he claimed. You could never be sure with Percy, when he got exuberant.

She should not have taken her eyes off him. He made a swift grab at her waist, secured it, and allowed his hands to stray downwards, to the accompaniment of a succession of passionate groans which she would have thought was beyond the range of any single human being.

'Pray leave my pants alone, Sir Jasper!' she said demurely, transferring his hands downward to her knees. It was a game they played from time to time, ever since the night when she had claimed that Percy's moustache reminded her of the aristocratic villain in a Victorian melodrama. The appendage was not long enough for him to twirl in the approved lecherous manner, but he mimed a valiant attempt to do so, then encircled her hips with his arms and began to stroke the front of her thighs appreciatively, with his moustache now clamped hard against the point where her buttocks began their separation. The groans began again, increasing in volume and intensity.

Whatever she did, she mustn't let him know that his moustache was tickling her there, and still less that she found it rather an agreeable sensation. She said as primly as she could, 'Pray desist from caressing my thighs, Sir Jasper!'

Percy removed his face reluctantly from her rear cleavage. 'So I'm not to touch your glorious bosom, m'dear, and I'm not to stroke your silk-smooth thighs, eh?' He leered into her face for a second, raising his eyebrows in what he thought a convincingly Victorian fashion. 'Then I'll just have to settle for the area in between the two, won't I?'

Which he promptly did, clasping her to him with strong containing arms, giving free rein to hands which were suddenly amazingly versatile in the things they could perpetrate. Lucy was giggling too much to put up effective resistance. She eventually extracted herself and slid between the protective sheets of Percy's double bed. Her lover went back to his normal voice and complained that it was totally unfair that a woman so well-rounded should at the same time be as slippery as an eel.

'You should be grateful that I'm warming the bed for you. It's bloody freezing in here, Percy Peach!'

Another mistake: he sprang upon her with the whoop of an Indian brave and set about warming her up.

Not such a mistake after all, though. When all the joking that passed for foreplay was over – and she liked the fact that she was never quite sure when the laughter ended and the serious business began – Percy was an effective and considerate lover, vigorous and tender by turns. Totally in harmony with her needs and her desires.

Twenty minutes later, she stretched luxuriously and said in the Lancashire accent which was another of their affectations, 'Eeeeh, that were champion, Percy Peach!'

'It were that, lass! I'd have a fag and study the ceiling, if I hadn't given up the habit to preserve my perfect body for young women like thee.'

They thee'd and thou'd each other for a while, comfortably intimate in the winter darkness. Then Percy claimed that this too was an aphrodisiac, and added almost apologetically, 'Sithee, I'll just have to roger thee again, now lass!' and proceeded to do just that, in more leisurely and less urgent fashion than in their first coupling.

She remembered nothing else until Percy was standing by the bed with a mug of tea in the cold grey light of Saturday morning. 'It's cold out here, lass,' he said pathetically.

It was obviously true. His feet were very cold indeed. And the place where he wanted to warm them up was quite outrageous, but she didn't see how she could complain about it to anyone else.

They drank their tea without haste. They were going to work, with a murder case demanding to be solved, but no one would expect them in at the normal time on a Saturday. It was whilst they were stretching luxuriously, in those last minutes in a warm bed before they braved the world outside it, that Percy Peach said quietly, almost lazily, 'You'll have to be thinking about making an honest man of me one of these days, Lucy Blake.'

It was Percy who had voiced the thought which had been drifting through her mind, not her. And this was the twenty-sixth of February, almost the twenty-ninth, that day when women were traditionally allowed to propose marriage – 2004 was a leap year.

She was glad that Agnes Blake, so anxious to be a grand-mother, had not heard those words from the man she was so determined to see as a son-in-law.

'There's a nun waiting to see you, sir.'

Peach glared suspiciously at DC Brendan Murphy. 'Saturday morning isn't the time for jokes, Brendan.' After the night of blissful sexual pleasure he had experienced, the last person he expected to confront in the cold light of a winter morning was a nun. The Catholic upbringing Percy had dispensed with many years ago was suddenly back with him. Sister Bernadette had rapped his fingers with a ruler for any illicit excitements he had enjoyed in his primary school. And the guilt complex built into him by clerics in his youth told him that pleasures as absolute as those enjoyed with Lucy Blake must surely be illicit.

Brendan Murphy had lived all of his twenty-four years in Brunton, despite his name, but his Irish background gave him a fair idea of the thoughts racing through his Chief Inspector's mind. He grinned. 'It's true, sir! She said she'd wait for you. She's complete with habit and wimple. Probably using her rosary beads to fill in the time while she waits. Can't think what you've been up to, sir, to bring a sister in here, asking for you personally.'

'Find out what she wants and get rid of her, please, Brendan.'
'She says it's connected with the Sunita Akhtar case, sir. Asked to speak to the man in charge. I didn't think she deserved Tucker.'
'Then I'll see her in my office. Immediately.'
She was a squat figure, made to seem even squatter by the black dress which reached almost to the floor and the white starched linen which encircled her forehead, making it seem broader than it would normally have done. When Murphy ushered her in, Peach stood up, moved awkwardly towards her and then stopped. He had been about to shake hands with her, but he hesitated to touch a nun.
'I'm Chief Inspector Peach. I believe you wanted to see me.' He slid a chair carefully behind her, anxious to avoid the accidental desecration of brushing against a nun's bum.
'Sister Josephine. And I won't break if you touch me. I'm not usually dressed like this.'
He realized that she was even more nervous than he was, and forced a smile. 'Childhood stays with you, Sister. I had some unfortunate experiences with a certain Sister Bernadette, a long time ago in another life.'
She smiled at him, a reaction which lit up her face all the more because he could see so little of it. 'We've most of us had experiences like that, if we grew up as Papists, Chief Inspector. If it's any consolation to you, wearing the habit comes almost as strangely to me as interviewing a nun does to you. I never wear it at work. Most of the people at the hospice don't even know I'm a nun. Not the patients, anyway. But the order still like us to wear the habit when we go out for any length of time. And it did get me a seat on the bus on the way here.'
He found it difficult to guess how old she was. He hadn't realized until now how much he relied on the lines in the forehead in assessing age. He said, 'DC Murphy tells me that you want to speak to me about the Sunita Akhtar case. Though I can't imagine what—'
'I was in that squat, Mr Peach.' She looked happy to have

got that fact out, as if she had taken the first and most demand-ing step in what was going to be a difficult process.

'At twenty-six Sebastopol Terrace.'

'That's the one. I was surprised you could still pinpoint the house when I saw how everything had been flattened.'

'The forensic people can do that. They identify even tiny fragments of wood as coming from a common source. And number twenty-six still had a front door and a number.' He did not know why he was telling her this. Perhaps they were both still a little embarrassed with each other.

'I see. Well, I heard your Chief Superintendent asking for people to come forward, and like a good citizen I came.' She smiled wanly at the idea of herself as a good citizen. 'I told you, I was in that squat.'

'You mean you visited it. When exactly would—'

'I mean I lived there. At the same time as Sunita Akhtar.'

With the experience he had by now, nothing should have shocked him any more. But he found the thought of this demure nun living in a squat hard to take in. She had mentioned working in a hospice, and he realized now that he had conjured up a Victorian picture of a charitable religious woman visit-ing the homeless in that squat, probably dispensing soup, with the New Testament in her other hand. He reached for a pad and a ball pen, giving himself time to come to grips with this strange idea. 'Forgive me, Sister, but I find the idea of you living in a squat rather difficult.'

'I wasn't a nun then.' Despite her nervousness, a smile came unbidden to her lips at his discomfiture, and he saw her for the first time as an attractive woman.

A phrase from Matthew Hayward came back to Peach, nagging at the edge of his consciousness – 'The women were called Jo and Emmy'. Was this that Jo, whom the pianist had remembered as a buxom girl in her early twenties, sitting in front of him now as the staid and sturdy Sister Josephine? He wracked his brain for any further details the man had given to him. Strong nose, he'd said, a good-looking face in a striking sort of a way.

Well, it fitted, once you stripped away the religious trappings from the face. Without that uniform of piety this could well be an attractive woman with a strong, striking face. Beneath those black folds of the habit she might even be a buxom woman in her mid-thirties. He tried not to blush at that thought and said, 'Thank you for coming here. You'll appreciate that we need to know everything you can possibly tell us about what went on in Sebastopol Terrace in the early months of 1991.'

'That is why I'm here.'

'We've already spoken to one of the other occupants of that squat.' No harm in letting her know that whatever she had to say could be checked against other evidence, even if she was a nun.

'Matthew Hayward?'

He was absurdly disconcerted by this prompt response, when he had thought to put her on her back foot. 'You're still in touch with him?'

'No. I've followed his career from afar. I heard him on the radio the other night, playing the Emperor concerto with the Hallé. A patient of mine wanted to listen. He said Matt was going to be one of the greats. I hope he was right.'

'He's probably right. We were in the Bridgewater Hall, waiting to speak to Matthew Hayward after that concert. He got a tremendous reception. Your patient has good judgement.'

'Had, Chief Inspector. He died the next morning.' There was at once acceptance and compassion in the simple statement, without a trace of sentimentality. Percy Peach had the absurd, irrelevant thought that he'd like to be nursed by this woman, if someone told him he was dying.

He drew the pad towards him and said, 'Tell me what you remember of Mr Hayward.'

'Matt. He'll always be young Matt, to me. Not that he was much younger than me, at the time. We were both pretty wet behind the ears, when I look back on it.'

'How did you come to be there?'

'My mother died of cancer when I was eighteen. I should

have been going to university at the end of that school year, but I missed a lot of schooling to nurse her through the last months. I'd never been as close to my dad as I was to her. When he started bringing home other women in the year after Mum died, I couldn't stand it. We had a series of rows and I moved out after the last one. I lived at a friend's house for a couple of weeks, but it was obvious that I couldn't stay there. Her mother kept trying to get me to go back home. I wandered around those deserted houses one autumn day and ended up in the squat. Matt moved in just after me.'

'And moved out a fortnight after Sunita disappeared. Is that correct?'

'Yes, I think so. About that time, anyway: she'd certainly disappeared before he went.' She wondered how much this calm man with the piercing black eyes and the startlingly bald head knew about what had gone on all those years ago. This was a completely alien world to her. She had never even set foot in a police station until this morning.

Peach nodded quietly. 'Do you think he killed her?'

It was shocking in its calm, matter-of-fact delivery. The figure in black on the other side of his desk looked very calm to Percy Peach, and that was a challenge in itself.

'No! Of course he didn't!'

'Someone did, Sister Josephine. Almost certainly one of the five people who were living with her at twenty-six Sebastopol Terrace.' He studied her coolly, reminding himself that even nuns could have awful secrets.

'I'm sure it wasn't Matt!'

'How sure? He was her lover, wasn't he?'

She felt a tremor at the thought of how much this man already knew, how difficult it would be to prevent him from discovering everything. 'Yes, he was, for a time. But not at the time when she disappeared.'

For the first time, she was looking at the desk, not at him. Perhaps she did not like discussing sexual liaisons. Too bad: this was a murder investigation. He said, 'Who broke off their affair?'

'She did.'

That was definite enough. 'Then look at it from our point of view for a moment. The boy was rejected by a girl who subsequently disappears, almost certainly because she was murdered. Her body is hidden in the deserted house next door to number twenty-six. A couple of weeks later, Matthew Hayward himself leaves the squat and never returns. Suspicious?'

'Yes. But I don't think Matt killed Sunita.'

'Then who did?'

'I don't know. I didn't come here to tell you that.'

He let a few seconds drag by, knowing that eventually she would have to look up into his face again. 'Did you kill the girl, Sister Josephine?'

'No.' She did not seem to find the idea as preposterous as it sounded to him.

'I had to ask.'

'And no doubt you will have to keep me in the frame, until you know otherwise. That's what you call it, isn't it? In the frame. I pick up all kinds of fragments in the television room at the hospice, you see!' She smiled at him, mocking him a little.

He had the uncomfortable thought that she certainly seemed cool and competent enough to be a murderer, if circumstances had required it. He allowed himself an answering smile. 'I think you had better tell me everything you can about the other people in that squat. Start with Sunita Akhtar, please.'

He was surprised how much this seemed to upset her. Perhaps it was just the thought of murder, of this girl she had lived with being violently dispatched by one of her fellow-residents. 'She was a disturbed girl, Sunita.'

'Can you enlarge upon that? First of all, can you confirm that she had left home because her parents wanted her to contract an arranged marriage?'

'Yes. She hadn't anyone else in mind at the time, but her father wanted her to marry an older man, whom she didn't like anyway. I think it was her father rather than her mother, but of course in her culture, fathers were powerful men, even more so thirteen years ago than now.'

'Would you say Sunita was emotionally disturbed whilst she was with you in that house?'

This time it was she who paused, taking the time to consider her answer carefully. 'I'd say she was when she first came there. Matt was a nice lad, but I think at that time she'd have given herself to any man of her own age who was sympathetic and attracted to her.'

'So you'd say she was unstable?'

'No, I'm not sure I'd say that. Did Matt tell you that she was?'

'He thought she might have offered her sexual favours around, after she finished with him. Even sold them, perhaps.'

'She didn't do that.' The reply was prompt, even terse.

'You're sure of it?'

'Yes. Sunita was desperate for money at times, but she didn't resort to that.' It was suddenly important to her to convince him.

'It's rather important to us, this question. You see, if Sunita was selling herself to people outside the squat, it opens up a new range of possibilities about her death.'

'She wasn't.' Again the reply came promptly on the heels of her questioner's words.

Peach wondered if this was prudery, whether she was embarrassed to talk to a man about sexual matters. But she hadn't seemed in any way inhibited previously. 'You must see that this increases the likelihood that she was killed by one of your friends in the squat.'

'Yes, I do see that. But it doesn't alter the facts. And I wouldn't describe all of them as friends. When you're desperate enough to be living like that, you can't choose your company. We were thrown together by a common need for a roof over our heads, not by anything else we had in common.'

Peach nodded. 'I understand that, Sister. And this is the kind of frankness we need if we are to find out who killed Sunita. Tell me what you remember of the other occupants of that house, please.'

'Matt you know about. Did he tell you about Wally?'

'A little, yes. But I need your impression. It may be quite different.'

'I doubt that. He was a bull of a man. When I look back at life in that place now, I think Wally controlled all of us. He certainly did exactly as he wanted to, and I don't think any of us would have dared to cross him.'

'How old do you think he was?'

'I think of him as much older than I was then. He probably wasn't. I'd guess now that he was then about twenty-four or five.'

'We need a description of him.'

She nodded slowly, picking words which came oddly from beneath a nun's headdress. 'Powerfully built, but not all that tall. Swarthy; he had a beard, which I think he grew whilst we were in that place. We didn't have hot water on tap, so shaving couldn't have been easy. And he exuded menace, physical menace – I always felt he'd fell me with a back-hander, if I upset him.'

'Did you see him hit anyone?'

'No. I think we were all a bit frightened of him, and that was probably enough. He was there when I got there: I don't know what had gone on with the others before then.'

'Accent?'

'Difficult. Not from Brunton, I'd have said, but probably Lancashire. Not Liverpool, definitely not a Scouser – I've nursed one or two of them since then and I'd know.' For a second an affectionate smile of remembrance lit up her smooth countenance.

'Have you any idea where he is now?'

'Not a clue, I'm afraid. I haven't even thought about him for years. Haven't wanted to, as a matter of fact, whereas I've been delighted to keep tabs on Matty Hayward's progress. I'd be pretty sure that Wally wasn't his proper name, by the way. He was there when I landed in that squat, and he was there when I left it.'

'Which was when?'

'May, 1991. About a month after Matt, or perhaps a little more. I went back to the school where I'd spent six years. The nuns gave me work in the kitchen, encouraged me to take a few exams. As you can see, I eventually decided to enter the order. But they've allowed me to do my own thing in the hospice for the last three years. I said I'd found my calling, that I was staying there, even if they took the habit away from me. So far, they haven't.' She lifted her arms a little beneath the black folds, let them fall back to her sides, and grinned at him. He saw in that moment the feisty, independent woman she had been, the difficult opponent she could still be.

'Two other people were in the house at the time of this death. I need everything you can give me about them.'

She nodded slowly. 'Billy. That was the other man. Very black, very sharp. Slung out by his stepfather. He was the youngest of all of us, but in some ways he knew more about surviving in a squat than any of us. He'd got used to living on his wits from when he was a kid of ten or so, I think.'

'What kind of relationship did he have with Sunita?'

Again he fancied she was frowning, but he could not see her forehead behind the white linen. Again he was forced to realize how much you needed the whole face to gauge how people were reacting.

She said, 'They were close. He educated her in the ways of the squat. Told her not to ask questions, how to make the most of the food we got, how to keep warm on winter nights.'

'Sexually close?'

'No. I think he was quite keen on Sunita. They were the two non-whites in the group, and I think Billy wanted her to feel a common bond. She was grateful to him for his help, but there was nothing sexual between them.'

He wondered for a moment how she could be so certain of that. But there was little privacy in a squat, where everyone was living from hand to mouth and the occupants tended to congregate in one room for warmth for a lot of the time. He said, 'But you think they were close to each other?'

'Yes. They were good friends.' Her face clouded a little.

103

'They used to go next door together, to what Billy called raves. At number twenty-eight.'

Percy Peach's heart sank. A new dimension to the crime, with God knew how many other people brought into its periphery. 'You'd better tell me what you know about these gatherings.'

'I didn't understand them at the time. Remember, I was a convent girl who'd led a very sheltered life, until I arrived there. I think now that there were drugs involved. Sunita came back high, and I know she didn't drink. I don't think they were "raves" at all, not as I'd understand the word. Things were very quiet, for a start. I think that there were only a few people there, and that they probably just sat around and smoked pot. I wouldn't know whether there was anything stronger available. Fourteen or fifteen years ago, drugs were around, but we weren't as conscious of them. But you'd know that!' She gave him a wan smile.

'I wasn't around here then, but no one thought Brunton had a major drugs problem at that time. Did any of the others take part in these gatherings at number twenty-eight?'

'No. Only Billy at first. Then Sunita went with him, not more than two or three times, as far as I can remember.' She paused, studying him closely. 'That's where the body was found, isn't it?'

'Yes. Do you know anything about the man who organized these meetings?'

'No. I've tried hard to dig something out of my memory over the last few hours, but I don't think I ever knew. Probably didn't want to know, at the time. I know that I didn't like Sunita slipping off like that, but it paid you to mind your own business, in a squat.'

'What else can you remember about this Billy?'

'He was average height, slim and athletic. Quite a sportsman, I think. He'd had a trial with the Rovers, but he reckoned he'd blown it by being unreliable.' Her face suddenly brightened with recall. 'Billy went off to Preston North End, though. That's just this minute come back to me. They took him on, gave him an apprenticeship, or whatever you'd call it in sporting terms. He said he was going to make a go of it this time. He was still very young, you know, probably only seventeen or eighteen at the time. And they fitted him up with digs in Preston, which got him out of the squat. Some time in the summer of 1991, that would be.'

It gave them a start. With average luck, someone would still be around at Preston who remembered a slim black boy named Billy arriving there, thirteen and a half years earlier. A boy who had apparently tried for a relationship with Sunita Akhtar, and been rebuffed.

Peach looked at his now encouragingly lengthy notes. 'That just leaves the other girl in the set-up.'

'Emmy. Tall, shapely, streetwise. Three or four inches taller than me, so probably about five feet nine. Twenty-one. I remember her announcing that it was her birthday, one bitterly cold day in January.' For a moment, she was back in that bleak world where she seemed to have been another person entirely. 'We weren't particularly close, Emmy and I. We came from very different backgrounds. She'd been brought up hard, with a mother who brought home a succession of different "uncles" for the girl to cope with. She had a low opinion of men in general, as you might expect, but she didn't have much time for me, either. I can understand why: I was still wet behind the ears, as I said earlier, and Em wasn't the most patient of women.'

'I'm told she was a blonde.'

She reminded herself again that she wasn't his only source of information about these people. 'Yes. I'm sorry, didn't I say that? I think she was a natural blonde, too. It wasn't easy to do anything sophisticated with your hair, in that place. In case you're wondering, I'm a brunette, under this lot!' She flicked her hand briefly towards her head.

'What about her relationships with the others?'

'She was a tough cookie, was Emmy. She even stood up to Wally, when she felt she needed to. Mind you, most of the time she kept herself to herself, like the rest of us. But she seemed to have more confidence that she was going to survive and go on to better things than anyone else in there.'

'How did she get on with Sunita?'

'I don't think she liked her much. Emmy had a contempt for her naivety, for a start – but she felt that for me too.' She paused, as if wondering whether to speculate further. 'But she seemed to resent Sunita being there at all, sometimes. She seemed to think she was a source of danger for us.'

'As she may have been, for someone. Someone who felt a need to remove her permanently from the scene.'

'Yes. I'm well used to death at the hospice, but I've never had to confront one like this before. Forgive me, but I find the thought of Sunita dying alone like that, with all her life in front of her, very disturbing.'

Suddenly she was weeping, dropping silent tears into a man's large white handkerchief which had arrived in her hand from nowhere. It was odd, after her previous composure.

Peach said, 'Thank you for coming in here this morning, Sister Josephine. I can assure you that what you have told me will be most useful to the team investigating this killing. All we can do for Sunita now is to find her killer and bring him to justice.'

She composed herself and stood up. 'I understand what you say, but I've become accustomed to thinking in terms of divine justice, which is sometimes rather different from the human sort in which you have to deal.' The handkerchief had disappeared as mysteriously as it had arrived. 'Thank you for being so considerate. I think I've given you all I can. If I think of anything else in the days to come, I shall be in touch with you.'

She was back in the privacy of her room at the hospice before she allowed herself to analyse what she had said to that strange, understanding Chief Inspector Peach. He seemed to think she'd been helpful to him.

She hadn't been able to tell him everything, of course.

Twelve

David Edmonds could not remember when he had last been in the office on a Sunday. Ten years ago at least, he reckoned, back in the days when he was a trainee negotiator. Before he had proved himself in the estate agency business. Before he had married the boss's daughter.

It wasn't a bad thing, opening up the offices of Ormerod's Limited and spending a quiet Sunday morning there alone. It gave you privacy. He enjoyed being a family man with three young children, enjoyed the image of wholesome respectability, but he had almost forgotten what it was like to have the luxury of being alone with your own plans for a couple of hours.

He had booked them all into a good hotel in Madeira, got quite a good deal with a late booking. He took one or two pictures of the swimming pool and the dining room off the Internet to show to the children; he would be greeted as a hero when he returned home at lunchtime. Then he rang his father-in-law to give him the news; no harm in letting the boss know that you were hard at work on a Sunday morning, when others were still in bed with the Sunday papers. 'I've arranged a couple of viewings for this afternoon,' he informed Stanley Ormerod. 'It's good to have time to myself in the office: I want to tie up all the loose ends before I go off to Madeira, as I said on Friday.'

There were four properties which were marked as 'Sold, subject to contract'. David Edmonds left memos for the staff concerned, instructing them to push solicitors for definite exchange dates, to harry the prospective purchasers a little to make sure they were serious. People talked about gazumping, but much more often it was the purchasers who let you down, in his experience.

On Monday morning, he would tell the staff in the office to stir things up a little, to let these people know that there were other people interested in buying these houses, whether that was actually the case or not. It wasn't strictly ethical, but it was what you had to do to hurry things along, to clinch sales. The younger people who worked for him needed to understand that, to learn how the world of property operates. But he'd remind them of it tomorrow, rather than include it in the memos: it wasn't sensible to put things like that in writing.

In fact, business overall was pretty quiet at this time of the year. No doubt it would pick up as usual around Easter, as he had told his father-in-law when arranging his fortnight away from the place. In not much more than an hour, he had cleared his desk and was wondering what else he could do to show his industry.

He made a phone call to an elderly couple who were threatening to take their Edwardian house off the market because they had not been able to find the bungalow they wanted. 'I understand your position, Mr Robinson, of course I do. This is probably the most important single decision you will make in the rest of your life.' He mouthed the words he had used so often before, forced the concern into his voice.

Flicking through the list of properties available, he half-listened to the frail voice telling him of sleepless nights, of how the situation was making this senior citizen's wife ill. Then he launched into his spiel. 'It's your decision, of course. But it's my duty to offer you the benefit of my experience in these things, which now stretches to many years. That's part of the service we offer. And I have to tell you, Mr Robinson, that I think you would be very foolish to with-draw from the sale at this stage. Very foolish indeed, in fact. We have secured a sale for you at very nearly the full asking price, and I would be less than honest if I did not state my opinion that you would be most unwise to turn away from that now.'

'I suppose we could fit into that bungalow we saw on Friday, if we got rid of most of our furniture,' the old man said uncertainly.

'It's an attractive place. Pleasant garden,' said David, reading from the details in front of him: he had never seen the property himself.

'Yes. It's rather overlooked, compared with the privacy we're used to here. But I suppose one has to make certain sacrifices, if—'

'Moving is all about compromises, Mr Robinson. Take my word for that!' David assured him confidently. 'No one gets exactly what he wants, unless he has millions to spend.'

'Well, I'll have another word with Edith, then. Tell her we ought to go ahead with the sale whilst we have the chance.'

'That would certainly be my advice, based on years of experience. I've seen too many people regret losing the courage of their convictions, believe me!'

'It's very good of you to take the trouble to ring us on a Sunday morning.'

'Not at all, Mr Robinson. I just thought I'd like to give you my full attention, whilst things were quiet here and there were no distractions.'

He smiled slowly as he put down the phone. With a bit of luck, he'd have the lucrative sale of their big house confirmed and the Robinsons lined up to buy that bungalow before he disappeared for two weeks on Friday. Nothing like leaving a tidy ship behind when you went away.

He was locking the door of the office when the voice behind him said interrogatively, 'Mr David Edmonds?'

He turned to look up into the fresh face of a man perhaps ten years or more younger than he was. 'I'm afraid we're closed for the day now. The office will be open from nine o'clock tomorrow morning, if you—'

'I'm Detective Constable Murphy. We'd like you to answer

some questions for us, in connection with the investigation of a serious crime.'

David Edmonds was not the only man at work on this last Sunday in February. Thomas Bulstrode Tucker had put in an unprecedented appearance at the Brunton Police Station. He was dressed in bright plus twos and a garish yellow sweater which his wife had given him for Christmas, which you could hardly call plain clothes. The Head of CID had been on his way to Brunton Golf Club, but had felt the impulse to pop into the station for half an hour, leave a memo for the absent Peach to show he had been there, and depart swiftly for his afternoon of golf.

The plan went wrong from the start. DCI Peach was already in the station when Tucker arrived there. And he came up to brief him on the Sunita Akhtar case, pinning his chief in his peacock garb behind the big desk.

'You don't know who was in charge of CID work in this particular district in 1991, do you, sir?' Percy Peach knew very well that it was Tucker, then a humble Detective Inspector, but it might be as well to remind his Chief Superintendent that he knew.

'Oh, I don't think there's any mileage in going back thirteen years, do you? Probably Harrison, I should think: he was the CID Superintendent at that time.' Tucker thought it was pretty safe to name a man who had been dead and buried for three years.

'Just curiosity, sir. One of the necessary attributes of the successful CID man, my first boss used to say. No one in the police seems to have paid much attention to the occupation of twenty-six Sebastopol Terrace by squatters at the time. An occupation which seems to have resulted in murder.' Peach shook his head sadly on the thought of this grave omission.

'I hope you're not trying to divert me, Peach. I hope you're not trying to disguise the fact that you're not making the progress on this case that you promised me when I went public to the media about it.'

Peach recalled no such promise. But that was par for the course; Peach consoled himself with a metaphor which reminded him that Tucker was a very poor golfer indeed. 'We're making steady progress, sir. But there's a lot more evidence to be unearthed yet! I say, that's rather good, isn't it, considering this case concerns a body buried for all those years?'

'Abandon the schoolboy humour and give me your report, please. I'm a busy man, you know!'

Peach stared pointedly at the empty desk in front of Tucker for a moment. 'We've found another of the people who were in that squat, sir. Another suspect, you'd have to say.'

'Indeed I would! And I hope a rather more likely one than the eminent concert pianist you produced for me on Thursday.'

'Matter of opinion, that, sir. Like to keep an open mind on these things. It's a woman, sir, this one.'

'Ah! Much more promising, I'd say.'

Peach wondered what the feminists who were now rampant in the police service would make of that. 'She seems to have been in the squat for the whole time that Sunita Akhtar was there, sir. Left a month or so after the girl disappeared.'

'Promising, Peach. A gut feeling tells me you may have chanced upon a prime suspect here. It may well be that—'

'She's a nun, sir.' Peach was rather proud of the timing of his deadpan delivery.

'A what?'

'A nun, sir. A Roman Catholic religious. They traditionally dress in—'

'Yes, yes! I know very well what a nun is, you fool. Do you take me for an idiot?'

Frequently, thought Percy grimly. It's one of the things which helps to keep me sane. 'This nun works in a hospice, sir. Very highly regarded, very dedicated and efficient, apparently. The secretary says the place couldn't exist without her. I made certain enquiries about her when she'd been in to see me, sir. Just as well I did, if you think she's now emerged as our prime suspect.' He kept his countenance studiously blank and fixed his gaze intently upon the white wall behind Tucker's head.

Tucker was already regretting his impulsive decision to come into the station. 'Have you any reason at all to think that this lady killed that Pakistani girl?'

'Not yet, sir. But I'm keeping an open mind, as I said. And now that I have the benefit of your overview, now that I know you consider her our prime suspect, I feel bolder about the situation.'

'Bolder? In what way?'

'Well, I thought I might rough her up a bit, sir. Give her a touch of the old third degree. Not exactly the Spanish Inquisition; no thumbscrews or—'

'You'll do no such thing, Peach!' Tucker's panic rang loud and clear through the almost deserted station.

'Not even the strong light shone straight into her face, sir?' Peach's disappointment was exquisite to behold.

'YOU WILL HANDLE THIS WITH KID GLOVES, PEACH! Is that absolutely clear?' Tucker gripped the edge of the desk in front of him and half-rose from his chair.

'Yes, sir. If you say so, sir. But it's difficult to get the information we need, playing things strictly by the book, isn't it?' Peach shook his head sadly at the restraints which were inflicted upon the modern policeman.

'If that's all you have to offer, I shan't waste any more of my time.' Tucker was already suspecting that the man was sending him up, that he had reacted to these suggestions about interrogating the nun in exactly the way that he had been intended to. But the wretched man kept such a scrupulously blank face that his chief was never quite sure of him. And you couldn't take any chances with public relations these days, especially where a sensitive area like religion was concerned.

'Sister Josephine did point the way to another suspect, sir,' said Peach tentatively.

Tucker settled back into his chair with a sigh. 'What have you produced this time? A bishop? A judge?'

112

'Very droll, sir. I like it!' Peach chuckled appreciatively. 'No, nothing like that. Rather a nuisance, actually, but it's got to be investigated. Another suspect, this time from outside the squat itself. A man called Dave, who held drug parties in the empty house next door.'

Tucker thought this was promising, but having risen once to Peach's bait, he was going to be more cautious this time. He nodded sagely. 'Drugs, eh! He could have been dealing, you know, this man.'

Good to see you haven't lost your talent for the blindin' bleedin' obvious, Tommy Bloody Tucker. Peach said stiffly, 'Yes, sir. That seems entirely possible. And diligent research has unearthed the fact that this man is still operating in Brunton today, sir.'

Tucker almost said that this sounded like a much more promising suspect. But once bitten, twice shy. 'We'd better have him in for questioning, then. Petty criminal, is he? Or has he gone on to larger scale villainy in the last ten years?'

'You could say that, sir, I suppose.'

'Dealing, is he?'

'Not in drugs, sir. He's an estate agent.'

'An estate agent?' Tucker's jaw dropped appealingly, in the reaction which Percy always thought denoted a small triumph for him.

He let go the chance to instruct his dumbfounded chief in what an estate agent did. 'Partner in Ormerod's Estate Agency and Auctioneers, apparently. Of course, he's no longer just Dave. The man now calls himself David Edmonds, Managing Director.'

'David Edmonds?'

'That's the chap, sir.' Peach brightened, his emotions moving in inverse ratio to Tucker's distress. 'You don't happen to know him, do you, sir?'

Tucker said dully, as if he had wandered into a nightmare, 'He was initiated into my Lodge last month.'

Peach allowed his delight to spread in a slow smile over his face. 'I didn't know that, sir.'

113

Tucker glared at him suspiciously. 'You didn't?'

'No, sir. I haven't even seen the rogue yet. DC Murphy has just brought him into the station.' Peach mounted his smile all over again, developing it into a growing excitement. 'But you realize what this means, sir? You're aware of my research which demonstrates that a Freemason is four times more likely to commit a serious crime in this area than an ordinary citizen. The fact that this Edmonds is a Freemason means that statistically there is an excellent chance that—'

'PEACH! Of course I am aware of this ridiculous so-called research of yours! I could hardly be otherwise, when you thrust it at me at every opportunity. And I have to tell you that I am sure that David Edmonds will prove to be a young man of complete integrity. He was proposed for membership by his father-in-law, Stanley Ormerod, who is a former Master of the Lodge.'

'By Jove, sir! The owner of Ormerod's himself. The oldest established property dealers in Brunton, as they call themselves! This would make the local headlines, if Edmonds did prove to be our man! Give us some very useful publicity that would, if we were able to make an arrest. We need good publicity, as you're always reminding us, sir.'

'Now listen to me, Peach. Listen very carefully. You have so far provided me as suspects with an eminent pianist, a compassionate nun, and a leading and well-respected local businessman. It's not an impressive list, is it?'

'Impresses me, sir. Intriguing, I'd say. And I must remind you that they were all in or around that squat in Sebastopol Terrace in 1991. That squat which no one in Brunton CID seemed to be interested in, at the time.'

Tucker breathed deeply, trying to still his annoyance. 'Take it from me that your killer will not be found among these three. You will need to look much further.'

'Yes, sir. You don't think it's worth my talking to this David Edmonds, then?'

Tucker attempted not to speak through clenched teeth. 'Of course you must speak to him. If he was really there at that time, which I find it difficult to believe, he may be able to throw some light on this crime.'

'Yes, sir. You wouldn't like to interview him yourself? Exercise your usual diplomacy, keep me from putting my foot in—'

'Of course not!' It was Tucker's automatic reaction to any suggestion that he might be involved at the crime-face. Then he thought of a rationalization. 'It wouldn't be appropriate for me to be involved directly, as a friend of David Edmonds. Or an acquaintance, I should say.' Better distance himself, just in case of the incredible possibility that this pleasant young man might be a killer.

'Very well, sir. I shall see him myself. Immediately, in fact.'

That announcement did not reassure Tucker, but he thought the best option was to be out of the place quickly. He cursed again his decision to show his face at the station on a Sunday. 'Yes. Well, you'd better be about your business,' he said.

He waited until a safe interval had elapsed after Peach's departure, then crept quietly to his door and opened it cautiously. He was feeling very conspicuous, in his yellow sweater, bright tartan plus twos and green stockings. But with luck, he should be able to slip out quietly: there was no more than a skeleton staff in the place on Sunday morning.

The coast seemed to be clear. He crept quietly down four flights of stairs and took the side door into the car park without encountering a single officer.

He had the door open, was about to slide his garishly clad frame into the driving seat, when a voice from above him said, 'Enjoy your golf, sir!'

Percy Peach was leaning out of the window of his office, wearing the widest and blandest of his vast range of smiles.

Thirteen

'I hope this won't take very long. I'm willing to help, of course, but I can't think what I can possibly have to tell you.'

David Edmonds had spoken as soon as they came into the interview room, before they had even introduced themselves. That meant he was nervous.

Percy Peach liked that. He gave the man a thin smile and studied him unhurriedly. Good suit; formal shirt and tie, even on a Sunday morning. Tallish, with well-groomed brown hair above a long head. Slim build, with just a little flab at the paunch and beneath the chin, probably from comfortable living.

He put a new tape into the cassette recorder, glanced at his watch, and announced, 'Interview with David Edmonds begins at 12.31. Present, Chief Detective Inspector Peach and Detective Sergeant Blake.'

There was no need for the tape: the man hadn't been cautioned, hadn't even been brought here under arrest. Officially, he was helping the police with their enquiries, of his own free will. But Percy found that being taped added a little pressure for interviewees, and he wasn't averse to that.

As if he read these thoughts, David Edmonds nodded at the recorder and said, 'Is there really any need for this?'

'Probably not, sir. But we find that people are less inclined to change what they have said to us when they are asked to sign a written statement, when it has been recorded. Do you have a problem with being taped?' He allowed his mobile black eyebrows to rise in surprise above the smile.

'No. No, of course I don't. I've nothing to hide, have I?'

David cursed himself for the nervous giggle which came unbidden on the end of his words.

'Remains to be seen, sir. I do hope not.'

David made an extravagant show of looking at his watch. 'I really should be home by now. My wife will no doubt be wondering where I've got to. I trust this won't take long.'

'Not very long, sir, if you co-operate fully. If it takes longer than we expect, you can always give Mrs Edmonds a ring. Let her know you're in the nick.'

Edmonds licked his lips, looked from this grim figure to the shapely girl with the chestnut hair beside him, and folded his arms. He had surprisingly big hands, with long, slender fingers. He said as firmly as he could, 'You'd better get on with it, whatever it is.'

'Much the best idea, I agree, sir. We'd like to talk to you about a house in Sebastopol Terrace. Number twenty-six, to be precise.'

'Did we sell this property? I'm afraid I don't recall it. I'm only in overall charge, you know, and we now have three branches at Ormerod's.'

It was a good reply, an expert bit of fencing. But Peach had seen the apprehension flash into the man's eyes when he had mentioned the name of the street and the number. 'You didn't sell the property, Mr Edmonds. It was condemned, eighteen years ago. The last legitimate residents were moved out of the house in 1989. It is the first few months of 1991 that we are concerned with.'

'I see. Then I can't see what I have to offer you.'

'How old are you, Mr Edmonds?'

'Thirty-seven. What is the relevance of that?'

'None. Except that I wouldn't expect someone of that age to be suffering from memory loss. I'm a year older than you, and I can recall perfectly well what I was doing thirteen years ago.'

It was insulting, but David's racing mind told him that he had much better swallow it. 'And so can I. I just don't see the relevance of this.'

'Don't you, sir? We have reason to believe that you were very familiar with what was going on at twenty-six Sebastopol Terrace. That you visited the empty house next door on several occasions and took part in what have been described to us as drugs parties.'

'I've never done drugs. I fear you've picked up the wrong man here, Chief Inspector. And I think you've wasted my time for quite long enough.' He tried to push back his chair and rise, but was disconcerted to find that it was bolted to the floor. And his own legs did not seem to be working as he would have wished.

Peach gave him a much grimmer smile. 'I do hope you're not going to refuse to co-operate, Mr Edmonds. Of course, if you feel that you need to have a lawyer present for this exchange, you are perfectly entitled to enlist one.'

David did a quick evaluation and saw the nightmare scenario of his wife, his children, his parents-in-law having to be told all about this section of his life. He said, 'Of course I don't need a lawyer! I'm sure I'm capable of clearing up this mis-understanding without any legal advice.'

'Misunderstanding.' Peach pursed his lips, then articulated every syllable of the word distinctly. 'I don't see any reason for any confusion here. We're saying that you were in that house at that time. That you brought drugs there for sale. Are you denying that?'

David wondered exactly how much they knew already. The man seemed very confident. Perhaps they were letting him tie himself in knots, and then would throw irrefutable evidence into his face, from someone who had been there at the time. He looked at the cassette, turning slowly, silently, incriminat-ingly. He wished now that he had objected to it in the first place, but it was too late to turn the clock back now. He couldn't see how he could do anything else but co-operate, or at least give the appearance of co-operating. He couldn't let them know everything, of course.

He said through dry lips, 'What is it you want to know?'

Peach nodded his approval of this change in attitude.

'Everything you can tell us about those parties at number twenty-eight, Mr Edmonds. And everything you know about the people occupying the squat next door at number twenty-six. So that we can put it together with what other people who were there at the time are telling us and see how far it tallies.'

'I deny that I was dealing in drugs, for a start.'

'Pity, that. There's a caution on record, you see. It reads to me as if you were very lucky to get away without a prosecution and a conviction at the time.'

'That wasn't at Sebastopol Terrace. That was months later, in the summer.'

'Your memory seems to be coming back quite well now, doesn't it? Very gratifying, that. Let me pinpoint it for you. You were cautioned for dealing in drugs on June the twenty-second 1991. You had been apprehended in the car park of a Brunton public house. Not in Sebastopol Terrace, as you now recall so vividly, though within a mile of it.'

For a wild moment, David wondered if he could deny it. He wanted to say that this man wasn't him at all, that this was a hideous case of mistaken identity, that the thick-headed police would be apologizing to him, when their error became obvious even to them. Instead, he heard himself saying dully, 'That was a long time ago, in another life.'

'Perhaps. Perhaps you could even demonstrate that to us, if we had the time. But it wouldn't be of any great interest to us, Mr Edmonds. Because it's that other life we're interested in, you see. And I think you know why that is.'

'The murder of Sunita Akhtar.' Again he hadn't meant to say that. The words had come unbidden to his lips.

'That is what we're investigating. Along with a team of almost thirty other officers.'

'I didn't kill her.'

'I'm glad to hear it. You won't expect us merely to accept that statement, however. It will need to be investigated. Which is what we are now beginning to do. You say you didn't kill her. So can you tell us who did?'

'No. I've no idea.'

119

'But you knew the girl.'

It was a statement, not a question. David wondered if he should have denied all knowledge of her, defied them to prove any connection between this caution he had received for dealing and the dead girl. But he didn't know how much they already knew, how much he could dare to lie. He said, 'I think I did. There was a Pakistani girl used to attend our little gatherings sometimes. I don't remember her name, not at this distance, but I'll assume it was her, if that's what you're telling me.'

You're lying, thought Peach. You know perfectly well it was Sunita, but you're trying to distance yourself from the girl. Why? I wonder. What else have you to hide? He leaned forward and said, 'It's my belief that you met Sunita Akhtar at number twenty-eight Sebastopol Terrace quite frequently.'

'I don't remember that. But it's too long ago for me to deny it. I've already said that I have only the haziest memories of the girl.'

'It's rather important to us that you start to remember more. Important to you as well, if you've nothing to hide. This is a murder investigation. We'd like to eliminate you from the list of suspects, if that proves to be possible.' Peach managed to imply that he thought this was very unlikely.

'She was one of a group. She didn't say a lot. She was quite attractive, I think. I can't remember much else about her.' He spoke tersely, picking his words like one anxious not to make any mistakes with them.

'We'll have to try to help that memory of yours, then.' Peach stroked his moustache and gave his man a sardonic smile. 'Describe your relationship with this murdered girl, please.'

David wished this truculent, muscular man wouldn't keep mentioning murder. It didn't help, when you were fighting to save whatever you could of your reputation. 'I've only the vaguest recollection of her. I didn't see her that often.'

'What was the purpose of these meetings in a deserted house?'

'We smoked a little pot, that's all. I'm not proud of it. It seemed like fun at the time.'

'Funny place to have parties like that. An empty house, with no heating and light. And most of the doors removed for fuel by the people in the squat next door, if my experience of squats is any guide.'

'We got by. I took an electric fire in with me to give us a bit of warmth, I remember. But I expect most of the meetings were in the spring and the summer. It's difficult all these years later to—'

'No electricity in the house at that stage of its life, was there? Made a mistake on that one, Mr Edmonds, didn't you?'

'Yes. I remember now, I used to buy one of those small bags of coal from a garage, on the way there. Well, it wasn't always me, I expect. Others must have taken their turn to buy the fuel, but—'

'Don't insult my intelligence, Mr Edmonds!' It was Peach who was terse now, dangerously so. 'At this rate, we're going to be here for a long time. So, let me shorten that time. I believe that it wasn't just cannabis involved at those meetings.'

'You forget how much more relaxed things are now than then. It may be regarded as just a recreational drug now, but in those days—'

'And I don't buy all this rubbish about meeting for parties. There was no heat in that place, and you didn't bring coal or any other fuel into it. You were there to deal, not smoke. And you were dealing more than pot. Heroin, coke, probably LSD in those days. Probably other Class A and Class B drugs as well.'

David Edmonds had taught himself to look people straight in the face as he had climbed the hierarchy at Ormerod's. It was important when you were selling property to have eye contact with people: it gave the illusion at least of frankness and sincerity.

Now he discovered that he could not look this odious tormentor in the eye. He found himself staring hard at the small, scratched table between the two of them and trying hard to summon up the convincing defence which would not come to him. He wanted to shout, 'Prove it!' at the man, to fling defiance into his face. But something told him that it would be foolish to provoke this man, to challenge him to come up with evidence. Perhaps, indeed, he already had that evidence, was just allowing his quarry to wander ever deeper into the mire. He shook his head and said heavily, 'It wasn't like that.'

In the tension of his struggle with Peach he had almost forgotten the watchful girl beside him. It was she who now said unexpectedly, 'Then tell us how it was, Mr Edmonds. We can only help you if you are prepared to help us.'

He looked up into clear eyes, which seemed green to him in the harsh fluorescent light of this square, claustrophobic room. 'You already know from that caution that I was dealing. But I was a small man in a big, dangerous world. I gave it up quickly after that caution. It scared me.'

She let that assertion hang unconvincingly in the air for a moment, as Peach had taught her to do when you got an improbable reply. 'I should think other people scared you far more than the police, Mr Edmonds. Drugs are a big industry: a lucrative, evil industry. There are some very big criminal fish in it. Fish who would devour a small dealer like you for breakfast. It's my belief that you were warned off by them.'

He nodded. They seemed to know far more than he had even feared. He wondered what they were going to do about it. 'I got out while I could. I've never been sorry about that. And you must admit that—'

'It's your dealings at twenty-eight Sebastopol Terrace which interest us. The house where the body of a murdered girl was hidden.'

She was almost as bad as his first torturer, this girl in the green sweater, with her pretty face and her soft curves and her gentle, persuasive voice. He said hopelessly, 'What is it you want to know?'

'Tell us about your relationship with Sunita.'

'I hardly knew her. She was living next door and she came in with someone else. She was only there a few times.'

'Mr Edmonds, we have already established that these weren't merely parties. Number twenty-eight was where you briefed people who were dealing for you, wasn't it?'

He shook his head, trying to find the words which would make a denial convincing. 'Sunita came in with someone else.'

It was at this point that Peach re-entered the exchange, like an official torturer giving the rack another and crucial turn. 'Not good enough, Mr Edmonds. These meetings didn't last long. You were expanding your activities in drugs. Moving from dealing yourself to creating your own network of small-time dealers. It was a good place to brief them, you thought. Away from the police and away from other and larger figures in the drugs industry. Sunita Akhtar was one of the people you recruited to work for you.'

He spoke with such certainty that no one would have known that this was speculation rather than established fact.

David Edmonds certainly didn't. He said, 'All right, I admit it. She was dealing for me, that girl.'

'Along with several others. Weren't you lucky to get away with a mere caution, in that year?' Peach dwelt a little on the last phrase, as though considering whether they might even now choose to prosecute, in view of his admission. 'So what went wrong with the empire you were building for yourself?'

'I told you. The police caution scared me off.'

'Not good enough, Mr Edmonds. That wasn't what stopped you.'

His eyes flashed desperately round the featureless green walls of the small room, came back to the relentlessly turning cassette in the tape recorder. 'I've a lot to lose here. I'm an established figure in a perfectly legitimate business now. Do I have your assurance that this won't go any further?'

Peach gave him the smile of a tiger poised over its helpless prey. 'You have no such assurance. No one could give you one, in the middle of a murder inquiry. If all of this proves to have nothing to do with this killing, it won't be made public by us. But you may of course be called as a witness in a murder inquiry, and questioned in court about your activities at that time. It should be obvious to you by now that your best chance of keeping the lid on all of this is to give us the fullest possible co-operation. So far we've had to wring everything out of you.'

It didn't feel like that to David Edmonds. He felt that he had hardly mustered even a token resistance. But by now he was in no condition to argue. 'All right. I'm sorry. Please understand that I thought all this was far behind me, that I'd never even have to think about it again, let alone talk about it. What is it that you want to know?'

'For a start, what it was which really stopped you dealing. It wasn't just a caution from the Brunton CID. That merely proved that they didn't know enough about what you were doing to charge you. If they'd had the evidence to show that you were setting up a ring of dealers, you'd have been behind bars. So who was it who warned you off?'

'Joe Johnson.' His voice was scarcely above a whisper, but the name was perfectly clear in the quiet, airless room.

'I thought so.' From a base in Brunton, twenty years ago, Johnson had created a drugs and betting empire which extended through the north-west of England. It had been Percy Peach's greatest achievement of recent years to put him behind bars a few months previously, for his part in the murder of a young prostitute. 'That's better. We're beginning to get answers which make sense at last. Now tell us about Sunita Akhtar, and what went wrong with your arrangements with her.'

'She came to me, you know. I didn't go out looking for her.'

'All right. Hardly matters, does it? What happened to her is the important thing. The reason why the three of us are buggering up our Sunday in an interview room at Brunton nick.'

'She came and asked to deal. Wanted the money. Said she couldn't do legitimate work for fear of her family finding out about it.' He looked up at them, flashing his troubled gaze from one earnest face to the other. 'Was that true?'

'It may have been. So you took her on.'

124

'Yes. She only wanted to do pot, and that was all I wanted to trust her with, for a start.' He shook his head and said with sudden bitter emphasis, 'I wish I'd never seen the damned girl!'

'I expect that was mutual, in view of what happened to her,' said Peach grimly. 'So what went wrong with the arrangement?'

'The attention she brought with her from next door. That's what went wrong! I should never have entertained using her. I didn't realize how little she knew about the dangers of the trade.'

'Wally.' Peach nodded sagely, as if he knew everything about a man who was no more than a name to him.

'Wally Swift. He knew far more than I knew about drugs. I was a novice.'

'I can believe that. I expect he warned you off.'

'He did more than that. He questioned Sunita, frightened her to death.' As the apposite nature of that phrase struck him, he shivered suddenly in the warm room. 'Swift pinned me in the corner of the pub car park and told me to get off his patch. I tried to say there was room for both of us, but he wasn't having that. He had me by the throat at the time and I wasn't going to argue. I thought that night that he was going to kill me, but he said there were other men to do that, that he didn't need to soil his hands with me.'

'He was working for Johnson?'

'I'm sure he was. It wasn't mentioned – you don't throw names about in the drugs trade – but I already knew Johnson was the big player in the area.'

'So you got out. Scared off not by a police caution but by Joe Johnson.'

David wanted to argue. Apart from anything else, it made him sound a wimp, and he wasn't used to that nowadays. He made an attempt to assert the worthiness of his present position. 'Anyway, they did me a favour, those people. I found a different and better way to make a living, in estate agency.'

Peach nodded and gave him the smile all of Brunton CID

125

would have recognized as dangerous. 'Yes. You took up a different kind of lying and distortion, some people would say. Not me, of course. Married the boss's daughter. Joined the Masons. Lived happily ever afterwards. Until someone discovered your murky past.' He studied the sweating man in front of him dispassionately for a moment, then rapped out, 'So what happened to Sunita Akhtar?'

'I told her I couldn't use her any more. I don't know what became of her after that.' David was fighting hard to convince them, to find words which would ring true, but he knew himself that he was far too shaken to be persuasive.

'And when would this be?'

'Some time in the spring of 1991. I can't be any more precise than that. It's a long time ago. And it's a part of my life I've put a long way behind me.'

Peach looked at him sourly. 'Let me put another scenario to you, Mr Edmonds. Sunita Akhtar knew too much about your activities. She'd already let you down with Wally Swift. She was a walking time bomb as far as you were concerned. So you put her out of the way.'

David Edmonds tried to control the panic he felt welling within him. 'No. I'm not a man for physical violence. I could no more strangle a helpless girl than fly to the moon. You'll see that I have no record of physical violence, anywhere in my life.'

That was true enough. But there was no need to concede the point. Peach said, 'You're not planning to leave the area, are you, Mr Edmonds?'

'I'm going away for a family holiday, that's all. We're off to Madeira for a bit of early spring sunshine.'

'And when would this be, Mr Edmonds?'

'Next Friday.'

'Recently arranged was it, this trip to Madeira?'

David heard the scepticism in the man's voice, wanted to scream at him that this had been arranged for months. But they could check on it, if they wanted to, couldn't they? And this man seemed to him all-powerful now. Certainly he seemed

126

to know far more about what had gone on in that squalid house thirteen years ago than David would have believed possible.

He was totally unconscious that he had added considerably to that sum of knowledge, that Peach had not even known Wally Swift's name until a few minutes ago, let alone his activities in the drug trade in 1991. He said, 'No, I only booked the holiday this morning, as a matter of fact. I find you get much better prices if you can leave it to the last minute. I'm lucky, I can do that, being the boss. Not that it's any business of yours.' He stuck this belated piece of defiance on the end of his defensive words, and immediately regretted it.

'It might be our business, Mr Edmonds, if we need to question you again in a murder investigation. But perhaps we shall be able to come back to you before Friday.' He gave his victim a final Torquemada smile. 'You're free to go now.'

David got out as quickly as he could, accelerating the BMW away from the police station in a flood of relief, as his pulse returned to somewhere near its normal rate.

It was not until he was composing himself to announce the joyous news of their holiday to his children that he realized that Detective Chief Inspector Peach should have been thanking him for his help. He had been voluntarily helping the man with his enquiries, after all.

Fourteen

The tentacles of great cities spread more and more widely as the years go on. Bolton, once a thriving Lancashire town in its own right, is now essentially part of Greater Manchester, and the urban sprawl has all but eliminated the sparse and unremarkable moorland country which once separated the two.

There are compensations. Bolton has caught some of the excitement and not a little of the prosperity which came with the redevelopment of the twin cities of Manchester and Salford around the turn of the century. There are new businesses growing up to replace or supplement the old manufacturing ones. In an era of high divorce rates and volatile relationships, one of the most lucrative of these is the introduction agency. The days when the activity was simply called 'dating' have long gone: 'introductions' imply more research and more careful matching, by the people who have taken upon themselves the task of organizing these meetings. And enable them to charge more.

It is an expanding market, but as always where there is money to be made and no formal training necessary, there is much competition. The best are doing very well, but the suspect agencies have recently attracted bad publicity to the industry. There have been newspaper articles warning lonely people to be careful, and researchers working for the BBC *Watchdog* programme have turned its spotlight upon some of the dubious practices and even more dubious charges which have occurred.

The Jane Watson Personal Introductions Agency in Bolton was not one of the dubious ones. It had a high street position, lushly carpeted and spacious premises, and privacy guaranteed in the interview rooms behind the main reception area. It had excellent literature, printed on expensive stationery, answering all the questions which diffident men and women might wish to ask before dipping their toes into the unknown waters of new relationships.

The brochure gave an account of the diligent checking and matching which went on before any attempt was made to bring people together, and stressed that the choice of whether to meet or not always rested ultimately with the client. People were reassured about most of their fears before they ever set foot on the premises. It was the proud boast of the owner that most of the people who came into the office to make tentative enquiries enrolled themselves as clients.

That owner was a working manager, who could usually be found upon the premises. The personal touch was another of the things which tended to promote success. In the area of social interchange, confidence is usually brittle or non-existent, and discreet guidance from a person with experience and insight is a vital ingredient in helping things along.

Jane Watson had both experience and insight in abundance. Not in introduction agencies, of course: that was a recent development. But about what men required of women and women of men, and of the infinite number of variations which existed in these complex webs of human relations, the proprietor of this particular introduction agency knew a thing or two.

For the retailers who surrounded the agency in the centre of Bolton, Monday morning was a quiet time, when you could play yourself back in slowly after whatever adventures the weekend had offered. Jane Watson found that her Mondays were very different; they were often the busiest day of the week.

Sometimes people who had finally broken up a relationship at the crisis time of weekend came in to register for fresh hopes and new excitements. More often, people who had spent a solitary weekend decided that they could no longer stand the trials of life alone, and took the plunge to come in and register themselves with an introduction agency.

At ten fifteen on this particular Monday, the last day of February, Jane was interviewing a woman of forty-three, who had completed her third divorce during the previous week. One of the advantages of experience was that nothing shocked you now: without raising an eyebrow, Jane took down the dates of three marriages and listened to the lurid details of the latest Lothario who had let the woman down.

The woman sitting opposite her was small and attractive, slim but shapely, with skilfully cut black hair framing a face with features which might have been shaped in fine china. The face was surprisingly unlined, for one who had been through the emotional traumas which she was outlining with such vigour. She looked much younger than her forty-three years, thought Jane, with a shaft of envy. Petite brunettes always seemed to age best.

Jane told her that quite bluntly. She even said openly that she was a little jealous of the fact: it didn't do any harm to bolster confidence, when people were looking for reassurance. The woman said, 'You think it's worth registering with you, then? I don't seem to have much talent for relationships, do I?'

'You haven't met the right man yet, that's all. Life's a complicated business. It's the purpose of a place like this to make it slightly less so.' Jane delivered the familiar phrases as if they had just occurred to her; she had long since decided that being an actress was as necessary a part of this game as of the others she had played in her time.

At least it seemed that she only needed to talk about men this time. She was getting an increasing number of people who requested same-sex partners, and even quite a few who declared themselves openly as bisexual, then asked what the agency could produce for them. 'It's necessary that you be absolutely frank with me, for your own sake,' Jane told this new client firmly. 'Once I know all about you and about your preferences in partners, I can begin matching you with a selection from hundreds of our male clients. The franker you are with me this morning, the better that match will be.'

The dark-haired, anxious woman opposite her nodded, admitting the logic of the argument. She was reassured by the appearance as well as the manner of this woman in charge. She looked a hard piece, with her neat, closely cut, blonde hair, her regular but rather blunt features, and the careful make-up which still could not conceal the crow's feet which were beginning to spread around her eyes. But a hard piece was what she needed, to sort out the emotional minefield of her life.

This Watson woman had a good figure still, even if there was an expensive bra shaping the breasts beneath that smooth mohair. She looked like a woman who had put it about a bit in her time. That was all to the good: if you were going to guide others, the more experience you had the better.

And everything about this woman spoke of experience, from her assurance that no detail of sexual history or sexual preference would shock her to the broad, competent fingers on the pen she was using to make notes. As if she read these thoughts in her new client, Jane Watson looked up and nodded encouragingly at her. 'All this will go into your personal, confidential file on the computer later,' she explained. 'I like to make notes and add comments before I put the final summary on the computer, so that I can make each entry as individual as possible.'

'I don't mind younger men,' the dark-haired woman blurted out with a sudden burst of intimacy.

'Don't mind or prefer?' The thin mouth beneath the broad nose dropped into an encouraging smile.

'Prefer, I suppose, really!' She felt herself blushing, despite her three marriages and her years of experience.

Jane Watson nodded, as if these and much more startling confessions were made to her every day. 'Meetings like that can be arranged. There are lots of young men who fancy an older, experienced woman. And you're still very attractive, fortunately.' She made a note which the older woman could not decipher. 'You should be aware that you may be taken for a ride if you get seriously involved. Most men are unscrupulous creatures at the best of times, in my experience. And younger men are likely to get you seriously involved and then take you for all they can get financially.' She looked back at her first page of notes. 'And you've come out of these marriages of yours quite well, financially at least. You must beware of becoming a target for a ruthless young man.'

You didn't call them fortune-hunters, these days. That would leave you open to the accusation that you should have rooted out such characters rather than put them on your books. And it was as well to remind this woman that she was quite affluent: the Jane Watson Agency did not come cheap, and she sensed that this lady was going to sign up for the fullest range of its introduction services. It was as well to cover yourself by warning foolish females like this one of the dangers ahead. Losers could sometimes refuse to pay their agency bills when in the midst of an emotional turmoil, and you needed to show that you were fulfilling the terms of the contract you had agreed, if it came to it.

She checked that the woman didn't have what she called 'Any sharp social preferences', and was assured that the reverse was the case. That meant that she was prepared to take on and enjoy a bit of rough, though of course you never called it anything as crude as that. Not to women, anyway; men were sometimes easily excited by phrases like that. Absurdly gullible creatures men were, when they sniffed sex in the air. Dangerous, but gullible.

The woman, as Jane had known she would, signed up for the full six months, rather that just the initial trial offer. 'I'm going to take my time over this,' she assured herself firmly. 'Once bitten, twice shy, that's me now. I'm not going to make any commitment until you've provided me with several introductions. Perhaps not even then.'

She believes it, thought Jane Watson as she listened to the cliches, hiding her contempt under a broad smile. 'That's the idea! Play the field for a little while. If I can just have your cheque, we'll get things moving right away.'

She watched the woman put her coat back on and leave the shop. Skirt a trifle short, and just a little too tight over the firm little bum. There'd be no problem in finding men ready to investigate a bum like that. And little Miss High Horse would be at it between the sheets within ten days, she reckoned, climbing all over some young stud and trying to convince him he had value for money. She might be well preserved, but she would be too randy and too conscious of the ticking clock to take her time, as she had promised herself she would.

Still, there was no harm in the Jane Watson Introduction Agency taking a generous slice of the cash she was going to fritter away. Good half-hour's work, that had been: Jane mentally toasted once again the infinite credulity of human nature.

She liked to do the first interview with people herself. She could afford good staff now, but she flattered herself that there was still no one who sold the services they offered quite as efficiently as she did. And prospective clients liked to be interviewed by the proprietor herself. It made them feel important that the head of an obviously prosperous concern should take a personal interest in their needs.

This meant that when a gangling, rather uncoordinated, young man came through the big glass door and moved rather uncertainly over the thick carpet, she moved swiftly forward. 'How can we help you, sir?'

She had seen hundreds like him, in her time. Had dozens of them for breakfast, in different ways. Wet behind their ears, but with their dicks bursting out of their trousers and their judgements consequently haywire. The trousers on this one were part of a dark grey suit, and he had a clean shirt and tie above it; probably he'd put on his most formal clothes to come in here, bless him. Tall, with his fresh face still unlined, with clear brown eyes and not a grey hair in sight for years, yet. Early twenties, she reckoned: certainly not over twenty-five.

Ripe for the plucking. She might even sell him that mobile little 43-year-old arse which had just pranced out, before the week was out. But there was no hurry: this young lad would go down well with lots of women. With his open, innocent face and his straight hair refusing to stay in place, there'd be lots of women who'd want to mother a lad like this. He wouldn't even have needed her services, if he'd had the confidence he so patently lacked. But of course she wouldn't tell him that.

'Emily Jane Watson?'

That careful enunciation of her full name gave her the first shaft of apprehension. 'I'm Jane Watson, the proprietor, yes. What can I do for you?' She reached for one of the brochures behind her, prepared to tell him to have a quick scan through it before they took this any further.

He looked her full in the face, as if it was important to him to memorize the details of it. Then he showed her a police warrant card, holding it rigidly still a foot from her face, as though to show how steady his young hand was. The card was genuine enough: Emily Jane Watson knew very well what they looked like. At least it was only a Detective Constable, and a raw one at that. She'd dealt with bigger police fish than this in her time. She said, her voice suddenly hard as steel, 'I'm carrying on a perfectly legitimate business here. You can see the books if you like. But I don't see why you should, DC Pickering.'

'I'm not interested in the books, Miss Watson. I'm not even interested in the business. But we need to ask you some questions.'

'And who are "we"?'

'Brunton CID. In connection with a serious crime committed in 1991.'

They had found her, then. And quickly, really, considering how she had covered her traces. She tried not to panic, told herself that she had always expected this, from the moment she had seen that idiot Tucker talking on TV about the discovery of that Paki girl's body. It was worrying, though, that they had got to her so quickly. She had thought about this meeting, and about how she should react to it, on each of the last three nights. Yet now, ridiculously, she found she needed time to think. She said, 'And suppose I tell you that I was not in Brunton at that time?'

'I should think we might challenge it. And if we found that you had lied about it, we should be forced to draw our own conclusions.'

She had underestimated this young man. That was not a pleasant realization. She said, 'Do you have a warrant for my arrest?' and immediately regretted it.

'No. Do I need one? Are you saying that you have committed a crime? Or that you are not Emily Jane Watson? All you are being asked to do is to help the police in the course of their enquiries, at the moment.' Gordon Pickering dwelt histrionically upon the last phrase: he hadn't been selected and trained by Percy Peach without learning to apply pressure.

'What exactly is it that you want me to do?' Both of them knew in that moment that she was going to co-operate.

'We can interview you here if you wish. I'll ring the man in charge of the case and get him out here. Tell him that you don't wish to come into the station.' He made that sound as if it would be a confession of involvement in this crime, which he still hadn't specified, though both of them knew perfectly well that it was the murder of Sunita Akhtar.

'And have police cars with lights flashing lined up against the kerb outside here? Lot of good that would do to a business which relies on discretion for its very existence! No, I'll come into your damned station, clear this up once and for all. Just give me an hour to reorganize my day, let me make a couple of phone calls. And please note that I haven't even admitted that I was in the area in the year you specified.'

But both of them knew that there was no mistaken identity here.

Matthew Hayward was on his way to play the Rachmaninov Piano Concerto Number Three with the Liverpool Philharmonic Orchestra.

135

'They're the official Classic FM orchestra, you know,' his agent had said. 'But it's the Third they want you to play, not that old war-horse the Second. But Classic will play your Beethoven recording and give you quite a few mentions on the air, in the two weeks before the concert. You'll probably find they're a bit populist, a bit vulgar, but the publicity will be good for us.'

Matt noted as he drove how his agent had changed from 'you' to 'us' since he had begun to enjoy success. Well, he didn't mind that, so long as the bookings came in. And he didn't mind the 'populist' approach from Classic FM, if the truth be told. It gave him a kick to hear his name mentioned in their publicity between records, and it meant that they chose to play him in preference to other pianists when he had a concert coming up with their chosen orchestra.

And since they had put his picture on the cover of their monthly magazine, a couple of people had actually recognized him when he was walking along the street in Brunton. That had been quite nice, really. You wouldn't want it all the time, of course, wouldn't want people stopping you wherever you went. But it was really quite pleasant to be modestly famous, to have strangers coming up to you to tell you that they had enjoyed your playing. Matt Hayward was human enough to enjoy the prospect of becoming that awful twenty-first century phenomenon, a celebrity.

It was perhaps because he was preoccupied with such musings that he never noticed the car which was following him.

Matt liked to be at the concert hall hours before the performance, principally to inspect the instrument on which he was to play, but also to get the feel of the place. He was still sufficiently star-struck, still sufficiently surprised by his own success, to enjoy looking round deserted concert halls, to enjoy letting his eye run slowly up the steeply tiered rows of seats and imagine them thronged with people bursting into thunderous applause. He might be almost in his mid-thirties now, but there was still a lot of the boy left in him.

But he would like a quiet lunch, somewhere where he could read his paper and forget about music for half an hour or so. It was half past twelve now. He would stop before he got even to the outskirts of the city sprawl around Liverpool. He pulled into what looked like a quiet pub in the roadside village of Rufford.

It was an old place, with a lot of alcoves, which had probably at one time been individual rooms. Matt ordered a bacon quiche and sat alone in one of these small enclaves with his copy of the *Guardian* and a half of bitter. He wouldn't allow himself any more alcohol than that, on the day of a concert.

He had not noticed the car which pulled in a few seconds after him and eased to the other end of the car park.

Matt ate his way slowly through a surprisingly good quiche and read in a few paragraphs at the bottom of the front page that Sunita had been strangled, then hidden away behind the chimney breast of a fireplace in one of the derelict houses near the squat. The police were getting to know more and more about how it had happened, it seemed. He shuddered involuntarily, trying to cast away the feeling of foreboding which dropped upon him with that thought.

Determined to think of other things, he turned to the accounts of the weekend football. As a boy, he had always wanted to score the winning goal for Rovers in the Cup Final, but he had slowly accepted that it would never happen, when he was invariably one of the last to be selected when the boys in his form picked teams. Being a concert pianist wasn't a bad second, he told himself, though he still fantasized about Wembley, not Carnegie Hall.

Perhaps in due course Carnegie Hall would be the reality for him, if his fame continued to rocket as it had in the last year. He sipped his bitter and vowed with a self-deprecating smile to keep practising.

The man slid silently into the seat opposite him and regarded him steadily. He was about thirty, with blue eyes which looked almost black beneath eyebrows which beetled over them. He did not smile; nor did he offer any form of greeting or intro-duction. He held a tightly rolled copy of the *Daily Mail* in his left hand, which he now put carefully on the table, like a spy delivering a signal.

Matt looked down at the paper, as if trying to read some impenetrable code. He said, 'If you want an autograph, I don't mind signing, but I don't really want to talk. I've a concert in Liverpool tonight, and I want to have a quiet lunch and compose myself.'

Now the man did smile. It wasn't a pleasant expression. 'Couldn't care less about your bloody concert, mate. I'm here to tell you what you have to do if you want to continue play-ing.' He looked at the slender fingers which were gripping the beer glass as if he were contemplating crushing them at this very moment.

Matt glanced nervously towards the bar, then back at the man on the bench seat on the other side of the small table. He wondered if the barman knew this nutter, if he was some-one who habitually came in and threatened customers. But the pub was unnaturally quiet at this Monday lunchtime, and the barman was nowhere to be seen.

And somehow Matt knew that calling for assistance would not be a good move.

And this man did not look like a nutter. Not like the kind of harmless nutter who might frequent a quiet country pub, anyway. He looked like something much more sinister, a crea-ture of the city, attuned to violence, and accustomed to using it efficiently when it suited his purposes. Matt found when he tried to speak that his voice would not work. He had to clear his dry throat before he could say, 'Who are you?'

The man gave a short, humourless laugh. 'That's for me to know and you to speculate about, young Matty.'

It was a long time since anyone had called him that. And this man was younger than he was, even if he was infinitely more experienced in the seamier ways of the world. Matt said, 'Who sent you here?'

'Doesn't matter, Matty me boy.' There was a hint of Irish

in the voice, but Matt couldn't be sure whether it was genuine or assumed. 'The important thing is that you have to watch what you say. That's the message.'

'Watch what I say? About what?' But suddenly he knew.

'About Sunita Akhtar. About that Paki lass you used to shaft at one time.'

'I loved Sunita!' The words were out before he could check them, without his ever being conscious of framing the thought.

The lips he could not take his eyes from curled into a sneer. 'Lovely, that. You should have stuck to your own kind, Matty boy. Might have kept you out of trouble if you had.'

'You're too late! I've already spoken to the police about Sunita.'

'I know that, you fool.' The cold contempt for his naivety came at him across the table like a shaft of icy air, and for a moment Matt thought the man was about to lay hands upon him. 'But they'll be back again. You're a murder suspect, young Matty. They'll be back.'

'I didn't kill Sunita!'

'You'd say that, wouldn't you? I would, in your position. But I wouldn't expect to be believed, unless I could prove it. And you can't, sunshine! So they'll be back. And when they do, you'll keep shtum about anything Sunita told you.'

'About what?'

'About anything she told you, mate. You might have killed her, for all I know. I don't care if you did. Just keep quiet about anything she might have told you about other people, that's all.'

'And why should I?'

Matt regretted his little flash of defiance immediately. The man leaned forward until his face was within a foot of his victim and gripped the collar of his shirt against the thin throat. Matt could smell his breath, see a filling within the irregular teeth, as he said, 'Because I'm telling you now, that's why. You could be fitted up for this murder, whether you committed it or not.'

139

Later, it seemed an absurd threat. At that moment, Matt felt this man and the people who were paying him could do anything, if they wished. He said hoarsely, cravenly, 'I won't talk.'

'That's better. You're getting the message now. Sensible man!' The man relaxed the pressure at Matt's throat slowly, as if it were a demonstration of great manual skill and strength to release his man so gradually. 'The people who sent me could snuff you out like a candle, mate. You could be dead meat in the Mersey in the morning, if they chose.'

'I told you, I won't talk!' Matt was anxious only to reassure the man, to get out of here and be rid of him for ever. He would have said anything just to get away. He had no idea what it was that he was supposed to know.

Belatedly, the barman was back at his post, making ready to serve a noisy party of office workers who had just arrived. The man did not look towards them, but kept his eyes beneath the beetling brows steadily upon Matt. 'I think you've got the message, Matty me boy! It's simple enough. Keep shtum, or someone will be back to shut your mouth permanently.' He gripped the top of Matt's arm for two seconds in fingers of steel, and then was gone.

It was some time before Matt Hayward was able to stem the trembling in his limbs and follow the man out of the pub. He drove slowly and carefully into Liverpool, putting on the radio to try to divert his thoughts from what had happened. It was the lunchtime request programme on Classic FM, introduced by the woman who treated you like a primary school child, patronizing you with waves of sugary pseudo-sincerity over the air waves.

Matt found himself shouting defiance at her, shivering with fury as he yelled out his frustration and fear in his warm moving cell of safety.

The people at the concert hall were surprised to see him so early, but they were kind, understanding, accommodating to his wishes. Above all, they were normal. He could almost think that what had happened to him a couple of hours earlier was a nightmare, that it had not really happened at all.

It was when he was changing into his white shirt and evening dress for the concert that he saw the livid bruising on the biceps of his right arm. That man had been real all right.

Fifteen

'Thank you for coming in to talk to us.' Peach began the interview with uncharacteristic low-key politeness.

'It was the lesser of two evils. I didn't want police cars lining up outside my business and police boots all over my carpets.'

Emily Jane Watson didn't like policemen and didn't see any reason to disguise the fact. She hadn't met either this pugnacious-looking bald man with the moustache or the attractive redhead beside him before, but they'd be the usual meddlesome nuisances no doubt, believing nothing she said and keeping her away from more important concerns.

'I believe you tried to enrol our young DC, Gordon Pickering.'

'We can accommodate anyone. Even coppers. There's lots of women who'd like to mother a daft young sod like your Gordon Pickering. Hardly knows a blow-job from a blow-wave, that one! Shouldn't think he's much use to you as a detective, though.'

'And there you'd be wrong, Miss Watson. But you have a business to run, so let's waste no more time on such pleasantries. We're interested in a murder committed back in 1991. In or near twenty-six Sebastopol Terrace, Brunton, where you were resident at the time.'

'Prove it.'

Peach sighed heavily. 'This is all going to take much longer if you are determined to be uncooperative. Do you deny that you were one of the people unlawfully occupying that house as squatters in the months at the end of 1990 and the beginning of 1991? Think carefully before you reply, please.'

He seemed very confident, seemed almost to be inviting her to deny it. What would he do then? Place her under arrest? Jane Watson did not know what her rights were in this situation. So she operated the way she had done for the last ten years and more. If there was some point in lying, she would be as brassy as anyone, but if there was no point, there was no use risking police hostility. And she could see no point here: they were going to pin her down eventually, however long she denied it. 'All right, I was there. I was in that squat, with a few others. But it's a long time ago and I don't remember much about it. OK?'

'No, it's not OK, Miss Watson. We need everything you can tell us about that period. We need to put it beside the evidence we are collecting from other people who were there. You were known at that time as Em or Emmy, a contraction of the first name Emily, which you now appear to have discarded.' He contrived to make that sound like a piece of criminal deception.

'I no longer use the name because it's part of a world I've left behind me. That squat's a long time ago, part of another life.'

That was a phrase they were getting used to hearing. 'Let's jog your memory, then. It was at that time, on the seventeenth of January, 1991, to be precise, that you received a caution for soliciting. In the name of Emily Watson.'

She felt her pulse racing, even whilst she told herself that she should have expected this. He was so calm, so matter-of-fact about it that she wondered just how much he knew about her life, how much else he had stacked up against her, just waiting to be brought out and thrown into her face like this. She said, 'Doesn't make me a murderer, does it, a caution for whoring?'

'No. Doesn't make you the Virgin Mary either.'

'And it didn't make the tosspot who arrested me a good copper, did it?'

Peach kept his face studiously impassive as he said, 'Mr Tucker was in charge of CID work in central Brunton in the mid-nineties.'

'He's a right wanker, your bloody Superintendent Tucker. I knew him when he was an inspector, and he was a tosser then. Didn't know whether he was coming or going. People made bloody great rings round him.'

She found she had dropped automatically back into the language she had used in the days when she had habitual conflicts with the police. She jutted her square jaw aggressively towards the man with the moustache beneath his startlingly white bald head, trying to provoke him with this assault upon his senior officer.

Emily Jane Watson did not know what music she was sounding in his ears with this denigration of the good name of Tommy Bloody Tucker. He wished now that he'd recorded this; he would certainly have found a suitable occasion to play the tape back to the man in question.

But Percy Peach did not even smile. Instead, he looked at Emily Jane Watson without emotion and said flatly, 'Tucker's a chief superintendent now, love. That's the way the world goes, you see. And I'm a chief inspector, in charge of the investigation into the murder of Sunita Akhtar. And you're running a prosperous business instead of whoring. You're also a murder suspect, until you or we can prove it otherwise. So tell us about the days when you were Emmy the squatter.'

There was something about his even tone which carried menace. She had better be careful with this man. She glanced for a moment at the woman with the gold ball pen ready beside him, then gave her full attention to Peach. 'There were six of us in that place. One or two others came and went, but, through that winter and into the spring, there were six of us who were permanent. It was a good squat, in that no one really disturbed us. It was on Tucker's patch, but he didn't want to know. We had an initial warning, but after that, the police more or less ignored us. We had more trouble from peeping Toms than coppers.'

So much for not being able to remember that period of her life, thought Peach. But he wasn't going to remind her of the contradiction with what she had said at the outset, if she was going to talk openly of the place. 'We've contacted some of those people already. We need to know everything you can add to what we've already discovered.'

Which included my whereabouts. I could have done without that. And now I'd better be careful, because I don't know what the others have said about me. Jane Watson said, 'You're welcome to what I know. I can't see that it's going to help you to find out who killed that stupid girl.'

'Stupid, was she? No one else has called her that. So, for a start, we'd like to know why you thought her stupid.'

'A Paki wandering into a squat with a lot of desperate English people? She had to be stupid, to take a chance like that.'

Lucy Blake said quietly, 'Maybe she didn't see any other option open to her. Maybe she was desperate.'

Emily studied the pretty, open face beneath the red-brown hair for a moment, wondering how much she knew about how life was lived at the bottom of the pile. She'd been introduced as a Detective Sergeant, so she couldn't be as young or as raw as she had seemed at first. Emily said, 'All right, maybe I shouldn't have said stupid. I didn't mean she was unintelligent. I meant she knew nothing about life. Nothing about people. She didn't seem to realize that people like Wally Swift regarded anything non-white as fair game, that if it suited him, he'd have her knickers off in the first couple of days, and rape her if she didn't go along with it.'

'And is that what happened?'

Emily realized that her impatience with this innocent-looking woman had led her to reveal more than she had intended already. 'I don't know. You minded your own business in the squat.'

Peach said, 'Wally Swift hasn't confessed to anything like that. Not so far.' She didn't know that this was only the second time they had heard the name mentioned; that they had not even known the name until they got it from David Edmonds twenty-four hours earlier; that Swift had never been questioned; that they had so far no idea where this increasingly sinister figure was at present. No wonder Lucy was busy with her notes.

The blonde woman on the other side of the table folded her arms and told herself to be more careful. The last thing she wanted was to find an irate Wally Swift back in her life, smashing up her expensive premises, wrecking her new respectability. 'He didn't rape her, no. All I was saying is that he could have done, if he'd wanted to, and very probably get away with it. I was saying that girl Sunita was asking for trouble, coming into a place like that.'

'And trouble is what she got, in the end. She became a murder victim. But she was there for at least six months before that happened.'

'Yes. She was lucky. At first, I mean.'

'In what way?'

'Other people looked after her. That other young fool, Matty, took up with her, for a start. Offered her his protection. There's no knowing how long she'd have lasted, on her own.'

'And why was Matthew Hayward a young fool?' Peach was quiet, matter-of-fact, asking for information rather than being confrontational.

She looked at him irritably, not used nowadays to having to justify her words. 'He was almost as wet behind the ears as she was. Lucky to survive as long as he did. Of course, the girl would have ended up going to bed with anyone who gave her a bit of sympathy and a shoulder to cry on. But he didn't see that. He thought it was some great love affair which was going to last.'

'You weren't surprised when they split up then?'

She wondered just how much they knew about what had gone on in that squat. She had better be very careful. She tried to curb her contempt for the girl as she said cautiously, 'No, I wasn't surprised. I'm pretty sure Sunita was a virgin when she came there, that Matty was her first man. It wasn't going to last. And perhaps she was the first woman he'd had, for all I know. That would explain why he cut up so rough when they broke up, wouldn't it?'

'It would be one possible explanation, yes. We'd like your version of the break-up now, please.'

'I think the Paki girl was bowled over by freedom. That once she'd got over the first thrill of being in the sack with someone, she wanted more, with different people.'

'And what reasons do you have for this view?'

She wanted to chant the words mockingly back into his smug face. Instead, she said, 'No reasons, except my own experience. I know a thing or two about sex, that's all.'

'And you're sure that it was Sunita who got rid of Matty, and not the other way round?'

'Quite sure. And I couldn't say I was sorry at the time. Cocky young sod had it coming to him.'

'And how did Matty react when Sunita wanted out?'

'He cut up rough, didn't he? Silly bugger should have seen it coming, but he didn't. And when she shacked up with a woman, he couldn't take that.'

Not a muscle moved on either of the two contrasting faces which were studying her hard, experienced features so intently. Not a flicker revealed that this was new and sensational news to them. From what she had said, the woman didn't mean herself. That left only one woman, however unlikely a candidate she seemed for the role. The woman who was now Sister Josephine.

Peach said evenly, 'I think you'd better tell us everything you can remember about this third woman in the squat.'

'Jo. High and mighty Jo. The woman who talked about principles, and lived in a squat. The woman who told me to keep my hands off Sunita, and then turned out to be a dyke.'

Seeing the two thirteen years later, Peach would have expected a personality clash between the woman he had seen only as the virtuous Sister Josephine, working her heart out in a hospice, and this stone-faced blonde who seemed to know so much about the seamier side of the world. Even when they were half-formed young women thrown together in the exigencies of the squatters' existence, he would have expected them to clash. That was no bad thing now: a woman full of

147

resentment was likely to reveal things she would otherwise have concealed.

He said, 'You're sure this relationship was sexual?'

'If you call sleeping together every night, if you call shutting themselves off in their own room, if you call moans of pleasure echoing through the house sexual, yes. Of course it was! That Jo was a dyke, talking high-flown rubbish about moral choices but just waiting for the chance to get a bit of Asian pussy under her blankets!'

Peach watched her breathing heavily, noting her vehemence with interest. Then he said calmly, 'You said this Jo warned you to keep your hands off Sunita. That implies that you had designs upon her yourself.'

'Not to get my hands on her, I hadn't. Jane Watson might have been around, but she's never been a dyke!'

He could see her suddenly with her coarse, indignant features as a man; one of those National Front thugs who had lately been causing so much trouble in the town, perhaps, with their homophobia and their racism. But this woman was more intelligent than those tattooed and unthinking louts. And probably as a result more dangerous.

Peach said suddenly, 'Why Jane? Em was good enough in that squat.'

'That's my business.'

'Possibly. But what you did as Emily Watson was ours.'

She'd suspected all along that they knew, that they were playing cat and mouse with her about it. She'd run rings round that Tucker bloke, at the time, but that wasn't going to happen now with these two. But there was nothing they could pin upon her, if she gave them nothing: she told herself that firmly. Make them work for everything, from now on. She used her haughtiest businesswoman's tone to say, 'I've no idea what you mean, Chief Inspector.'

'I think you do. Within two years of leaving that squat in Sebastopol Terrace, you were running a disorderly house. Operating a ring of prostitutes. Living off immoral earnings.'

'Prove it! Your Superintendent Tucker never did, and he was around at the time.'

Percy Peach was used to picking up the pieces after Tommy Bloody Tucker. But not pieces from before he was even on the scene. 'I don't have to, Miss Emily Watson! Fortunately for you, I'm not interested in doing so, at this distance in time. I'm interested in a murder which took place three years earlier, and your possible part in that.'

'Guilty until proved innocent now, is it?'

Peach answered her sneer with his most impudent grin. 'Not a bad motto for an investigating officer, that, when the evidence is thin upon the ground. We're paid good money to be suspicious buggers, in CID!' He paused to register how eminently satisfying he found that thought. 'It's my belief that you were not only operating as a prostitute yourself early in 1991, but that you tried to recruit Sunita Akhtar to go on the game.'

It was a hit, a very palpable hit. She snarled, 'Prove it! I defy you to prove it!' at him, but it was no more than a ritual defiance. She was wondering furiously whom he had talked to, who it was that might have passed this on to him.

'I don't have to prove it. And fortunately for you, I'm not interested in doing so at this moment. I'm interested in who killed the poor girl. Perhaps she resisted your suggestions, and you killed her when she refused to comply.'

'I didn't.' But she was staring at the edge of the square table in front of her now, too shaken to look into the piercing black eyes of this odious man.

'So who did?'

'I don't know. I'd tell you if I did. Get me off the hook you seem so determined to put me on, wouldn't it?'

'It might, if I felt I could trust a word you said. Tell me about Wally Swift.'

Emily thought quickly. He wasn't a man to grass on, Wally. Not even now, after all this time. But with her own neck on the block, she hadn't much option. She said in a low voice, 'He was a vicious bugger, Wally, even then.'

Peach nodded. 'So everyone tells us.'

149

Even Lucy Blake, sitting beside him and preparing to record whatever she could pick up about this still shadowy figure, was almost convinced at that moment that they had gathered accounts of this man Swift from various other people. Percy was making bricks without any straw at all, this time.

But Watson just nodded her agreement. 'He had his own schemes going, whilst the rest of us were just surviving in that squat.'

'Drugs.' Percy made it a statement rather than a question, though his only source was the dubious one of David Edmonds.

'Yes. He was dealing himself from when I first knew him. By the time Sunita died, he had others working for him.'

'Including her?'

'I don't know. He may have tried to recruit her. This bloke who was holding his meetings next door certainly did.'

David Edmonds, who had already told them that Sunita was selling for him. Apparently she didn't know the name. Perhaps she really didn't know it, wasn't aware that he was now a prominent local estate agent. If he proved in the end to have no connection with this murder, they wouldn't bring his name into it.

Peach said, 'Do you mean that this man operating from twenty-eight Sebastopol Terrace actually succeeded in enlisting Sunita to sell drugs, or that he merely attempted it?'

She ran a hand briefly across her forehead and the top of her broad nose, as if she was checking that she wasn't sweating. 'I don't know. I thought she was working for him, at one time. She suddenly seemed to have more money than she'd had before. I'd always thought she was sponging off Jo, until the last month or so.'

'Do you think that Wally Swift might have killed her for working for someone else rather than him?'

She paused for so long that they thought she was not going to reply. Then she gave a tiny shrug of her square shoulders and said in a low voice, 'I don't know. It's possible – I told you, he was a vicious bugger, was Wally, if you didn't do what he wanted. If he'd got her working for him and she transferred to this other bloke, he'd have taken that very badly. You can't let that kind of thing happen to you, if you want to be a big player in drugs.'

That rang true enough. They were going to have to find this man, and quickly. Peach said casually, 'And where is Wally Swift now?'

The square jaw dropped. She had thought they had already questioned Swift, whereas it seemed they didn't even know his present whereabouts. How much else had she given away that she might safely have concealed? She said dully, 'I don't know. I haven't had any contact with him since we were together at Sebastopol Terrace. We went our separate ways.'

'Separate criminal ways, it seems.' No harm in reminding her of that, if they wished her to continue to co-operate. 'Do you think it was Billy who killed Sunita?'

Again that abrupt switch, catching her off guard when she had been preparing herself to fend off more questions about Wally Swift. She hadn't even thought about the young West Indian, until now. 'I don't know who killed the damned girl, do I? I've told you that.'

'So it might have been Billy?'

'It might, yes.'

'Keen on her, wasn't he?'

They knew that much then. They might be trying to trip her up here. 'Yes. He seemed to think because they were the two non-whites that he had a right to bed her. She didn't go along with that. He was very black, Billy; I don't think she liked his colour. They can be as racist as anyone, you know, the Pakis, but no one makes a fuss about that, do they?'

'Did Billy take it badly?'

'I think he did, yes.' She couldn't actually remember, all these years later, but anything which spread suspicion away from herself was worth using.

'Like Billy, did you?'

'What sort of question's that? We were interested in surviving, in that place, not liking or disliking each other.'

'But you've already expressed certain thoughts about the others. So what about Billy?'

Had they been asking the others how they felt about her? And what had they said? She wished after all this time that she hadn't been quite as vicious with Jo and Matty as she had at the time. Not to mention Sunita. She said cautiously, 'I didn't mind Billy. He was black but he knew his place. And he was streetwise for his age, knew how to look after himself. He wasn't asking for trouble or likely to bring it on the rest of us, like Matty or that dyke Jo.'

'Or Sunita.'

'Or Sunita. She got what she was asking for in the end, that girl.'

They let her go on that. Let her go back to her legitimate and lucrative business. Let go this woman who had run a brothel and might be a murderer.

Sixteen

'I want to speak to Mr Swift.'

'Who is that?'

'It's an old colleague of his. Billy Warnock. He'll speak to me.'

A pause. Then, 'He's not available, I'm afraid. But I'm his manager here. Empowered to deal with all matters. What is it you want, Mr Warnock?' The voice managed to put a faint stress of bored contempt into its pronunciation of the surname. It was a male voice, heavy with menace beneath the polite words. The tone which carried those words was saying that Mr Swift was a powerful and important man, who paid well to keep unwanted calls and unwanted callers out of his life, that this anonymous voice from the past had much better forget the attempt to contact him.

'He'll speak to me. He'll want to know about this. We go back a long way, Wally and me.' Billy tried to keep his voice firm as he mouthed the once familiar forename, to answer menace with menace. This man couldn't know that he wasn't as powerful a man as Wally, that he didn't employ underlings of his own to keep people at arm's length.

Another pause. Billy wondered if this smooth and anonymous heavy had his hand over the mouthpiece, whether he was speaking to someone else. Then the baritone voice, bereft of all accent and therefore conjuring no visual picture for Billy beyond its sound, resumed with what was nearly a drawl. 'I'll pass on your message, Mr – Mr—'

'Warnock. Billy Warnock.'

'Mr Warnock, yes. Well, if he wants to ring you back, no doubt Mr Swift will do so.'

153

'He'll ring me. Tell him it's urgent.' Billy forced a little impatience into his voice.

'Yes. Perhaps you should know that he is now universally known as Walter. To those few people who do not address him as Mr Swift, that is.'

The phone went dead.

Billy Warnock, who had nerved himself for three hours to make the call he did not wish to make, found that he was sweating profusely, in the unheated room where he had gone for privacy, on the twenty-eighth of February.

'We've located another suspect, sir.'

It was a grey Monday afternoon, with flurries of tiny snow-flakes passing the big window in the Chief Superintendent's office. DCI Peach felt in need of a little light relief, on such a bleak day.

'Another pillar of society, is it?' Tucker was pleased with the sneer he managed to inject into the words.

'Can't control who gets himself into trouble, can I, sir?' Peach allowed himself a moment of outraged innocence.

There didn't seem to be any answer to that. Tucker had to content himself with a peevish, 'Well, you'd better get on with it, Chief Inspector. I haven't got all day, you know!'

'No. sir. Absolutely not, sir. I can see that.' Peach allowed his dark eyes to sweep slowly across the immaculately empty surface of the big desk between them. 'Well, this one's not a Mason, sir.'

'I'm glad to hear it. You seem to me to be obsessed with sullying the reputation of as fine a—'

'Restrictive rules wouldn't permit this one to join a Lodge, sir. Though I dare say there's some as wouldn't mind view-ing this suspect with a bared breast. It's a woman, sir.'

'Ah.' Tucker gave such a weight of understanding to the meaningless syllable that it might have denoted a serial rapist or multiple poisoner. 'This sounds much more promising.'

Peach wondered what Lucy Blake would make of that; she was sure to think he was exaggerating when he retailed this to her. 'This is a woman who was in that squat in 1991, sir. I'd hazard a bet that she was acting as a part-time prostitute at the time. We're certain that she's run a brothel since then.'

Tucker leant forward, solemn and portentous as an Old Testament prophet. 'My feeling is that this is our killer. Just a gut feeling at the moment, mind; you'll need to get on and gather the evidence. But remember that you heard it first here, Percy.'

'Yes, sir. I certainly shall, sir.' It always disturbed him when Tommy Bloody Tucker addressed him as 'Percy'. He said hastily, 'This is the benefit of your overview of crime, sir. Sometimes we people working on the ground can't see what should be staring us in the face.'

'Indeed.' Tucker waved an arm, magisterially and vaguely. He said generously, 'Of course, I shall give you full credit in all my reports to the Chief Constable, at the conclusion of the case.'

Peach, who knew that this was a brazen lie, mustered his widest and most innocent smile. 'It's good to hear that, sir. I'm sure you'll be as generous as you always are to your team.'

Tucker, who had an ear deaf to irony, said, 'Excellent work! Tell the rest of your team that they've done well, will you? It's good to know that a woman who has been involved in criminal activity for so long is finally going to—'

'She's a prosperous businesswoman now, sir.'

'Who is? You mean . . .' The same hand which had lately swept broadly and generously in front of Tucker now pawed feebly at the air.

'Emily Jane Watson, sir. Known as Em or Emmy when she was in that squat in Sebastopol Terrace in 1991. She seems to have dropped the Emily now, sir. Understandable, with a past like hers.'

'But you say she's now running a successful business?' The confidence drained out of Tucker's voice word by word as he spoke. 'You're sure this isn't a case of mistaken identity?'

'We are, sir. We're confident that this is the same woman who was in the squat. But she's a brassy piece, prepared to deny any knowledge of the murder and any connection with it. And as I say, she's now running a very successful and legitimate business, as she was only too eager to point out. An introductions agency, in Bolton, sir. High Street position, very expensive and prosperous-looking premises, DC Pickering assures me. She'd very likely be in the Masons by now, if she were a man.' He nodded happily on that thought.

Tucker hastened to backtrack in the face of this new information. 'She may just have had an unfortunate start in life, Peach. People do, you know.'

Percy was glad to hear his surname back in use. 'That's the kind of argument she's sure to put forward, sir. And she won't easily be diverted from it. Quite capable of pulling a few strings and creating quite a stink, I should think. It's good to know that you're so certain she strangled Sunita Akhtar.'

'Now wait a minute, Peach. I never said—'

'Gut feeling, sir,' Peach quoted happily.

'I know, but—'

'Benefits of your overview, sir. I often tell the lads and lasses at the crime-face just what your overview is worth to us.' He smiled contentedly, his eyes consistently on a line three inches above his chief's head.

'What I'm saying, Chief Inspector Peach, is that you must keep all your lines of enquiry open. Never jump to conclusions without proper evidence. It's a basic rule of detection, that.'

And as unvarying as your talent for stating the blindin' bleedin' obvious, thought Peach. 'This means that we have found and interviewed three of the five people who were in that squat with Sunita Akhtar. Matthew Hayward, now a concert pianist, Josephine Ingram, now Sister Josephine in a hospice, and Emily Jane Watson, owner and manager of the successful Watson Introductions Agency.'

Tucker nodded glumly. 'None of them seems a very likely candidate for murder.'

'There's also the man who met Sunita in the empty house next door, and possibly tried to recruit her to push drugs for him. The man who is now Chief Executive for Ormerod's Estate Agency.'

'David Edmonds? He wasn't even residing in that squat at the time, and he's now a pillar of Brunton society.'

Peach pursed his lips. 'Member of the Freemasons, sir. And thus four times more likely to be guilty of a serious local crime than—'

'Peach! For heavens sake stop quoting that ridiculous statistic at me!'

'Very well, sir. I suppose I'm just proud of my research.' Percy looked suitably hurt.

'This means that there are two people you haven't yet unearthed.' Tucker was pleased with his arithmetic. 'Why not?' He jutted his jaw aggressively at his odious subordinate: it was time to press rank.

'Covered their traces well, sir. But we are making progress in their direction. We now have a name for the one they all seem to have been frightened of at the time, Wally Swift. Whereabouts at present unknown, but I have feelers out with other forces in the north-west and with the Drugs Squad. And a man at present only known as Billy. Black man, sir.'

'Aah!' This time Tucker elongated the syllable, and oozed a weight of satisfaction into it.

Before the man in charge of Brunton CID could display another of his prejudices, Peach said hastily, 'I'm planning to interview a man we hope will prove to be Billy tomorrow morning, sir.'

'Good. Very good.' Tucker put his elbows on the desk and steepled his fingers. 'You must keep an open mind, as I said. But it's my belief that your murderer will turn out to be one of these last two.'

Peach, who thought that Tucker might very well be right, could nevertheless hardly credit such an unashamed volte-face. He rose and turned to leave, then stopped just before he reached the door, like an actor determined to make the most of an exit line. 'There is just one more thing I think you should know, sir. To keep you fully in the picture, I mean.'

Tucker, dropping back into the role of overworked executive with Peach's anticipated exit, said wearily, 'And what
might that be?'

'Sister Josephine, sir. Apparently she was enjoying a lesbian
relationship whilst in that squat, sir. With the dead girl.'

He carried the appealing picture of his chief's goldfish-wide
mouth away with him into the winter night.

Music was a friend in need to Matthew Hayward.

He was nervous right up to the moment when he walked
out into the welcoming applause of the audience for the concert
with the Liverpool Philharmonic. He had been uptight about
any following cars on his way into the city. He had even
watched edgily as the audience filed into the hall to take their
seats. He had been apprehensive in his dressing room as the
orchestra played the overture which preceded his performance
of the Rachmaninov Number Three concerto. These were not
the normal stage nerves which he felt before every performance, but something more sinister, which ran directly back to
that exchange with the man who had threatened him in the
pub over his quiet lunch.

But music dispelled all that for him. From the moment when
the orchestra began the introduction and he made ready to lay
his fingers on the keys of the Bechstein, concentration took
over. He heard nothing but the accompaniment of the players
around him, saw nothing but the conductor and the smooth
ivory beneath his fingers, thought of nothing but the rhythm
of performance and the passage which was coming next.
Actors spoke of Doctor Theatre curing other concerns; for
him, it was Doctor Music which took him over.

He had that wonderful feeling that he was at one with the
instrument, that he had become himself an instrument, at the
disposal of the composer and totally subject to him. It lasted
right through the concerto, as the difficulties flashed past him,
disposed of with triumphant ease. He could scarcely believe
that it was over so quickly, that the applause was for him. It
was not until the conductor came forward and led him from

his stool to acknowledge the swelling tumult of that applause that he rejoined the normal world, bowing shyly to acknowledge the wonderful uproar, which should by now have been familiar to him, but which still came as a surprise.

His problems began after the concert was over.

He had visitors after the performance. That was becoming the norm, with his increasing success and his rave reviews, but he hadn't yet mastered the art of receiving their adulation nonchalantly and getting rid of them swiftly but politely, an art which his agent assured him he would need to acquire. That meant that the car park was almost empty when he left the now deserted concert hall.

Every shadow seemed to him to carry the menace of a human shape. He found himself looking over his shoulder repeatedly, even whirling suddenly in response to some unidentified but innocent sound. He even checked the back seat of the Vectra to make sure it was empty before he slid into the driver's seat and turned the ignition key. He called a goodnight to the attendant as he went through the exit, happy to hear the sound of a cheerful answering voice through the darkness.

At least the city was quiet by this time, and Matt knew the route he was going to take. On his way to Liverpool, he had dawdled his way round Preston on the old A59, knowing that he had plenty of time before the concert. But somewhere along that route, his menacing lunchtime companion had picked him up and followed him. He had told himself repeatedly over the last few hours that the man and the mysterious force behind him wouldn't be interested in contacting him again: they had got their message across, and that was that.

Nevertheless, Matt took the motorway route home. He drove swiftly along the M58 to the junction with the M6, then north to Bamber Bridge, then westwards along the M65 until he had passed Brunton, keeping a wary eye on his rear-view mirror. When a car appeared to be following him, he put his foot down hard and took the Vectra up over the ton, wondering what the police would think of his explanation if he was stopped.

159

The car did not follow him.

The route he chose was considerably further, but not slower. He felt the tension build again when he had perforce to leave the motorway for the last few miles, but it was half past eleven now, and no headlights followed him through the lanes to Waddington.

The cottage looked very black against the hillside in the light of the thin moon. For the first time in months, he wished that he did not live alone. It would have been nice to see a welcoming light within the low-roofed old building, to hear a friendly voice acknowledging his opening of the front door.

He went swiftly through the place, switching on every light as he went, turning the cave of darkness into a box of bright light. There was no one in the house. Of course there wasn't. He had never expected that there would be, had he? He made himself a pot of tea and sat behind drawn curtains, listening to a recording of Brendel playing Mozart, telling himself that he had always intended to wind down like this when he got home.

The episode at lunchtime seemed like a bad dream now, though he could remember every detail of the man's appearance and what he had said. He wondered what it was that these people were so anxious that he should not reveal. But he didn't want to think about that now. At least it seemed they didn't know where he lived. That was a huge relief.

And he wouldn't talk, if they didn't want him to: he had no plans on being a hero.

He washed his cup and checked for a second time that all the doors were locked before he went up the narrow staircase. In the low-ceilinged room beneath the eaves, it took him much longer than usual to get to sleep. He told himself that it was the excitement of the concert and his reception after it, but he knew that it was what had happened earlier in the day which was keeping him awake. At least he was secure here, in his cosy village retreat. It was three o'clock before he fell into a fitful sleep.

He awoke later than usual, to the sound of his post coming

through the letter-box. Quarter to nine. He was usually up a good hour before this. There was nothing today from his agent. He had received so much good news lately that it was a disappointment when there were no new offers. He picked up the letters and the paper, went into the kitchen, reached for the cereals and filled the kettle. He would read the *Guardian* review of his concert over his breakfast. It was a mark of his increasing maturity that he no longer felt compelled to race feverishly through the pages to find what some critic had said about him.

He thought at first that the envelope with the Lancs postmark would be a circular: it had the computer-printed label with his address which such communications usually carried. He slit it methodically with the rest of the junk mail and carried it to the table with him.

At first he thought the envelope was completely empty. It was only when he turned it upside down and shook it that the single scrap of newsprint fell out. It was not even one of those messages cobbled together with individual letters cut from newspapers and glued to a sheet of paper. This was just a single word in inch-high black print, cut from some headline Matthew Hayward would never identify.

It said simply: 'REMEMBER'.

They knew where he lived, after all.

Seventeen

Peach and Blake parked discreetly by the training field.

It would be March tomorrow. The snowdrops had almost finished, the crocuses were blazing, and the early daffodils were making a brave show on this sunny morning, insisting that spring was just around the corner.

But this was a bleak place. You could immediately see that the prevailing wind was from the west, from the way in which the stunted hedges bent all one way, as if cowed by the gales. Or as if craving alms of the sun, thought Lucy, who was a romantic at heart and remembered her *Wuthering Heights*. But the wind today was from the north-east, and it chilled their hands and their ears instantly as they emerged reluctantly from the warmth of the unmarked Mondeo and took in the scene.

Money was short at Preston North End Football Club, as it was at most clubs in the Nationwide League. The first team squad had a designated and well-equipped training centre, but the juniors took their chance where they could, which meant enduring arctic conditions on a day like this. Yet only two of them wore gloves as they ran up and down on the half-frozen surface: when you are still a teenager, you are ridiculously reluctant to show any sign of physical weakness to those who employ you.

They were playing nine-a-side on a full-sized pitch, which at least meant they had to run about and keep the circulation going. The man in charge was very black, though a two-inch-wide patch halfway up his face was the only skin which could be discerned. As if in deference to his ancestry, he was as well protected against the glacial conditions as it was possible to be. His tracksuit trousers were tucked into thick football socks, the top part of his head and his ears were insulated under a knitted bobble hat, his hands were invisible beneath thick-knit mittens. His instructions to his charges were made indistinct by a black and white club scarf, wrapped twice around his mouth, with the ends trapped securely within his tracksuit top.

He urged on the youngsters with emphatic arm gestures, though it was difficult to discern from the touch-line that his instructions received much attention from the enthusiastic players. He nodded as he passed the only two spectators he had on this Siberian morning, muttering some remark about their sanity which was mercifully unintelligible.

Percy Peach took advantage of the ball going out of play for a throw-in to flash a warrant card in frozen fingers and yell into the gale, 'Billy Warnock? Brunton CID. We'd like a word, as soon as you've a minute. Which had better be soon, on this brass-monkey morning.'

Billy nodded. They had come, then. He had known they would, of course, so there was no need to be surprised or fearful, was there? He wondered if they had tracked down Wally Swift yet, whether they had spoken to him. What would Wally have said? He didn't fancy contradicting him. He could still see Wally's wolfish face in the shadows of that dimly lit house, even after all these years.

He lowered the scarf an inch, said as confidently as he could, 'I'll be with you straight away. Let's go into the changing room over there, shall we?' Then he turned and yelled at the juniors, 'You're on your own for a few minutes, OK, lads? And remember what I said about discipline and positions. Most of you are just chasing the ball and forgetting your main jobs!'

The changing room was no more than a wooden hut, with a single oil heater in the middle of the floor and two showers which were inoperative because the water was turned off at the main. Billy pulled up three rickety chairs as close to the heater as it was possible to get them and sat down opposite his two visitors. 'Sent you up from Deepdale, did they?'

163

'Not exactly.' What the Secretary of the football club had actually done was given them the man's second name and his job description, and confirmed that he had originally come to the club as a triallist thirteen years ago. 'We want to ask you a few questions. In connection with your presence in a squat at twenty-six Sebastopol Terrace in Brunton, in the winter and spring of 1990–91.'

He didn't deny it. There seemed little point, when they had the details so precisely. He mustered a big grin from his wide mouth, displaying the rows of very white teeth which his wife said were his best feature. 'You got me banged to rights there, guv'nor. How can I help you?'

'You could tell me who committed the murder of Sunita Akhtar, your fellow-resident in that squat, if you're really anxious to be helpful,' returned Peach with equal cheerfulness.

The grin vanished abruptly. 'I know nothing about that. Nothing beyond what I've read in my paper and heard on my television.' When they continued to stare at him, he added feebly, 'I can't remember much about those months in the squat. It's a long time ago, now.'

'So everyone tells us. So let's see if we can prod that reluctant memory of yours a little. Tell us what you can remember about the other people who were with you in that house. Detective Sergeant Blake here will be only too pleased to record a few notes for posterity!' He nodded to Lucy, who produced her gold ball pen from some intimate recess of her clothing and gave Warnock an encouraging smile, exhaling a soft cloud of white vapour from a face which seemed as pale as his was dark in that freezing hut.

'I don't remember much about them,' said Billy defensively.

Peach gave him the smile of a hungry polar bear. 'Really? They remember quite a lot about you, Billy Warnock.' You had to stretch the truth a little at times, to encourage reluctant talkers.

'Well, there was Wally Swift.'

'That's better! Tell us all about Wally, then.' It was interesting that he had begun with the man they most wanted to hear about. 'Friend of yours, was he, Wally?'

'No!' The response was too immediate, the tone too vehement. He tried to rescue things. 'I remember him best, because we were all a bit scared of him, I think. He was older than us, and he seemed to know what he was about.'

'Which was what?'

He could scarcely believe that he had led himself here, into the area he least wanted to talk about, the most dangerous area of all for him. 'I don't know quite what he did.'

'I think you do, Mr Warnock. And I think you'd better tell us, don't you? Unless you want to get yourself into even deeper waters.'

Billy hadn't realized he was in water of any kind, but this dapper figure in the dark suit and tie and the leather jacket seemed very certain about it. 'I think Wally was probably into drugs of some kind. I think he was dealing.'

Peach nodded. 'This is better, Billy. You're beginning to sound more convincing, now. In the light of what we've heard from the other people who were in that squat.'

Billy didn't like the way this was going at all. He had planned to be very vague, to dissociate himself completely from Wally and this killing. But he felt as if a net had been thrown over him: it had been loose at first, almost undetectable, but now he found it being drawn more tightly around him, cramping his limbs for movement when he wanted to lash out wildly. He wondered just who they had been talking to, what damage the others might have done to him with their evidence about those events he thought had been buried for ever. He said desperately, 'I didn't kill her, you know. That Sunita.'

'We haven't accused you of that, have we, Billy? Not yet.' Peach nodded thoughtfully, as if wondering exactly when that accusation might best be made. 'I think the best thing you can do now is to give us your recollections of the other people who were breaking the law with you in occupying that house. Don't you think so, DS Blake?'

'I think that would be much the best thing for Mr Warnock

165

to do, yes.' Lucy eased back the hood on her anorak a fraction to reveal her lustrous red hair and gave their man an encouraging smile.

Billy was grateful for the smile. He wished he could talk to this softer creature alone, but he knew that that would be quite impossible. He swallowed and said, 'There were two other girls there, as well as Sunita.'

'Jo and Emmy, yes. You'd better tell us what you recall of them, I suppose.' Peach sounded suddenly bored, as if he already knew about these two, but was prepared to go through the motions of collecting all available evidence.

That was a pity, thought Billy, as he felt on safer ground with them, and had been prepared to speak at length. 'Jo was nice. She had dark hair and a good figure. I wouldn't have minded – well, I wouldn't have minded getting closer to her, but she wasn't interested in me. She was kind, though. Thoughtful, like, and prepared to share food, when she saw I was hungry – I was very young when I found that squat and moved in. I'd had trouble at home for a long time, before then.'

'And you'd learned to fend for yourself, because you'd had to. Done a bit of shoplifting, I shouldn't wonder. Run a few errands for dubious people. Learned to live off your wits. You knew quite a lot about how to survive, for a seventeen-year-old.' Peach nodded thoughtfully, as if Billy had just confirmed all this for him. 'Difficult to see what Jo could offer, to a streetwise lad like you. I'd have thought it would have been you showing her the ropes.'

'I was only seventeen. She gave me good advice. Even gave me confidence. Said I should make the most of whatever God had given me. We'd both been brought up to go to church by our mothers, see.' He offered the last sentence almost apologetically, as if he needed to apologize for the mention of God.

'And what particular talent do you think she was referring to, in your case?'

'Football. I'd had one chance, with the Rovers, and I'd blown it. Jo told me if I really wanted it, I could get myself another go. That's how I got myself out of the squat. No one really wants to live in those places, you know.'

'So you got yourself a trial with Preston.'

'Yes. North End took me on during the close season. I was just eighteen, by then. Old enough to get a contract, and wages, with bonuses for appearances at different levels. It wasn't much, but I'd never had a regular wage until then.' His eyes were dreamy with the memory of that unexpected Garden of Eden.

'I saw you play, Billy. About ten years ago, it would be. In the first team. You were good.'

'I was quick. And I had a good first touch. Improved a lot, that did, when I was training full time with North End.'

'So what went wrong?'

'Injury. Bastard brought me down when I was right through on goal and going like the clappers. Did my knee ligaments. I needed an operation and eight months off. I recovered, but I was a yard slower, and that made all the difference. I was small and quick, see. I couldn't compensate with other things, like Alan Shearer did when he lost his pace. But North End were good to me. They kept me in the stiffs for a couple of years, bringing on the youngsters. Then they gave me this job, in charge of developing the juniors. We're bringing one or two good lads through now.'

'Good to know you've made it as a law-abiding citizen,' Peach said dryly. He turned suddenly grim again. 'Resent it, did you, when Sunita rejected your advances?'

Billy forced himself to smile. 'When you're as black as I am and brought up where I was, you get used to rejection. Besides, it wasn't just me. Turned out she wasn't interested in men, was she, Sunita?'

'She wasn't?'

'No. She took up with Jo, didn't she? Didn't upset me: I was glad just to be mates with the two of them, to have friendly faces to talk to. It was Matty who got upset about it, not me.' It felt good to be able to defend himself against something.

'Yes, we gathered that. Cut up quite rough, didn't he?'

167

'I think he did, yes. I kept out of it, mind. It was nothing to do with me. Sunita was his bird. They came to the squat almost at the same time, those two, and neither of them knew anything about life, if you ask me.'

'We are asking you, Billy. We need everything you can tell us. We're asking everyone else as well, mind. So you'd do well to give us the whole truth and nothing but the truth.' Peach was back into predator mould again, metaphorically circling his prey. His leather jacket was as black as his eyes, his moustache and the fringe of hair beneath his bold dome; Billy found himself wishing there was something about this man which was not black. 'Do you think Matty killed Sunita because he was jealous when he saw her in the sack with Jo?'

'No. Well, I don't know, but I wouldn't think so. He seemed a nice lad, even if he was infantile when it came to squats.' Billy was pleased with that word 'infantile'. The Chairman of the football club had used it, when he had been annoyed with the behaviour of one of their stars. Billy had picked it up for use with the young lads he handled, who were just kids really, and mustn't get swollen heads. He used it quite a lot now.

'Nice lads commit murders, Billy. Sometimes.'

'All I'm saying is that I don't think Matty did. He's a concert pianist now.'

'Yes, we know that, Billy. We've spoken to him. Twice. Surprised you've followed his career like that, though. Is it because you thought he might be a murderer?'

Billy wished he wouldn't rap out questions like that on the back of what seemed innocent sentences. 'No. I liked Matty, that's all. He was dead keen on football, for one thing. We got out of the squat at about the same time, and we both seemed to be making a go of it, in our different ways. Until I got injured in 1997.' He was suddenly sad with the memory of what might have been.

They could hear the urgent sound of young voices calling to each other outside the hut, as they played the game Billy loved. Lucy Blake said gently to him, 'But you don't know that Matthew Hayward didn't kill Sunita, do you?'

168

Billy shook his head unhappily. It seemed odd to have Matty's full name rolled out like that; it was as if he was being reminded of what different worlds the two former squatters now inhabited. 'No. But I don't think he did. Jo would have been more likely to kill her, if you ask me, when she saw the girl going off the rails. She'd stood up for her in the squat, and I think she'd grown very fond of her.' You didn't mention love, he thought, when you were talking about dykes.

'And Sunita rather let her down, didn't she?' This girl's voice was soft and persuasive, convincing him that she already knew everything that had gone on in that squat. Far more than he did, probably, if they'd spoken to all the others. 'Yes. She went off talking to that bloke who brought the drugs. The one who was operating out of number twenty-eight next door.'

'Do you think she was pushing stuff for him?'

He made himself think. It could help to get him off the hook, this, if he played it right. 'Yes. I think she probably was. I heard Jo having terrible rows with her, and I can only think it was about that.'

'Was Sunita pushing drugs for Wally Swift, as well?'

It was like a blow in the face, bringing him back to Wally when he thought he had been leading the questioning away from him. He said sullenly, 'She might have been, I suppose.'

As soon as the words were out, he realized that he had admitted that he knew Wally was pushing drugs. But they must surely know that already. There was a pause then, and he looked from the soft features of the girl who had been questioning him into the face of the man at her side.

Peach looked like the cat who had won the cream. A very large and dangerous cat: a tiger, perhaps. He smiled at Billy and said, 'Running an extensive network of dealers was he, by the time you left?'

'Wally?'

'Who else? Sounds to me as if Sunita was torn between working for this man who came next door and Wally Swift. Of course, I wasn't there at the time. But you were, Billy. What do you think of that idea?'

169

'Sounds possible, I suppose.' That sounded woefully weak, even in his own ears, and he was moved to add, 'I didn't know much about what was going on in the place, you see.'

'Really, Billy? A streetwise young lad like you?' His voice hardened from incredulity into accusation. 'I'd have thought that you'd have known exactly what was going on. More quickly than anyone else in that squat, apart from Wally Swift himself.'

Billy had gone straight for so long now that he felt he had lost the capacity to deceive. He had possessed it abundantly as a seventeen-year-old, and even earlier as a streetwise urchin. He said unconvincingly, 'I don't know what was going on. I didn't have anything to do with Wally Swift.'

'So how did you earn your living in those months in the squat, Billy. How did you survive?'

All invention suddenly deserted him. He should have had an answer ready for this one, should have prepared the ground for it in advance. Now, with those unblinking dark eyes seeming to peer into his very soul, he could not even think on his feet, as he had been able to do all those years before. 'I can't remember, now. It's a long time ago. We weren't paying rent, so we didn't need a lot. We helped each other out. I did bits of part-time work, wherever I could get it.'

Peach smiled and shook his head. 'Not what other people are telling us, that, Billy.' He leaned forward and spoke as if he was iterating an established fact. 'You were working for Wally Swift, and he was pushing drugs. Beginning to establish a network in the town.'

'No.'

'And this man who came next door was a threat to that network. And Sunita Akhtar was a foolish girl who got caught between the two of them.'

'No!' He was shouting, now, trying to stem the flow of this stream of accusation.

'Did you kill Sunita, Billy?'

'No! I don't—'

'Did Wally Swift kill her?'

'No.'

'Do you know that?'

He almost said that he did, then realized that that would be the same as telling them that he knew who the killer was. He said slowly, 'I can't *know* that Wally didn't do it, can I, without knowing that someone else did it? I'm saying that I don't think he killed her.'

'He seems the likeliest candidate, doesn't he? A man with a history of violence. A man making his way in the drugs industry, where violence, lethal violence, is a tool of the trade.'

He repeated dully, 'I don't think Wally killed her. That's all I'm saying.'

'Might not have done it himself, a man like that.' Peach seemed to be thinking aloud now, directing his words to the woman next to him rather than the man opposite. 'Much more likely to have employed an underling to do his dirty work for him. Someone like Billy Warnock here.'

Lucy Blake nodded her head, then looked sadly at the apprehensive black face. 'Don't you think you should tell us everything you know about Wally Swift, Billy? Whilst there's still time?'

Billy spoke like a man who no longer expected to be believed as he said, 'I don't know anything else. I wasn't working for Wally.' He wondered what came next, whether they knew about the phone call to Wally he had made on the previous day, whether they were merely allowing him to condemn himself out of his own mouth.

There was a long pause, during which the shouts of the youths outside seemed unnaturally loud, as if they were about to invade the scene in the icy hut. Then Peach said, 'There were two women there as well as the murder victim. Tell us about the other one.'

He tried not to show his relief at the switch. 'Emmy. I don't know her other name. She was a hard piece.' He found that it was difficult to get the words out.

'Hard in what way, Billy?'

'She knew what went on in the world. She took whatever

171

she could from the rest of us. Gave very little back. As little as she could get away with.'

'I see. And what did she do to survive in the place?'

He looked up, but found Peach's face inscrutable. 'Haven't you spoken to her?'

'We have, yes. We'd like your opinion.'

'I think she was selling it.'

'On the game, you mean?'

'Yes. I don't mean she was a regular prostitute. She wouldn't have needed to stay in the squat, if she had been, would she? I mean that she sold it around, when the opportunity came up. I expect that she went on the game when she moved out of the squat. But I don't know that. She was still there when I left.'

'You're probably right. We know that a couple of years later the woman you knew as Emmy was running a brothel, organizing her own group of tarts. Do you think she tried to recruit Sunita?'

'Yes. I remember her telling the girl that there was a big demand for Paki women in the town.'

'And do you think that she might have killed her, if she refused to work for her?'

He shook his head as if trying to clear it. 'I don't know. I wouldn't have thought so, but she didn't like it when she didn't get her own way, Emmy. And I said, she was a hard piece.'

Lucy nodded slowly and said softly, 'Yes. If Sunita agreed to operate for her and then didn't cough up her share of the takings, Emmy wouldn't have taken kindly to that, would she?'

Billy grasped at it like a man being offered a lifeline. 'No. She had a hell of a temper, Em. And if someone had tried to double-cross her, there's no knowing what she'd have done.'

They asked him if he could offer them anything else about any of their suspects, then released him, sending him outside to blow a long blast on the whistle and bring in his charges.

They caught a last glimpse of Billy Warnock as they drove away, standing motionless with his arms folded in the doorway of the hut and looking after them.

They were back on the main road to Brunton before Peach said, 'He learned to deceive early in life, that lad. I wonder if we've got everything he knows out of him.'

Eighteen

Police undercover work is a specialized and highly dangerous occupation. It requires special skills in acting and deception and an extraordinary level of nerve. No one can be compelled to undertake it. Senior officers think long and hard before putting their colleagues in danger, and are required to make it absolutely clear that anyone undertaking such an assignment has to be a volunteer. Strict regulations ensure that anyone who declines to work under cover will not be penalized for the refusal.

Undercover work in the illegal drugs trade is the most dangerous operation of all.

Mike Allen was twenty-eight, a sergeant in the Drugs Squad, which is the most highly trained specialist unit in the British police service. Like almost every officer who opted to take the risks of assuming a false identity, he was single and without any long-term partner. He had been operating under cover for almost four months now.

Mike had thought he understood what he was taking on when he had volunteered for the assignment. It took him less than a week to appreciate that the dangers were far greater and more continuous than he had anticipated. You were at risk for every hour of the day and every day of the week. Even when you were asleep, you were not safe. People went through your belongings when you were asleep, listened to anything you might mutter in your exhausted rest, heard any revealing words you might blurt out in that dangerous period between sleep and consciousness, when you stirred into life without always being aware of where you were.

Mike knew that the only solution was to live the part, to become the drop-out and the petty drug-dealer you were supposed to be. After sixteen weeks of tension, he was unshaved, unwashed and unkempt, with the stale smell which drug users, careless of everything but their next fix, carry upon them. He lived rough, shivering through the winter under a couple of thin and filthy blankets, eating little beyond stale bread and beans spooned cold out of tins.

And Mike hoped that he looked even rougher than he felt. He took a daily intake of coke, though only a quarter of what his new masters thought he was taking. You couldn't simulate the symptoms of addiction without taking a certain amount of the stuff. He wondered how easily he would be able to kick the habit when all this was over. He had found himself counting the hours to his next snort of the white powder in the last fortnight. They had offered him crack last week, cocaine in rock form, 'cooked' with baking powder. That was the most terrifyingly addictive form of coke of all. He had said he could not afford it: at forty pounds a rock, it was too expensive for him.

That had got things moving. It had been suggested to him that there were ways of paying for his habit without cash changing hands. He knew what that meant: they were considering using him as a dealer. Things were coming to a head. One way or another, his situation was going to be resolved.

In the darkness of the night, the only time when Mike Allen could collect his thoughts and remember what he had been in the days before he volunteered for this assignment, he often wondered whether he would ever get out of this alive. This was the reality now; that 'normal' world outside it, where he had worked with normal people, seemed increasingly a dream-world, a land of lost content which would never be available to him again.

In these last months, he had joined so often in the ritual condemnations of the police and the law that he was confused: sometimes he felt that *this* was his real life now, that the obscenities he screamed against the pigs were bitter and heartfelt. He had been warned that it would be like this, that feeling as he did was a sign of success in the role he was playing. But he felt only confusion and danger. And isolation. He wondered how much the regular intake of coke was affecting him.

Sergeant Allen wondered if when the moment for decision came he would recognize it, or whether he would perish in a cock-up of his own making.

You were hamstrung anyway by the police rules: they wanted you to pose as a drug-pusher, without actually pushing drugs. That was the most ridiculous thing of all. If you actually sold drugs to addicts, you would be committing a crime, whatever your reasons for doing it. The lawyers wouldn't have that: it would compromise the legal case against the men higher up the chain that you were trying to trap if you were enticing them into crime.

It was all right for the bloody lawyers, sitting smugly in their comfortable, warm, Crown Prosecution offices and making the rules for those who took the risks. Making the rules for a world they did not know and did not want to know; ignoring the dangers of that world because it suited them to do so. Mike Allen could do quite a speech about lawyers, without needing to act at all.

Normally he was glad when it went dark. He found it easier to be convincing, to play the man he had to be, after nightfall. It seemed the natural setting for this desperate cast-off from society, this piece of flotsam who must float helplessly along currents controlled by stronger criminal men. He was glad that they would be into March tomorrow, with its promise of increasing warmth in the sun. But he found that he resented the increasing daylight, because that seemed to carry the threat of exposure. He was like a mole that operates under the earth and cannot reveal itself in the glare of the day.

But it might all be over tonight, if things went as he hoped. Even if they didn't, in fact. He tried not to think of his days here ending in exposure and the squalid death which would inevitably follow that. He had seen enough of the drugs trade and the men who operated it to remove any delusions about survival if things went wrong. Sometimes your body would be found in some anonymous city dumping ground, beneath a motorway flyover or in a disused canal. More often, you would simply disappear, removed from the face of the earth without any sign that you had ever existed upon it.

He dragged his feet unwillingly through the Manchester streets, moving like a much older man. Now that the moment which would bring release or oblivion was approaching, he was reluctant to move towards it. That impulse for survival, that instinct which means that even the most determined of suicides by water finish by fighting the river with bursting lungs, made him reluctant to move towards this rendezvous with the greatest danger of all.

He had taken the coke an hour ago, as his cover demanded that he should. Normally it gave him a lift, made him for a time more confident and optimistic, even though he knew in his heart that this well-being was an illusion. Tonight he found as he slunk along the almost deserted streets of Moss Side that the high had not lasted, that he felt less rather than more secure.

Would his reactions be slowed, would he be unable to act and react to events as swiftly as he surely must if he was to survive?

He told himself that he would have the backing of the firm. Tonight, for the first time in months, he would have the bene-fit of police support, of colleagues who were anxious to secure his safety. That thought gave him no comfort. He struggled indeed even to comprehend the idea. He had immersed himself for so long in the culture of the underworld which he had made his natural habitat for the last four months that he could not regard the network which was supposed to extricate him from this as anything other than an alien force.

Mike Allen had ceased to think like a policeman.

The building loomed ahead of him, massive and black as a setting for a horror movie. But it was worse than that: his fevered brain, so full of unwelcome thoughts, told him that. This multi-storey car park, tall as an office block, black as

Satan's palace, was worse than any *Psycho* motel. It was bigger, blacker, more threatening in its massive anonymity, than any cinema mock-up could ever be.

To see so large a building so dimly lit was the worst thing of all. Some of the university buildings were only half a mile away, their size making them seem even closer through the darkness. Some of them were much higher than this one. But they were brightly lit, teeming with a life that was innocent and ongoing. Mike put up the collar of his anorak against the straggling hair at the back of his neck and turned away from them.

The man, whoever he might be, would not be there yet. That was the way it operated. He forced himself to move beneath the big concrete arch of the entrance and into the cave of darkness.

The basement smelt of rotting wood, of urine, of a host of other dank smells he did not care to identify. There was a tiny scratching at the far end of it, thirty or forty yards away from him. Rats? Mike was a Winston Smith when it came to rats; he feared that he would run screaming from the place if anything ran over his foot. But the sound was not repeated. Mike Allen forced a long breath of the damp and icy air into his coke-narrowed lungs, then put his shoulders and his back against the damp concrete of the wall. This wait would be the worst time of all. You had to try to close your mind against the possibilities of the next half hour.

The minutes stretched like hours, the sounds of the city outside sounding muted and distant, as if reminding him that he was isolated here, that he was alone with the evil forces which would dictate his destiny. He thrust his hands deep into the pockets of his grubby anorak, trying not to register the tremors which began to run through his limbs as the effects of the cocaine wore off and the damp cold of this place began to take its toll on his thin body.

He should have been glad to hear the car, to know that his vigil was coming to an end. Instead he felt only fear. Fear of himself, as well as what was coming. Fear that his body would be so rigid with terror that his limbs would be unable to move, his brain unable to act out the part it had played so successfully for months. Fear that in this climax of his ordeal, his nerve would fail him and he would collapse in suicidal confession at the feet of the man he was supposed to trap.

The Jaguar purred softly into the car park and down to the basement, fixing him like a rabbit in its headlights, threatening as it eased silently towards a stop to pin him against the dripping wall. Mike Allen's knees were shuddering against the front bumper when the long vehicle stopped and the illumination switched abruptly to side lights. Mike had thrown up the back of his arm in front of his eyes, blinded by the fierce white light after the darkness of his waiting.

He was conscious of a heavy man easing out of the passenger seat and standing over his crouching form. The driver and another figure from the back of the car got out and stood slightly behind their leader, one on each side, the heavies providing the protection he would never need from Mike.

'Good evening, Mr Smith,' said Mike obsequiously. He was glad that his voice at least was working. You called them all Smith; no one in the hierarchy revealed his name, and the less you knew the safer it was for you.

The man did not reply. He studied the form in front of him for a few moments, then reached out a toe to Mike's leg and turned him from a sideways cower to a position facing him directly. 'So, Michael Allen, you want to work for us. You want to deal.'

'I do, Mr Smith.' Mike had caught a touch of Irish in the voice. It was irrelevant, now: he wasn't a detective, not in this situation. He was bait, dead as a dodo within minutes, if the men who might not even be there did not intervene to save him. Yet he was glad he had picked up the bit of brogue: it showed that his brain was working, when he had most need of it. He whined, 'I need to deal, see. It's the only way I can get my supplies, innit?'

It was the way most people became dealers at the bottom of the chain, the way the barons were assured of their loyalty.

Once you became an addict, you were no longer employable in legitimate work in the world outside. You needed your coke or your heroin in ever larger doses, but you no longer had the money to buy. You had to deal, to get your supplies.

'Cokehead, are you?'

Mike could hear the contempt in the voice. He thought for a moment that the man who had come to vet him was going to touch him again with his toe, to give him a kick perhaps, just for the pleasure of it. Instead, he stood motionless, studying the abject figure in front of him: Mike could hear the sound of his breathing, smell stale cigar smoke on his camel coat. He pleaded, 'I'm not an addict, Mr Smith. I'm in control still. I'm a user, not an addict. I won't let you down, when I deal.'

'*If* you deal.' The check came promptly, as if he had touched a nerve. This man enjoyed the power he wielded; it wasn't just the wealth which interested him. 'Can you shift horse?'

'Horse and coke. LSD as well, if you've got it.'

'And E?'

Mike could hear the voice ticking off the list of the most lucrative drugs for the suppliers. 'Yes. I can shift Ecstasy, plenty of it. The middle classes want that! And speed. And as much rohypnol as you can supply!'

The laugh came back at him harshly through the dimness. 'Everybody wants the date-rape drug! Everyone can shift that! Symptom of our decadent society that is, Michael Allen.'

'Yes, Mr Smith.' He stood with head bowed, feeling the weakness now in his knees, wondering where this was taking him, how long he could keep up his part if no one intervened to save him.

'We'll be looking to you to turn over a thousand quid a week initially. Two thousand a week, once you get going. Think you can do that?'

'Yes. Yes, I'm sure I can, Mr Smith. So long as you can make sure that I get what I need for myself.'

'You'll get that, Michael Allen. And perhaps commission for yourself, when you begin to shift the right amount. There's money in this, you know, for those who keep their mouths sealed and get on with shifting the stuff.'

That was the nearest he would come to a pep talk. Most of these pathetic instruments did not survive more than a year before their own addiction caught up with them. That did not matter to the Smiths of the industry, so long as those who failed knew nothing about the men above them.

'I'll shift them all, Mr Smith. I know I can do it. I'll be one of your best operatives, once I get going.'

Smith's laugh rang loud in that quiet, echoing place. He had heard it all before, knew that these contemptible creatures really believed what they were so desperately telling him. 'I like that word: "operative". Comes from a different world, that does. I like it. Well, Michael Allen, you'll be delighted to know we're going to give you a trial.'

'Thank you, Mr Smith. I won't let—'

'A couple of weeks to start with. You'll get your own intake, which you're not to exceed, and quantities to shift. We'll be watching you, mind. If we find you satisfactory, you'll be given more dope and an extended period.'

'Right. I'll make sure you—'

'You won't see me again, Michael Allen. I don't deal with the likes of you.'

'No. No, I wouldn't expect to—'

'But I'll be watching you. Don't you worry about that. So don't you step out of line.'

He had never taken his eyes off the submissive figure against the dripping wall in front of him. He did not do so now as he nodded to the man behind his right shoulder. The man opened the boot of the Jaguar and bent to lift the box from inside it. The boot light gleamed unnaturally bright in the darkness around it, throwing the man's features into a goblin profile as he stooped and straightened again. He waited for another nod from Smith before he came forward and held out the box to the man with his back to the wall.

It was at that moment that hell broke loose.

Arc lamps flashed bright and blinding, throwing up the

group by the Jaguar as if they were on a stage, freezing the cameo into stillness as the police sirens blared and the vehicles screamed in to block off the exit for the Jaguar.

There was a confusion of yelling voices, telling the men caught in the lights not to move, that armed police had their weapons trained upon them, that they should keep perfectly still. Seconds later, the three men who had so terrified Mike Allen were against the side of the Jaguar with their hands above their heads and their feet splayed, as expert hands ran up and down their bodies in search of weapons.

Mike slumped against the wall, scarcely realizing that salvation had come, scarcely hearing the torrent of oaths and obscenities pouring over him from Smith as he realized he had been betrayed.

The officer yelled into the man's ear that he was being arrested for attempting to supply illegal Class A drugs, that he did not need to say anything now, but that it might prejudice his defence if he failed to reveal evidence which he might later rely on for his defence in court.

All Mike was interested in was the strong police arms which held Smith in check as he tried to launch an attack on the exhausted figure in front of him.

It was only when the big frame was being arrested and flung into the back of the police Rover that Mike heard that his real name was Walter Swift.

Nineteen

February the twenty-ninth. A day of great significance, in the minds of some people.

Frivolous people, Lucy Blake told herself firmly. Forget all about the date and enjoy the evening, that was the best approach. It's not every day that Percy Peach takes you to a posh restaurant. She'd offered to go Dutch, but he'd rejected the suggestion, with a lordly wave and an expression wholly inappropriate for the delicate ears of a young lady. As Lucy had decided that at twenty-eight she was now no longer either young or a lady, she did not make even the attempt to blush.

She wondered whether to pretend that she had eaten duck à l'orange of this quality on many previous occasions, then rejected that idea also. Percy Peach had a disconcerting habit of seeing straight through any pretensions of that sort. More importantly, she was pleased to find that she no longer wanted to deceive him, that they had gone beyond the point where they played silly games of that sort with each other.

The silly games they did play with each other were much more enjoyable.

Percy seemed to be having to search much harder than usual for words. Perhaps the immaculate linen on the tables and the gleaming cut glass inhibited him. Or perhaps he was inhibited by the fact that at the beginning of the evening he had forbidden any shop talk, any observations on the baffling case of the murder of Sunita Akhtar.

Percy was at his most trenchant and most amusing when he spoke off the record about the suspects involved in a case. It was his involvement in his work which was one of the things which had attracted her to him, in the first place. Try finding that in the ten most important factors in a relationship, as listed by *Cosmopolitan.*

He kept filling up her glass with the Shiraz. It was a good one, and he even threatened to order another bottle. When she refused, he insisted on ordering brandies at the end of the meal. She shuddered to think what the evening was costing him. He can afford it, as a single man on a chief inspector's salary, she told herself firmly.

Peach lingered uncharacteristically at the end of the meal. He was usually far too impatient to spend more time than was strictly necessary over anything. Well, almost anything. You couldn't count sex: all men were prepared to spend inordinate amounts of time on that. But certainly food was not normally one of Percy Peach's major concerns. And this lingering, this running of his finger thoughtfully round the top of his glass, this series of soulful glances into her eyes over the latter stages of the meal, was quite untypical. Unnerving, in fact.

He said suddenly, 'You've got very beautiful eyes, you know. Blue or green, according to the light. Or something between the two, a shade which can turn strong men's knees to water.'

'Ultramarine,' she said dryly.

'Is it?'

'You told me all about my eyes the first time we went out. Ultramarine, you called them then.'

'Did I really? I congratulate myself on that. I had great discernment, in those days.' He shook his head sadly, as if they were thirty rather than three years behind them. He'd be going in for the full nostalgia trip next, recalling their first, tentative advances to each other as if they had been Romeo and Juliet. It was all quite perplexing, especially when you hadn't much of a head for alcohol.

Lucy realized that weakness when the cold night air hit her outside the restaurant. Percy asked her, 'Your place or mine?' as the taxi drew up. That was disconcerting, too. He normally had it all worked out, was looking forward with relish to the romp ahead of him, whether in her warm bedroom or in his freezing one.

Lucy looked up at the thin moon, caught the frost on the grass, and said firmly, 'My place, I think!'

'Much the best idea,' Percy agreed. 'I like a woman who can take important decisions!'

He made it sound heavy with import, and it was so far from his normal attitude that she wanted to take issue with him. But he darted his mobile right hand straight to her thigh in the darkness of the back seat of the taxi, and she was soon giggling her way through much more familiar battles. Normal service had apparently been resumed.

Yet he was not as anxious as usual to get her into the bedroom. He accepted the offer of another coffee and sat in the big armchair looking through her CDs, making desultory conversation. He seemed to be at a loss until she mentioned the England cricket team, whereupon he enlarged at great length and with great expertise on the length of the England tail and the inconsistency of their bowling. Her mother would have loved it.

Lucy Blake wondered whether Percy was beginning to go off her.

That awful idea was quickly dispelled when they made their tardy retirement for the night. Percy held her at arm's length and looked soulfully into her eyes before they left the sitting room, an uncharacteristic delay at this particular moment. But once she began to undress, all was busy activity. She was reassured, even as she employed the nimble side-step which was a necessary skill during this part of the evening.

Percy seemed as usual to have at least two pairs of hands, both of them highly active. 'You're a fetishist!' she told him breathlessly. 'I've never seen anyone turned on so immediately by the sight of a pair of pants.'

'I've always been into knickers,' Percy agreed happily. 'Even more so since I got into yours!' Suiting the action to the word, he fell upon her with a warrior's whoop and deployed his four hands at the back and the front of the blue silk garment.

185

'Now that's what I call a backside!' he said with a long sigh of pleasure. 'I warmed my hands specially for this.'

'You were always one to bowl a girl over with your consideration,' said Lucy, deciding that the line of least resistance was the only possible one here and making for the double bed she knew would soon be in disarray.

It was some time before Percy Peach said anything else. When he did, it was the mystic but simple 'Bloody 'ell, Norah!' which was his usual seal of approval on their carnal exchanges. It was warm and muffled, from somewhere beneath the bedclothes.

They had eaten and drunk too well and exercised too strenuously. At two thirty in the morning, Lucy Blake found herself staring at the ceiling and reviewing the curious events of the earlier part of the evening. Indigestion. She must be getting old: she needed a tablet.

It was a mistake. It was whilst she was stretching for her handbag beneath the bed that the man she had thought deeply asleep beside her fell upon the ample backside he had so admired and ravished her anew. For certain, his ardour was not diminishing.

She sank happily back upon her pillows. 'Bloody 'ell, Norman!' she murmured admiringly.

It was over the stark simplicity of the breakfast bar in her small modern kitchen that she puzzled herself again about the events in the restaurant on the previous evening. 'You weren't your usual self, my man,' she said, as lightly as she could. 'You were polite, even romantic. It's not your style.'

'I'm a romantic at heart.' Percy stared bleakly at his muesli and imagined a full fry-up. 'And I'm ten years older than you. I'm not allowed to presume.' On that gnomic utterance, he delved his spoon resolutely into his healthy cereal and ate.

'Nearly ten years,' she corrected him. 'And I didn't notice any decline in energy during the rest of the night.'

Percy smiled in spite of himself, looking rather like a schoolboy who has just received praise for getting his sums right. 'Nevertheless, I am a modest man, Lucy Blake. I do not

186

presume.' He sighed rather theatrically. 'I'm disappointed, but not surprised. It's a pity, because I'm very fond of your mum – she talks a far better cricket game than you ever will. But there it is.' He sighed again and resumed his meditational munching of muesli.

An alarming thought gnawed its way into the back of Lucy's mind. 'You're surely not saying that you expected me to – to propose to you?'

Percy gave the slightest of nods at the now empty bowl in front of him. 'February the twenty-ninth, yesterday, weren't it, our Lucy?'

She loved the way he dropped into Lancashire talk for their most intimate moments. Loved the way he thought that it would be presumptuous for him to propose marriage to her. Loved the way that he had hoped she would take advantage of the date that came only once every four years to propose to him. Loved Percy Peach and everything he meant in her life.

Bloody 'ell, Norah.

'Wally Swift. Been looking for you for quite some time. In the deep doodoos, aren't you? The very deep doodoos.'

That thought obviously afforded Percy Peach deep satisfaction. He switched on the cassette recorder and announced that the interview with Walter Arthur Swift was beginning at 0912, with DCI Peach and DS Blake in attendance. 'Expect you'll want your brief here for this.'

'No. Nothing for a brief to do. I've been fitted up.' Swift knew the form. You said nothing. If the barons thought you were worth the effort, they'd make sure you had a lawyer, in due course. The best. Meantime, you kept shtum. It was more than your life was worth to name names, especially from anywhere higher up the chain. With luck, and a good brief in court, you'd get a hefty fine or a short custodial sentence for dealing.

All three of them in that warm cell of an interview room knew the score. They would all go through the motions, utter their well-rehearsed lines, and then he would be taken back to his cell and left there, whilst they struggled unsuccessfully to get more evidence against him, a better idea of the chain above and below him. That bastard Mike Allen had trapped him, but he surely couldn't know enough to get the big boys. It was a bloody nuisance, but these buggers couldn't touch the million and more that Wally Swift had stashed away in off-shore funds. There was nothing they could do about that.

Percy Peach was about to surprise him.

'Best thing you can do is to be perfectly frank with us, Mr Swift. I don't expect you'll see it like that, but that doesn't worry me. I'll be quite pleased to hang a man like you out to dry.' Peach gave him a first smile, a dazzling of white teeth against the dull green of the room's walls.

'I was fitted up. You Drugs Squad blokes are at it all the time. Surprised you think you can still—'

'Not Drugs Squad, this, Wally. Mr Swift.' Peach managed to convey a sneer on what seemed a routine repetition of the surname. 'Drugs Squad will probably have a go at you when we've finished. After you've been hung out to dry.'

Swift had been determined to play it cool, to let nothing ruffle him. He'd dealt with plenty of pigs before, knew their tactics in interviews. But now he was shaken. This man was changing the rules, before they'd even started. And he looked so smug, so confident. It was years since anyone had called him Wally; he would not have thought it possible that a single word could be so unnerving, but it seemed to have happened. He said aggressively, 'No one hangs Walter Swift out to dry, Chief Inspector.' He tried to get the same kind of sneer into the title that Peach had visited upon his name, but he couldn't quite bring it off.

'Sounds like a challenge, that, Wally.' He turned to the woman at his side. 'Wouldn't you say that sounded like a challenge, DS Blake?'

'It did to me, sir, yes. A very ill-advised challenge, in view of the evidence we've gathered over the last week.' She gave the man on the other side of the table a different kind of smile from Peach's, the sympathetic smile reserved by nurses for those disappearing to the theatre for serious surgery.

Swift was already regretting not having a brief. But it would be a climb-down to ask for one now. And Walter Swift did not do climb-downs. Another mistake.

He said, 'I've issued no challenges. I'm here on a trumped-up charge of dealing drugs.'

'Correction. The very serious drugs charge will be dealt with in due course, by the relevant officers. Who happily know a lot more about your organization than you think they do.' Peach smiled happily at the ceiling and nodded a couple of times on that thought. Then his smile vanished abruptly as he said, 'We're here to talk about something much more interesting, Wally. Murder.'

'Murder?' Even for a man as steeped in criminality as Swift, the word carried a grisly glamour which stilled his tongue.

'The murder of Sunita Akhtar.'

'I've never heard of her.' But he felt the colour draining from his face, even as he kept his brown eyes resolutely on Peach's black and sparkling pupils.

'Mistake, that, Wally. Another mistake. Her name's been all over the papers for the last week. Of course you've heard of her. But let's play your game and refresh your memory. You lived under the same roof as Sunita Akhtar for at least six months, at twenty-six Sebastopol Terrace, Brunton, during the winter and spring of 1990 and 1991. Are you denying that?'

'Well, what if I did? You can't go—'

'At the end of which period, she was murdered.' Peach nodded happily, as if ticking off another stage in the assembly of a cast-iron case.

'I can't be expected to remember what happened in 1991 in Brunton. It's a long time ago.'

'They all start off by saying that. But it's surprising how much comes back to them, when they think seriously about those months. When they're trying to avoid a murder rap and give us the man who really killed Sunita.'

189

Swift found himself licking his lips. He didn't fancy asking who these others were, finding out exactly how many of the inmates of that squat where it had all started for him they had been able to find. And what they'd told these two smug pigs about him. 'I didn't kill that Paki girl.'

This time Peach allowed his grin to develop into a chuckle. He had to shake his head over the silliness of it all. 'You won't expect us to accept your word on that, though, will you, Wally? Not a man with your vast experience of police procedure.'

'What happened to "Innocent until Proved Guilty"?'

Peach shook his head sadly. 'Indeed, what happened to that, Wally? Nice idea put about by the lawyers, I think. Funny buggers, lawyers. Don't suppose the idea ever had much clout, for blokes like you.'

Swift wished again that he'd gone for the brief when he'd had the chance. He was sure this cocky little bantam of a policeman wouldn't have got away with this attitude, with a brief around. He said doggedly, 'I can just about remember those days in the squat. I can just about remember the Paki girl, but I didn't kill her.'

Peach nodded happily, as if this was exactly the line he had expected. 'Twenty-six Sebastopol Terrace, Brunton. Unlawfully occupied as a squat on a regular basis by you, Wally Swift, and by five other people.'

'I don't—'

'All of whom we have now interviewed. Just needed you to complete the set, you see, Wally. And you walked obligingly into our hands. Well, into the hands of the Drugs Squad, to be strictly accurate. But murder takes precedence even over serious drugs charges, so here we are.' He smiled widely and happily at that situation.

'I don't know what these other people have told you, but—'

'Quite a lot, Wally, as a matter of fact. Quite a lot about you, too. It's been most illuminating, hasn't it, DS Blake?'

'Very illuminating indeed, sir. I felt I almost knew Mr Swift, long before this meeting.'

Peach nodded happily. 'That's the advantage of our organization and our methods, you see, Wally. We plod along – get criticized for plodding, at times – but it produces surprising results. We know, for example, that you were deep into criminal activity, even in those days.'

'And who told you that?'

Another chuckle from Peach. 'You wouldn't expect us to reveal that, Wally, would you?' He leaned forward. 'But now's your chance to tell us about the others in that squat. Get yourself off the hook. If you think that's possible.'

Walter Swift looked at him with a face full of hate. But hate didn't help you to think. To think rationally. That was what he needed to do, in this situation. He was surely a match for any plod. He said, 'There weren't just the people in the squat, you know. There were others came next door. One other, anyway. And he knew Sunita Akhtar.'

'Good, Wally. That's good. You see, you're remembering things already about Sebastopol Terrace. Obscure things, like who came next door occasionally. You wouldn't by any chance be trying to divert our attention away from what went on at number twenty-six, would you?'

'He was trying to get that girl to work for him.' Swift furrowed his brow and pretended to think. 'Edmonds, he was called. Dave Edmonds. You should talk to him. He tried to get that girl to sell drugs for him, if I remember right.'

Peach regarded these efforts with some distaste. 'We have talked to Edmonds, Wally. We have a statement from him.'

Swift was shaken for a moment. He wondered just how much this cocksure little sod did know. If it was true that he was the last of those who had lived in the squat to be interviewed, perhaps his card was already marked. Perhaps they were wanting to hear him condemn himself out of his own mouth. He said, 'If she wouldn't work for that Edmonds or went back on her word, he could have killed her for that. People dealing drugs don't mess about.'

He wished he hadn't spoken those last words, as soon as they were out. Peach grinned delightedly. 'Good motive, that.

Only snag with it is that it applies to you as well, Wally. I think it sits better on you, though. You had already established a trade in drugs, and Edmonds was stepping on to your patch. If he poached a girl who was one of your pushers, I wouldn't like to have been in her shoes.' He spoke as if testing the theory to see how it sounded, then nodded approvingly. 'I like that. It's quite convincing, to me. Not going to confess, are you, Wally?'

'Of course I'm not bloody confessing!' But the motive had indeed sounded terribly convincing as this odious adversary had outlined it, all the same. Wally said desperately, 'There were others in that squat, you know. Others who might have done it. There was that wanker Matty, for a start!'

Peach turned to the woman at his side. 'Memories are coming tumbling back to him now, aren't they, DS Blake?'

'Almost miraculously, sir, when he's prompted a little. Just like all the others were, isn't he?'

'Indeed he is. All coming back to him now, isn't it? Liars need good memories, you know. Some sod in the seventeenth century said that, and it's still just as true today.'

These two were dancing mental rings around him when he needed to think. Swift said, 'That bloke Matty was Sunita's boyfriend, before she threw him over for the dyke. He was bloody annoyed about that. Might have killed her, I'd say.'

'Would you indeed, Wally? Well, I can't say that that surprises me. Any other gems to offer us?'

Swift wondered what Matty Hayward had said about him, whether he had offered them anything which might be damning. He said furiously, 'There were two other women there as well as Sunita, you know. There was the dyke – I think she was called Jo – and a blonde bint.' He found himself dropping back into the words he had used all those years ago. Well, that probably wasn't a bad thing. It might give authenticity to what he was saying. 'Emmy. She was a hard piece, Emmy. She was tarting, even then, even from that squat. She'd have been capable of killing the girl, if it suited her.'

That was an opinion Peach had already formed himself,

after speaking to Emily Jane Watson. But he forced incredulity into his tone as he said to Swift, 'And why on earth should it suit her to kill an innocent girl like that, Wally?'

Swift's eyes narrowed; his mouth pinched with the craftiness of a criminal fighting to save his own skin. 'I reckon she'd tried to recruit the Paki to sell it on the streets. Emmy was after starting her own whorehouse, if you ask me. She was done for it a couple of years later, you know.'

'We do, actually. We've talked to the lady about it. And about lots of other things, including you, Wally.'

'Well, if Sunita refused to work for her, or threatened to grass on her, she wouldn't have taken kindly to that. Not Emmy.'

'You're saying now that Emily Watson killed Sunita?' Peach made it sound quite ludicrous, as if it damned this man even further rather than got him off the hook.

Swift said sullenly, 'All I'm saying is that Emmy was a woman well capable of killing, if you got on the wrong side of her. And so was the dyke. They get very involved, you know, dykes. Turn very nasty if their partners decide they've had enough.'

'Really? Well, it's good to hear from an authority on these things.' Peach nodded absently for a couple of seconds and then snapped, 'Did you kill her, Wally?'

Swift was shaken: he had been busy devising motives for others, and the pig had caught him by surprise. 'Of course I didn't!'

'No of course about it, Wally. A known criminal, who's just been arrested on a very serious charge. Who's going down for a stretch anyway, before we even consider him for murder. Wouldn't like to be in your shoes, I'm afraid.' Peach pursed his lips and whistled noiselessly, then shook his head sadly. 'You wouldn't like to make a clean breast of it now? They tell me that confession provides a huge relief. The greater the crime, the better the relief, presumably.'

'I didn't kill Sunita Akhtar.'

'All right. Interview terminated at 0940 hours.' He switched off the recorder. 'The Drugs Squad officers will bring you out of your cell again in due course. Give you quite a going over, I should think. Not all policemen are as civilized as me. But you'd know that, with your record.'

They played the tape back again, when Swift had been taken away. At the end of it, Percy looked at Lucy Blake with his head on one side. 'What do you think?'

'I think he's scum. I'd like it to be him.'

'Doesn't always work like that, though. On the whole, he wriggled just as I'd have thought he would. There was one interesting thing, though.'

'And what was that, oh master?'

'He tried to implicate everyone else around him, as you might expect of a man in his position. Even brought in the man who wasn't in the squat, David Edmonds. But he left out one candidate. Billy Warnock. I wonder why.'

Twenty

This place didn't smell of death, as she had expected it to. It was full of smiling faces, of people who carried a joy with them which she seldom saw in her life outside this building.

Emily Jane Watson waited in the corridor outside the room on the upright, uncomfortable chair someone had brought for her. Probably they thought she had a parent in here. She had never been in a hospice before. She was discovering that it was one of the few places which could still make her feel uncomfortable.

Through six inches of gap in the doorway, she watched the movements of the woman beside the bed, watched in particular the actions of her powerful hands. She muttered low words of consolation as she turned the thin body beneath the blankets, dabbing the ointment on to the bedsores with a touch as light as a butterfly's wing. When she had finished her ministrations, she tucked the clean white sheet expertly under the patient's chin and smiled down at him.

Jane was surprised to see that this was a man, with thin grey hair cut neatly above his exhausted, emaciated features. He said something to his nurse, his voice no stronger than a whisper, so that she had to put her ear above his mouth to get the sense of it. Then she smiled down at him, nodded, lifted an impossibly thin arm from beneath the blankets, and lodged the skeletal hand between her strong ones.

At first there was no sound from the pair, just a gentle rhythmic swaying from the strong figure in blue on the edge of the bed. Then a thin vein of melody arose from the pair, the soft keening of a tune Jane Watson vaguely recognized

from the dead, forgotten days she had spent with the grand-
father who had died when she was twelve.

> *'Kathleen Mavourneen! What, slumbering still?*
> *Oh hast thou forgotten how soon we must sever?*
> *Oh hast thou forgotten this day we must part?*
> *It may be for years, and it may be for ever,*
> *Oh why art thou silent, thou voice of my heart?'*

It was softly sung, even as it gathered towards its emotional
climax, and Jane strained her ears to catch the words. The thin
reed of the voice from the bed rose with a strange power as
the lines proceeded, whilst the voice from the woman who
held his hand blended so softly and gently with it that from
the corridor it was difficult to distinguish from whom the sound
was coming.

When it was over, the nurse looked tenderly down at the
closed eyes on the immobile face for a moment, reflected the
slight smile on the bloodless lips with an answering one of
her own, and slid the hand she had clasped so lightly back
beneath the sheet. She waited for a moment, making sure that
the paper-thin eyelids were not about to open again, then stole
softly away from the bed.

Jane, standing hastily as the woman she had waited for came
through the doorway, wished suddenly that she had not
witnessed this tiny musical interlude, that she had not intruded
on anything so private and so intimate. But instead of apologizing, she found herself saying with uncharacteristic tender-
ness, 'That was beautiful!'

It was banal, but it was sincere, and the woman in blue
accepted it as such. 'He used to sing it to his wife when they
were young,' she said, her voice surprisingly matter-of-fact in
explanation. 'She's been dead for twenty years and more, but
we all go back to our youth in the last days.'

'You're good at this, aren't you? I'd no idea that you'd be
so good.' Now that the time had come to begin, Jane Watson
couldn't find the words to do it.

'You get to know a lot of the old ballads, when you work with the dying. I know all the words to "I'll take you home again, Kathleen" now. I tend to think of my favourite singer, Kathleen Ferrier, who was a local girl anyway.' Jo Ingram looked up at the high ceilings of the old Victorian house, as if she wondered whether the immortal Kath might have sung in this very place. Then she turned to the woman standing awkwardly beside her and said, 'Are you a relative?'

'No. No, it's you I've come to see, actually. They tell me you're Sister Josephine, nowadays. I'm Jane Watson.'

The nun's eyes narrowed, but there was no recognition in them. She looked at this blonde woman with the coarse features and the expensively cut short hair and decided that she came from a very different world from her. A professional woman, probably, from the look of her fashionable dark blue trouser suit and the shoes that had probably cost a hundred pounds. 'I'm sorry. You'll have to—'

'You might remember me better as Emily. As Em or Emmy, in fact. And you were Jo, then!'

Josephine Ingram looked at her without speaking for a long three seconds. Then she said, 'We can't talk here. You'd better come into my office at the end of the corridor.'

She shut the door carefully and motioned to the armchair beside the big desk. She did not go behind the desk herself but sat down in the armchair opposite her visitor. 'Have the police been to see you?'

'Yes. Well, I went to see them, actually. An Inspector Peach and a girl sergeant.'

Jo Ingram nodded. 'That was the man I spoke to. Not a lot escapes him, I'd say.'

'I agree. We need to be careful.'

Jo ought to have asked why they should need to be careful. Instead, she said nothing. They eyed each other up, with two sharp brains working furiously behind their unrevealing faces. Their minds were slipping back thirteen years, to that squat in Sebastopol Terrace, a spot scarcely a mile from this place, but a world away in every other respect.

197

They had been chalk and cheese then, and there was no reason for either of them to think that things had changed since then. They were thrown together now as murder suspects, but it was not a natural alliance. It was Jo Ingram who eventually ended a long pause. 'I didn't lie to them. I may have been a little – well, a little economical with the truth.'

'You concealed things.' Jane gave her a mirthless smile. 'I'd be willing to bet you didn't tell them about you and Sunita.'

'I didn't, no. It didn't have anything to do with her death, so I didn't see the relevance of it.'

'And it wouldn't sit easy with the image of Sister Josephine, would it?'

Jo Ingram felt herself blushing. In this place where she was so much in charge, it was a long time since that had happened. She said quietly, 'Both Sunita and I were sexually inexperienced. We fell into each other's arms because she was looking for protection in that squat.'

'And thoroughly enjoyed the experience. I remember the way you used to be with each other, you know.'

'And I expect you told those policemen all about it.'

It was Jane Watson's turn to be discomforted. You didn't grass to the police, in her book. And she had done just that. It had been self-defence, of course, but she couldn't admit that to this pious cow. She said stiffly, 'I did, yes. For what it's worth, I got the impression they already knew all about you hitting the sack with the girl.'

'I see. I didn't tell them about your trying to recruit Sunita to go on the game. Perhaps I should have.' Jo was appalled to find how much she relished this waspish rejoinder.

Jane controlled her anger. There was no point in their falling out. It wasn't going to help either of them if this exchange descended into a slanging match. She was certain that she could outswear this woman, could beat her in a physical fight, if it came to it. But it mustn't do that. She said, 'I got the impression that they already knew about that, as well. I didn't admit to it, of course. But other tongues from that squat have been wagging. We need to stick together, you and I.'

'And why would that be?'

This time it was Jane who took her time, gathering her thoughts for a convincing reply. 'Get real, Jo. We're both in the frame for a particularly nasty murder. I'm sure I've had more dealings with the police than you have. I know that they won't hesitate to charge either of us with that killing, if anyone gives them a case for it. And remember, they've been talking to everyone who was in that house with us. Every one of them will be wriggling like a fish on a hook, looking to implicate someone else. Which might be either of us.'

Jo regarded this tough street-fighter and told herself she mustn't underestimate her superiority in the ways of this world, which Sister Josephine thought she had left behind. 'You might have killed Sunita, for all I know.'

Jane hadn't expected her to come out with it, straight into her face like that. She forced herself to speak calmly, 'And so might you, Sister Holy Josephine. Jealous dykes often turn violent.'

They regarded each other steadily for a moment, each breathing heavily enough to show the emotion she was trying to conceal. Somewhere in the distance, a piano was being played, exuberantly but inaccurately. 'They lose their inhibitions, when they're mortally ill,' said Jo with a thin smile. 'The music room is very popular with the dying.'

Jane refused to be distracted by this glimpse of a world which was totally unknown to her. 'Who do you think killed Sunita, Jo? You must have been thinking about it.'

'I've thought about it a lot, in the last week. Matty Hayward was very cut up when she ditched him. But I couldn't see it being him, myself. He's a concert pianist now, you know.'

Jane smiled grimly at such naivety. 'You and I both think we know who killed her, don't we?'

'Wally.' The word was out before Jo knew it was coming. She should have been appalled at herself. Instead, all she felt was a relief that this other woman should be leading her this way.

'Wally Swift.' Jane nodded her satisfaction that they should at last be getting to the point. 'He was the man in that squat who knew what he was doing. He was the one ruthless enough to kill someone who got in the way of his plans.'

Jo knew she should be asking where the evidence was, asserting that you couldn't go round making wild accusations like that unless you could substantiate them. Instead, she said tersely, 'I've been thinking that, too.'

Jane Watson smiled. 'We've got to tell the police what we think. And we've got to give them things that will make it stick.'

Jo felt a belated stirring of conscience. 'What kind of things?' She wanted to say that she couldn't tell lies, even if they were in a good cause, but she knew how prissy that would sound. So she said nothing.

'Nothing too extreme. Nothing they could trip us up on.' Jane Watson tried to sound as if she was thinking on her feet, as if she hadn't worked all this out before she came here. 'We only need to be quite frank about what we know about Wally, about the things he did in that squat.'

The mention of the squat brought back to Jo the memories of how she had fought with this woman in those days, how she had bitterly resisted Emmy's attempts to take Sunita away from her, to lead her into the ways of sin. How quaint and holier-than-thou that phrase seemed to her now, when both of them were fighting for their freedom because of the death of that poor, dear, dead girl all those years ago.

Jo Ingram turned what might have been an accusation into something more neutral. 'We all did things we wouldn't be proud of, whilst we were living in that house.'

'Maybe. But Wally's the one who killed Sunita. I'm certain of it.' Emily Jane Watson's lips set into a hard line above the square jaw.

Jo knew that she should be asking for the hard evidence to prove that claim. Instead, all she said was, 'So how do we convince the police of that?'

Jane noted that she had the woman's agreement now. A nun, on her side, putting her case for her! It was ironic, something she could never have envisaged happening to her. But desperate circumstances needed desperate solutions, and this one seemed to be working. She hastened to nail down the support of this unusual ally. 'We tell them everything we know about what Wally was up to. About him recruiting Sunita to push drugs for him. About the man who moved in next door with a rival enterprise. About Wally's fury when Sunita threatened to desert him for this new dealer because he paid more.'

The accusations came tumbling out so quickly one upon another that Jo was not sure what was true and what was fiction. She made her protest. 'We can't be sure of that. Not all of it.'

'*I'm* sure of it. Most of it is fact. What isn't fact is a reasonable assumption from the facts. Intelligent deduction, I'd call it.'

'And am I supposed to ignore the fact that you were trying to entice Sunita into whoring?' Jo put a great emphasis upon the ugly word. It was the excuse for the things she knew now that she was going to accept about Wally Swift. 'Am I supposed to conceal the fact that you were trying to recruit her as a prostitute?'

Damn the woman! Damn her good life and her worthy work and her sisterhood! Couldn't she see the fix they were in together and what they must do to protect themselves? It was all very well being other-worldly, clinging to your integrity, but what did you do when there was a crisis in the real world?

Jane controlled herself and spoke more calmly than she felt. 'I didn't kill Sunita. But I'm no angel. And as far as the police are concerned, I've got a record. They'll fit me up for this, if they can. All I'm asking you to do is to tell them what you know about Wally. And what you know he was capable of. With what they're getting from other people and what their forensic people are turning up, that should be enough to put a guilty man behind bars.'

It was persuasive. Especially to Jo Ingram, who wanted to be persuaded. After all, she had always thought Wally Swift was the likeliest man for this killing. She said, 'All right. I'll tell them everything I can remember about Wally. None of it's good. He seemed an evil man to me, even then. Whenever I've thought about it over these last few days, ever since I went into Brunton police station to talk to that CID Chief Inspector, I've kept coming back to Wally as my murderer.'

'That's all I'm saying. That's what we must tell them.' Emily knew enough to leave it at that, knew that she had got the biggest commitment she could from this very different woman.

The two women who had survived life in that squat were now united against Wally Swift.

Twenty-One

'It really isn't convenient, you know. There'll be clients visit-
ing the office and I'm really very—'

'We'll do this at the station, if you like. I can make it clear
to your staff that you're not under arrest when we take you
away. Not yet, anyway.' Percy Peach looked round at the
brightly lit estate agency, with its attractive colour pictures of
property on offer, its suited young men and women at their
desks.

David Edmonds strove to retain control of his temper. 'There
is no need for that attitude. If you really *must* do this now,
you had better come into my office, Inspector. But I can't
think that Superintendent Tucker would be pleased to hear
about your attitude.'

'It's Chief Inspector, sir. And he's Chief Superintendent,
now. I can give you his work phone number if you'd like it.'

'That's all right. It's just that life's a bit hectic at the
moment.' David Edmonds gave them a wide grin, waved his
hand towards the two armchairs, and attempted unsuccessfully
to recover the panache he found so easy with clients.

'I expect life must be hectic for you at the moment, yes.
I'm surprised you're able to leave the country for a holiday
in two days' time, in view of that.'

Edmonds gave him a sickly smile, which he transferred to
Lucy Blake when he found that Peach was not responding to
it. 'One needs a break. One of the advantages of being in
charge is that you can take a holiday and a little winter sun
when you need it.'

'Really, sir. On impulse, as you might say. Well, we'd

better get this out of the way before you disappear from the face of the earth, hadn't we? Or the face of Brunton, at any rate.'

'Of course I want to help. But I told you everything I could remember when we spoke on Sunday.'

'We'll need to jog your memory again then, sir. I seem to recall that we managed to help you quite a lot in that way, on the occasion of our last meeting. This is a follow-up interview, in the light of information we've gathered from other people since we last spoke together. No need for us to record it, though. You're simply being a good citizen and helping the police with their enquiries, at present.'

Edmonds wondered just whom they had spoken to and exactly what they had learned in the last three days. Which was exactly what Peach intended. He said, 'I can't think what I can add to what I told you on Sunday.'

'When was the last time you saw Sunita Akhtar?'

So there it was, baldly stated, after all the preliminary fencing. The challenge knocked him off balance, though he knew he should have been ready for it. 'I can't say. Well, not with complete accuracy, when it's so long ago. I suppose it would be some time around the end of March in 1991.'

Peach looked down at the sheet in front of him. 'That tallies fairly well with the information we have from other people.' He nodded thoughtfully three times. 'And where did this meeting take place?'

David licked his lips. This man could make the simplest statements sound like dynamite. 'At twenty-eight Sebastopol Terrace.'

'And what was the nature of your exchanges?'

'I – I can't accurately recall what was said. Not at this distance.'

'No. That is why I asked what was the nature of your exchanges, rather than asking you to recall the actual words said.'

'I'm afraid I can't recall that.'

'Then let's try to prompt you. We established that you were

trying to get her to work for you, as a pusher of drugs. Cannabis initially, you said, with a view to expansion into the market for harder drugs in due course. But it turned out that Sunita had already been recruited by the man next door, Wally Swift.'

David wasn't sure that they had established all this at their last meeting, not as clearly and unequivocally as this. But he couldn't find a detail to refute in what the man was saying. He said, 'All right, I've admitted to dealing and to trying to use the girl. That's all I've admitted and all I'm going to admit.'

Peach gave him a sudden dazzling smile, which blazed like an arc lamp into his face. 'Badly phrased, that, sir. It implies that there's more that you could tell us, if you chose to. Did you have an argument with Sunita at this last meeting?'

'No.'

'Did you cut up rough when she told you that she wasn't going to work for you?'

'No.'

'Did you find out that she'd been talking about your little drugs ring to the man next door, when you'd told her to keep it secret?'

'No!' He found himself yelling out this third denial, could picture the shocked faces of his employees in the room outside. He tried to control his breathing as he said through clenched teeth, 'You're making this up. There was no argument. I never laid a finger on the girl.'

'No one suggested you did, Mr Edmonds. I was just trying to prompt your reluctant memory into action, that's all. You still don't recall the date of this last meeting with the dead girl?'

'No.' Another denial. David sought desperately for something which would make it look as if he was trying to co-operate, without incriminating him. 'It would be about the end of March in 1991, I suppose, as I said. It might even have been on the last day of the month.'

'A Sunday, that would be. Did you meet on Sundays?'

'I think we did, yes.' David was shaken by this detail, even though he didn't see how it could affect him.

'That tallies with the information we have. No one seems to have seen Sunita Akhtar alive after the end of March.' Peach paused, letting the simple statement make its full effect.

'I didn't kill her.'

'Then who do you think did?'

'I don't know, do I? Someone in that squat with her. The black boy, perhaps. He was upset when she wouldn't sleep with him, according to what she told me.'

'Keep thinking, Mr Edmonds.' Peach stood up. 'Unless you hear anything from us, you're free to leave the country on Friday. We have your address in Madeira.'

David wondered how this man managed to turn the simplest statement into a threat.

'It's the first of March, Peach. High time things were moving. I'm being pressed by the media for a result.'

Superintendent Tucker was at his most petulant.

'Thirteen years, sir, that body lay undiscovered. Considering how cold the scent was, I'd say we've discovered quite a lot in nine days.' Peach was understandably testy.

'But you are nowhere near an arrest, despite all the support I've given you.'

'I wouldn't say that, sir. I can't say an arrest is imminent, but we've made considerable progress. I'm pretty sure that our killer is one of the people I've spoken to myself in course of the investigation.'

That sounded impressive. Tucker decided it wasn't. 'I really can't be put off with these prevarications, you know. I'm sure the Chief Constable wouldn't be taken in by them.'

'Really, sir? He seemed quite impressed by our progress, when DS Blake bumped into him on Monday.'

Lucy was a member of the same gym as the CC, and they occasionally met there by chance, though they rarely spoke about their work. Tucker did not know what to make of this. He peered suspiciously at his DCI, but found Peach's

Dusty Death

expression inscrutable and his gaze fixed as usual on the wall above his chief's head. 'But you've said yourself that you're nowhere near an arrest.'

'No, sir. I said I wouldn't claim that an arrest was imminent. Different thing, sir, with respect.'

'Have you produced a prime suspect yet?' Tucker jutted his chin aggressively.

Peach considered the question, but did not answer it directly. 'I've just come from a man who's a very good prospect, sir. Statistically, that is.'

Tucker looked at him doubtfully again. 'Statistically? I hope you're not going to come up with this ridiculous statistic about a Mason being more likely to commit a serious crime than other—'

'Four times more likely, sir. In the area of East Lancashire, that is. My survey does not extend beyond our immediate environment. Not yet.' Nor would it ever do so. Peach's treasured statistic stemmed from the pinning of eight fraud and peculation offences on the same hapless company accountant two years ago, but if this lazy old fool couldn't work that out for himself, why should he be enlightened?

Tucker looked at him sternly. 'If you're still trying to make out that David Edmonds is a leading suspect for this killing, I would have to tell you that I consider that most unlikely. He wasn't even in that squat in 1991.'

At least he remembers something, thought Peach. He tried to sound as solemn and portentous as he could as he said, 'But he met Sunita Akhtar in the house next door, sir. And apparently recruited her to push drugs for him.'

'This all seems most unlikely, to anyone who knows what a fine young man David Edmonds is. And even if you are correct in your contention that he had this wild youth, the idea of him as a murderer is quite preposterous.'

'Let's reserve judgement on that, sir, shall we? I have to admit that there are other people who are superficially more likely candidates.'

'Ah! This might after all be a useful discussion.'

207

Tucker wasn't much good at irony. Peach looked at him impassively and said, 'There's a nun, sir, Sister Josephine, who's running a hospice magnificently, according to all the reports we have. And there's a successful businesswoman, Emily Jane Watson, who's running an introductions agency in Bolton. A very prosperous one, apparently. Apparently you interviewed Ms Watson yourself, sir, during a previous life. When she was running a brothel.' He was pleased by the casual way in which he managed to drop this bombshell into their exchange.

'There was never enough evidence available. The Crown Prosecution Service would never have taken it on.' Tucker's reaction was swift and predictable. Ms Watson had run rings round the lazy sod: Peach had read the files in the Brunton basement.

'Emily Watson might have recruited Sunita Akhtar to work for her on the streets. Or tried to recruit her. Or seen her off when the girl reneged on their agreement. Ruthless, I thought she was, when we spoke to her.'

'You need to be ruthless to be successful in business, you know, Peach. You probably exaggerate her criminal proclivities. Just as you do with David Edmonds, if I may say so.'

'You may indeed, sir. Part of your overview, that would be. What about another ruthless occupant of that squat, Walter Swift?'

'Ah! Different kettle of fish altogether. A man who hasn't reformed his ways. A man who was a lieutenant to Joe Johnson. A man who has built up a lucrative drugs business of his own.'

'A man who was laying the foundations for it, even then, sir. A man who had a capacity for violence; a man whom everyone in that squat seemed to be afraid of, if we can trust what they're saying to us now.'

Tucker jutted his jaw again. 'You're right. In my view we have the man who committed this murder in custody at this very moment. All that is necessary is to document the case against him. That's your job, Peach.'

'I thought it might be, sir.' Percy, who thought there was a very good chance that Tommy Bloody Tucker might for once be right, was uncharacteristically at a loss for words. He said, 'He's wriggling hard, is Swift. Trying to implicate everyone but himself in that killing in 1991.'

'Sure sign he's guilty, that. I have a certain feeling for these things. You may have noticed it.'

I've noticed your talent for the blindin' bleedin' obvious, thought Percy. Repeatedly. 'Nevertheless, we must leave no stone unturned, sir,' he said, flinging one of his chief's favourite clichés back at him. 'I'm off to see Billy Warnock this afternoon, sir.'

'Good for you, Peach, good for you!' Tucker nodded absently, his thoughts still on Wally Swift and the announcement he would eventually make to the television cameras. Then his jaw dropped. 'Who is Billy Warnock?'

'Suspect, sir. The fifth person in that squat at the time of this death. Currently in charge of the youth team at Preston North End.'

'Ah! Well, don't waste too much time on him. I want this one wrapped up by the weekend, you know!'

'He's black, sir.' Percy couldn't resist experimenting with that gratuitous fact.

'Ah! I suppose that puts a different complexion on it.' Tucker was quite unaware of any pun. 'Most of the crime in our capital city is committed by blacks, you know.' He shook his head sadly and gazed from his penthouse window, now in elder statesman mode.

'Yes, sir. This is Brunton, sir.'

Tucker gazed at him suspiciously, suspecting insubordination. But Peach was as inscrutable as a statue of Buddha. 'You must do whatever you think is necessary, Peach. I never interfere with my staff, as you know. All I'm saying is that I want a person charged with the murder of Sunita Akhtar by the weekend.'

'Yes, sir. Whether black or white, sir. I know that political correctness has no part in your thinking, sir.'

209

J. M. Gregson

Peach left a suitably worried head of CID on that enigmatic note.

But events were moving faster than even Peach could have anticipated. Whilst he was reporting to Tucker, the CID section had a visitor. Lucy Blake called up DC Brendan Murphy and the two of them took him into Peach's empty office.

Matthew Hayward was on edge. He looked over his shoulder nervously to make sure that the door of the room was shut, as if he feared that even here his actions might be witnessed and punished. He said, 'I've been threatened. I – I thought you should know about it.' It sounded cowardly to him, somehow. He was glad that the Chief Inspector with the piercing eyes and the aggressive manner wasn't here to make it seem more so.

DS Blake said, 'In that case, you've done the right thing to come here and tell us about it. You don't think anyone saw you coming in?'

'No. I'm pretty sure I wasn't followed. Probably there's no need to be afraid. I expect they think I've been frightened off and they don't need to do anything else—'

'Much better to take these things seriously, though. You'll need to tell us all about it.' She gave him an encouraging smile, and her face lit up beneath the auburn hair, so that Matt could scarcely believe that she was a police officer.

'Well, it was on Monday. Monday lunch-time, actually. I was on my way to give a concert with the Liverpool Philharmonic.' He still hadn't got used to delivering statements like that as if they were run-of-the mill, and he found himself shrugging away his fame self-consciously. 'I stopped for a light lunch in what seemed a quiet pub between Preston and Liverpool.'

Brendan Murphy was suitably unimpressed. He said, 'And why didn't you report this threat to us immediately, Mr Hayward? Why did you leave it for two days before you came in here?'

'I – I don't know. I suppose if I'm completely honest, I was

210

scared. The man told me specifically not to speak to the police, I think.'

'Always best to be completely honest, when you want our help,' said Murphy dryly. He hadn't worked for two years with Percy Peach without learning how to put a man on the back foot.

'Yes. It's just that nothing like this had ever happened to me before, and I was thrown off balance.'

Lucy Blake gave him that wonderful, encouraging smile again. Why couldn't the girls who were beginning to wait for him after concerts be more like this vision? She said, 'Understandable. But as DC Murphy points out, the sooner we hear about these things, the more likely it is that we can nip any threat in the bud. Better tell us all about it now.'

He couldn't very well tell them that he had determined to keep shtum as the man had so forcibly commanded him to, that it had taken two sleepless nights to make him come in here and ask for protection. So he told them everything he could remember about that sinister figure who had accosted him, who had gripped the collar of his shirt and snarled into his face, in that quiet pub in Rufford. 'He had dark blue eyes. Very dark – nearly black. Dark hair, cut very short. And beetling eyebrows. He was a big man, very powerfully built, and he – well, he seemed like a man who was used to using violence. He was carrying a copy of the *Daily Mail*.' Matt grinned in embarrassment at the feebleness of this last detail. 'I'm afraid I can't remember much else about him. He took me completely by surprise.'

'And how did he threaten you? Try to recall for us exactly what he said.'

'He said he didn't give a damn whether I'd killed Sunita or not. All that mattered was that I was to keep shtum about anything I'd learned at the time. About anything she'd said to me about what had been going on in that squat.'

'So he thought you knew something which could damage someone else who was in or around the place at the time. Something Sunita had said to you, perhaps. What would that be?'

'That's the puzzling thing. I haven't been able to recall anything she said which would be damning to anyone.'

'You know that there had been an attempt to recruit Sunita to act as a prostitute?'

'Yes. Emmy tried to get her to do that. I think she even toyed with the idea. She might have even tried it out.' His face was tortured with the recollection.

'And she was pushing drugs, wasn't she?' Lucy's voice was gentle as a therapist's, encouraging him to spit out secrets he needed to be rid of.

'Yes. I think she tried that out, as well. Tried working for this man who came into the house next door to set up his operation. She was frightened of taking proper employment in case her parents found out where she was, you know.' He found he wanted to defend his lost love, even after all these years.

'And what about Wally Swift? Was she working for him?'

Matt shook his head hopelessly. 'I don't know. She'd stopped talking to me about what she did by then. She – she was with Jo.'

'Yes, we know that.'

'But I think she was probably working for Wally when she died. I'm pretty sure he stopped her pushing drugs for this man next door. Billy Warnock might be able to tell you: he was pretty thick with Wally by that time. I know that Wally had Sunita in tears in a corner one day, had everything out of her about what this other man was doing.'

'Yes.' She gave no sign that these were new details to them, new additions to the picture of the life in that squat which had preceded a murder. 'Mr Hayward, it's obvious that this man who threatened you on Monday wasn't acting on his own behalf. Who do you think it was who retained his services to try to silence you?'

He couldn't know for certain, of course. But they had asked him what he thought. And there was only one man he could think of who would have sent a man to threaten him like that. Matt said, 'I think it must have been Wally Swift.'

Lucy nodded slowly, then decided that she could offer this frightened man a little consolation. 'You might like to know that Walter Swift is currently in custody. He was arrested last night in connection with serious drug offences, and will probably be charged with them in the next few hours. He has already been interviewed in connection with the murder of Sunita Akhtar, though no charges have been preferred against him as yet in connection with that crime.'

Matthew Hayward found that the sun had come out whilst he had been inside the big new police station. And the whole world felt a brighter place with the news he had just heard within it.

Twenty-Two

The snooker balls looked very bright under the brilliant white light.

Billy Warnock rolled the red in expertly with a bit of stun, then watched with satisfaction as the cue ball rolled slowly behind the black. He made thirty-four before he narrowly failed to double the last red into the middle pocket to keep the break going. It was good enough to clinch the frame from the eighteen-year-old lad with acne and an expensive haircut. You had to show these youngsters who was in charge, even when you could no longer keep up with them on the pitch.

'Sign of a misspent youth, my dad used to say,' said Percy Peach. 'I expect you keep this place going, you and your football lads.' He grinned with satisfaction at the way the startled Warnock whirled round. Then he looked round the rather depressing scene in the snooker hall, which at three in the afternoon was peopled largely by the unemployed of Preston. The brightly lit tables were rectangles of light in the long, low room. The walls were lined with bench seats, on which a few people sprawled whilst they waited their turns to play. Otherwise there were few furnishings and fewer conversations.

'I have to come in here to keep an eye on my lads. Make sure they don't join the drinking culture, see? It's not like it was in your day, Mr Peach. We do our best to make sure these lads stay on the straight and narrow, now.'

He made it sound as if it was forty rather than twenty years since Percy was a teenager, but the DCI knew what he meant. You had to have the right diet and the right lifestyle, as well as the skills and the luck, to succeed in football, these days.

He looked at the youths with their Diet Cokes and said, 'Need a word, Billy. In private.'

Warnock looked for a moment as if he would resist, then caught the glint of Peach's dark eyes in the half-light above the table. He followed the DCI without a word out into the car park. A moment later he was sitting in the passenger seat of the unmarked police Mondeo, with a blank brick wall six feet ahead of him the only thing he could see. He could not even see the top of it; it was like a prison wall, hemming him in, crushing his spirit.

As if he understood all of these things that he could not possibly know, Peach allowed the feeling of claustrophobia to build for several seconds before he spoke. 'You weren't completely frank with us yesterday, Mr Warnock. That was a mistake.'

Billy wasn't used to this formal mode of address. Amidst the informality of a football club, you rarely got a 'Mister'. It unsettled him far more than he would have expected. He said without hope, 'I can't think what you mean, Mr Peach.'

'I think you can, Billy. And I think you're going to change your tactics and tell me everything you know. Right now.'

'There's nothing else I can think of which—'

'Wally Swift's in a cell, Billy. He's going down for quite a stretch. Whether we pin a murder on him or not.'

Billy Warnock wondered if it was all bluff, if this man with the quiet, menacing voice was spinning him a yarn to make him say things which would get him a severe beating or something much worse from Wally. He said stupidly, 'I don't believe it. You'll have to give me proof of—'

'I don't have to give you proof of anything, Mr Warnock!' Peach's voice was suddenly harsh, with Billy's title appended this time as a sardonic afterthought, as if it were a prelude to charging him. 'Drugs Squad officers are interrogating Wally Swift at this very moment. They've waited a long time for the right moment to net him. Serious charges will certainly follow. And I've already spoken to him myself about the murder of Sunita Akhtar.'

Billy wished unexpectedly that he had been facing Peach, looking directly into those dark, hostile eyes. This strange set-up where he could not look at his interrogator, where both of them sat staring ahead at the blank brick wall, was even more unnerving than confronting the man directly. He said falteringly, 'It's a long time since we were in that squat. Difficult to remember things. I – I might have made the odd mistake when I spoke to you yesterday.'

'Oh, you did, Billy, you did! Not so much in what you said as in what you didn't say.' Peach stopped for a moment, as a gang of noisy youths came out to a van behind them and drove noisily out of the car park, their voices more raucous than ever in the quiet around them. Once they were through the gates and away, the silence dropped back like mist into the car park which enclosed the pair in the Mondeo. Peach's voice began again, quiet and insidious. 'You helped Wally Swift to set up his drugs operation, when you were in that squat in Sebastopol Terrace, didn't you, Billy?'

This time it was Billy who paused, seeking desperately for words in which he could frame a denial. No words offered themselves. 'I gave him a bit of help, yes. I didn't know exactly what he was about at the time.'

'You sold drugs for him, didn't you?'

'No. I'm not saying I did that.' He could hear the desperation in his own voice.

'You might get away with this, Billy, if you come clean now. Unless you killed the girl yourself, that is.'

'No! No, I didn't do that! And I didn't see Wally kill her! I've not been hiding that!'

'Lot of denials, there, Billy. You'll need to convince me, won't you? And the best way to do that is to come clean. I keep telling you that, don't I? Keep giving you another chance. But my patience isn't inexhaustible, Billy.'

'I – I just fell into it. Really I did. I was using myself: mainly pot, but a bit of coke as well. Anyway, it wasn't easy for me to get any sort of job when I was in that squat, being black and a user. I started running errands for Wally. Then I helped him to set up his first small ring of dealers – I knew some other users, see. Knew some who were desperate enough to become sellers. He paid me when no one else would. Not a lot, but—'

'Paid you to put the frighteners on Sunita, I expect.'

'No! He did his own frightening in those days, did Wally. He was good at that. Enjoyed it.'

'I see. Enjoyed violence too, didn't he?'

'Yes. We were all frightened of him, even then. He could have got out of that squat earlier than any of us, could Wally. I think he stayed there because it suited him, because he could get hold of the people he needed for his set-up.'

'People like you, Billy. People who could offer a little violence where it was useful to him.'

'No! Honestly, Mr Peach, I wasn't much good at violence, even then. I don't expect you'll believe that, but it's true. I got out as soon as I could. North End gave me a second chance at football, and I wasn't going to screw up on that!'

He was desperate to convince now. Peach contemplated the excellence of the brickwork in the wall for a few seconds, feeling the tension building in the man beside him. Then he said very quietly, 'Did Wally Swift kill Sunita, Billy?'

Billy Warnock tried to control his breathing, which sounded very loud in that confined space. 'I think he did. I didn't see him do it. He was very annoyed that the girl had been working for that man who came next door and offered her better terms. I know he made her tell him all about that. I saw her afterwards and she was very upset and frightened. And – and that was the last time I saw her. I assumed she'd been frightened away, when she disappeared so suddenly. I think we all did. Even Jo – and she was closer to Sunita than any of us.'

It sounded like the truth. When you were surrounded by lies, it was difficult to tell, but this sounded right to Peach. He said as casually as he could, 'And when would this be, Billy? This last time that you saw Sunita Akhtar alive?'

'End of March, 1991.'

'You can do better than that, Billy.'

'I can't, Mr Peach. It's too long ago! That's God's honest truth! End of March is as near as I can get.' He was desperate in his need to convince.

Another pause. Another agonizing few seconds in which Warnock wondered whether he would be believed. Then Peach said casually, 'Kept in touch with Wally Swift, have you?'

Billy gasped. His torso listed to one side, away from the muscular man in the driving seat, like a ship holed below the Plimsoll line by this unexpected salvo. 'It's more that he's kept in touch with me, Mr Peach. He used to ring me up, ask how I was getting on.'

'Very touching! But he wasn't concerned with your welfare, was he, Billy? He was asking you to recruit for him, I expect.'

'He was, yes. Only a very few lads make it in professional football, you know. The majority simply haven't got the skills and the pace required to play it professionally. But there are other reasons why people miss out, too.'

'Drugs.'

'I was going to say temperament. But that's part of it. You have to have the temperament to resist things like drink and drugs and gambling. Lots of young men haven't, especially when they get big money too early.'

'And you fed the names of lads like that to Wally Swift. Lads who you knew were users. Lads who might become pushers in one of Swift's rings of dealers.'

'He threatened me, Mr Peach. Said he'd reveal things about my past to the bigwigs at Preston North End, things which would make sure that I lost my job. I need this job, Mr Peach! I'm good at it, and it's the only thing I can do.'

'Good with the kids are you, Billy? Perhaps you are. Except that you've delivered some of them into Wally Swift's clutches. I can't think they'd thank you for that.'

'I hadn't a choice! Honest I hadn't! I was scared.'

'Scares a lot of people, Wally, doesn't he? Scared people even back in those days you spent in the squat together. The question is, did he kill Sunita Akhtar, as you think he did?

218

And is there any way you could be charged as an accessory to that murder? For withholding information, for instance.'

It was no more than a final twist of the tail, for Peach was privately convinced that he had got everything this man had to give. But he was wrong.

Billy Warnock spoke so quickly that it was difficult to distinguish the words as he said, 'I rang him. Tried to speak to him on Monday. Tried to tell him that you might be on to him. I was scared, see. I left a message, but he never came back to me.'

There was yet another pause, whilst the two men in the car considered the implications of this latest revelation. Then Percy Peach said, 'Probably a good thing for you that Swift didn't get back to you, Billy, I'd say. I know where to find you, when I need you. You can get back to your snooker now.'

Wednesday night on the first of March. A new month, with a hint of spring in the mild air and the first brave daffodils bursting from bud into flower in Brunton's Corporation Park.

The battered corpse of the girl who had died thirteen years ago lay in the mortuary, not yet released for burial. The people who knew her in the months before she died, who thought she had disappeared for ever, tried to continue their lives, whilst wondering how much the police now knew about the manner of her death.

Matthew Hayward locked all the doors and windows of his cottage as darkness closed in. Normally, he loved the solitude, and the wildness of the moor behind him, rising towards the navy blue of the night sky. But since he had been threatened so unexpectedly with violence two days earlier, he had felt lonely and vulnerable, and those emotions rose in him again as darkness closed in upon the village below him. He told himself that Wally Swift was safely under lock and key, that the threat must surely have come from him. But he knew that Swift's brutal instruments were still at large, and even wondered if they would blame him for

219

Wally's arrest. And Peach had made it clear to him that as Sunita's discarded and resentful lover, he was still a murder suspect.

He sat down at his grand piano and tried hard to concentrate on the slow movement from Beethoven's first concerto, which he was due to play with the Birmingham Symphony Orchestra in two days' time. For once, music failed to distract and engross him. He could not remember when that had last happened. He wished increasingly that he was not alone.

David Edmonds was not alone. He was surrounded by his boisterous family, looking forward eagerly to their holiday in Madeira in two days' time. He would like to have been alone, to collect his thoughts and deal with the image of that chimney breast at 28, Sebastopol Terrace, the container within which the body of Sunita Akhtar had been entombed for all those years.

It was an image which had risen to haunt him on each of the last three nights. In his detached and luxuriously furnished house, David Edmonds wished with ever-increasing fervency that he had never set foot in that place, had never tried to set up a network of drug-dealers, had never seen that brown, attractive face which now threatened his rest each night.

Billy Warnock was also at home with his wife and children. He did not long for solitude like Edmonds. His girl of seven and his boy of five were a welcome distraction to him. Their joyous and innocent black faces shone brightly through his anxiety, convincing him that all would be well, that this uncomplicated and healthy life he had built for himself in football would surely not be snatched away from him now.

It was only when they were safely in bed that his thoughts turned again to his actions in that other life, half-forgotten until they had been brought vividly back to him with the events of the last week. That was when he bitterly regretted the things he had done for Wally Swift all those years ago. He had always wondered what had happened to the body. It had been clever of Wally to hide it in a derelict house like that. He'd got away with it nicely at the time, and would have got away with it for ever if it hadn't been for that damned wrecking ball.

Billy Warnock wished that he had never set eyes on Wally Swift.

In the hospice, Sister Josephine worked hard and long, staying with a woman dying with ovarian cancer far into the night, upping the morphine when the pain rose, holding the woman's hand in both of hers long after she knew that she must be unconscious. Jo Ingram was happy to sit here in near-darkness.

She had thought she had got over Sunita, long ago. But the discovery of the body had brought it all back to her. She tried to utter a prayer for the girl she had loved, but the right words would not come to her. The God with whom Sister Josephine had of late been so familiar had withdrawn beyond the thick clouds of this starless night.

Jane Watson was trying to enjoy a dinner in Bolton's best restaurant. She was here with a man who had put money into her business, a married man who was twenty years older than her. He would want to slide into her bed at the end of the evening. Both of them knew the score, and normally that didn't worry her. She had taken him on as a sleeping partner, in both senses of the phrase, and got her money interest free as a result. And she had seen that he got his money's worth: she knew how to pleasure a man by now.

But ever since Peach had brought back that other name, that Emily she thought she had discarded for ever, she had been disturbed. She would have backed herself to carry this situation off better than anyone, before it happened. Yet it had disturbed her more than she would have thought possible, to the extent that she was frightened that she had given things away. She kept going over what she had said to the police, trying to convince herself that she had given them nothing which would allow them to pin this death upon her.

She had said that girl was trouble from the start, had done her best to get rid of her early on. If pious bloody Jo hadn't taken her into her bed, she'd have gone, too. Emily had told everyone that she was trouble. But she hadn't expected her to come back like this, all these years later.

Emily Jane Watson said to the man on the other side of the expensive wine, 'You won't be able to come back to my place tonight, I'm afraid.'

In his cell in the bowels of the police station in Manchester, Wally Swift was exhausted, but he couldn't sleep. The events of the day revolved in his head like a manic merry-go-round. When Peach and that girl had finished with him, he'd had two hours with the Drugs Squad detectives. He'd had a brief with him for that, sent in by the men above him in the drugs hierarchy, and he hadn't given away more than he needed to. But he'd been shaken by how much they knew, by how far their undercover man had penetrated into the organization. They were on to bigger fish than him, and they had the evidence to send them all down, as far as he could gather.

Wally tried to banish his depression by telling himself that they couldn't keep holding him like this. They'd have to charge him or release him tomorrow; the good old English law was always on the side of the criminal, as his brief had told him with a chuckle before he left.

But Wally knew that he wouldn't be released. He'd be remanded in custody and locked away in Strangeways. There'd be serious drugs charges, and he would be going down for a long stretch.

That was bad enough, but it wasn't the worst. You got life for what he was going to be charged with. With the cards stacked against him like this, with him locked in here and unable to put pressure upon anyone, Wally Swift was convinced that the filth were going to charge him with the murder of Sunita Akhtar.

Twenty-Three

David Edmonds arrived at work early on the morning of Thursday, the second of March. He hadn't been able to sleep, and he couldn't face a conversation with his wife over the breakfast table.

Nor did he fancy the children bringing him the pictures of the hotel in Madeira, with its swimming pools and its gym and its restaurants and its views over the Mediterranean. They would be there in thirty-six hours now, as they kept telling him, and able to see for themselves. He could not tell them that their father had a superstitious, unreasonable feeling that the more he talked about the brilliant blue of that sea the less likely he was to see it.

He told himself repeatedly on his way to the office that this was a silly and illogical idea. Yet the first event of his morning proved to him that instinct was a surer guide than logic in this. Detective Chief Inspector Peach was standing unsmiling beside the window display of properties for sale as David Edmonds emerged from the private car park at the rear of the building with his keys in his hand.

David tried aggression. 'This is an imposition, you know. It's really not convenient. I've a lot of work to get through before I go on holiday tomorrow. That's why I've come in early, to get a bit of privacy.'

'Bit of privacy's what we'll need for this, I reckon. Your wife said you were missing at home, that we'd likely find you here.'

David tried conciliation. 'Well, I suppose you've a job to do, like the rest of us. I hope you've been making good progress with your enquiries into the death of that poor girl.' He smiled at Lucy Blake, whom he had not at first noticed behind Peach.

'Very steady progress, since you ask.' Peach's dark eyes had not left the estate agent's face since he had appeared on the scene.

David accepted the inevitable. 'You'd better come inside. Hopefully we can get this out of the way before any of my staff come into the office.'

'Hopefully we can, yes. It shouldn't take too long, if you behave sensibly.'

David Edmonds didn't like the sound of that. He turned the key in the lock, noting with relief that his hand was very steady, and threw open the door. He went and switched off the alarm, cutting off its insistent bleeping without haste. He was suddenly aware that he must take his time, that he must marshal his thoughts carefully if he was to outwit this calm, watchful opponent.

Peach for his part was aware that the evidence as yet was thin upon the ground. The more he could get from the man here, the better the case they would be able to mount. He watched the tall, rather handsome man of thirty-seven as he put his car coat inside the cupboard in his office and waved his hand towards the armchairs beside his desk. A nice office, this, with a good carpet and prints of Chester and York on the walls. Not as dramatic a view as from Tommy Bloody Tucker's penthouse office in the new Brunton police headquarters, of course. But then probably a lot more work went on in here, a lot more useful business was transacted.

Detective Sergeant Lucy Blake sat in the armchair beside him and studied their man just as intently as Peach. It was a shame, this outcome, in many ways. David Edmonds was probably a good father and an excellent family man. His wife would be terribly shocked, his parents-in-law even more so. His three children would have to carry this with them through the rest of their lives.

Edmonds decided it was much too early in the day to get the whisky bottle out. That was a pity, because he could have done with a generous double to see him through this. He kept telling himself to keep his professional smile on his face and brazen it out. Whatever they had come here for, they could surely not pin that old, forgotten murder upon him. It had been a shock when the wretched girl's body had turned up like that, but he had grown accustomed to it now. If he kept his nerve, it would be over soon and he could look forward to the rest of his life. By tomorrow night, he would be in Madeira, gazing out over the Mediterranean, and this would be no more than a bad dream.

He became aware that Peach was watching him, studying him with as little embarrassment as if he had been a slide under a microscope. He wondered if he could let the silence stretch, challenge this man who seemed so at home with it. But before he was even aware that he was speaking he heard his voice say, 'Come to give me an update on the case, have you?'

'In a manner of speaking, yes.' Peach gave him a small, mirthless smile.

'Got that Swift bloke under lock and key yet?'

'As a matter of fact, Wally Swift was arrested in Manchester on Tuesday night. I understand he is still in custody. In view of the serious nature of the charges against him, he has been refused bail.'

David tried not to show his relief too obviously. 'I'm glad about that. The rest of us will be able to breathe a little more easily now. Swift was a bad lot in 1991 and he hasn't improved since, from what I've heard on the grapevine.' He glanced from the watchful and impassive Peach to the more agreeable female face beside him and decided to address his remarks to DS Blake. 'If it doesn't sound too sycophantic, I'd like to congratulate you on the efficiency of your investigation of this crime. The police get a lot of—'

'Wally Swift will go down for a long stretch, for serious offences in connection with the trafficking of illegal drugs. But not for life. He hasn't been charged with murder.' Peach's voice cut through the thin skin of Edmonds' strained affability like a barbed whip.

'No?' David felt suddenly that he knew what was coming. He strove desperately to keep up his front. 'Well, you know your business best, of course, but I must admit that I'd rather assumed that he'd killed that Asian girl.'

'Sunita Akhtar!' Peach rasped the name like an accusation, suddenly outraged by the way this man had dismissed his victim into anonymity. 'She had a name, Mr Edmonds. That girl you throttled without mercy. That girl you killed and then calmly stowed away like so much baggage behind a chimney breast. Sunita Akhtar!' He found himself quivering with fury on behalf of this girl he had never known, who had died so many years ago, in a house he had never visited.

David felt his pulses racing as he saw this rare flash of temper from Peach. He told himself that he had always expected this, that they could prove nothing if he kept his nerve and played out this game of bluff and counter-bluff. He was pleased to hear how steady his voice sounded as he said, 'That is a wild accusation, made without reason. You have not a shred of proof. You may regret saying these things in due course, particularly as I have a witness to your rashness.' He shone his full professional smile into the face of Lucy Blake for a moment, then turned his attention back to his adversary. 'There are laws about such things as slander, and they apply even to detective chief inspectors.'

'Forensic science has moved forward in the years since you murdered Sunita Akhtar. Material has been gathered from the corpse, even after all this time. Hairs which did not come from Sunita's head, Mr Edmonds. Fibres which did not come from the clothing which Sunita was wearing.' Peach found that he relished his repetition of the girl's name, sounding it as if it were a challenge from the grave, a cry for justice from this pathetic, forgotten victim.

'That sounds rather feeble, if I may say so.' David found he was very cool, in what he now recognized as a crisis. Keep up the front, keep dishing out scorn, and this implacable, gimlet-eyed man would be reduced to the bald-headed clown which was his real status in life.

'Once we have charged you with murder and are holding you in custody, we shall be able to take DNA samples from you. I have no doubt that we shall find a match or matches with material gathered from Sunita's corpse and from the site where it was discovered.'

David felt the first prick of fear through the adrenalin which had been insulating him against it. He wished Peach wouldn't keep mentioning murder, as if it were a recurring chorus in his attack. He could not keep the same degree of confidence in his voice as he said, 'I've already admitted to you in our previous meetings that I saw the girl, that she said she had been working for me. In other words, I've admitted to an association with her. The discovery of material like that upon her would imply nothing more than the connections which I have already declared.'

'A lawyer would argue with that view, I'm sure. And I'm sure you'll have the very best lawyers, when the time comes. We'll wait and see whether the forensic material from the corpse is conclusive. It will certainly add to the sum of the case against you.'

Peach sounded as dry and dispassionate now as a lawyer in chambers. His calmness was disconcerting. Edmonds said, 'I can assure you that it will reveal nothing.'

Peach studied him for a moment, noting the strain evident in the face, which belied the calmness the man still maintained in his voice. 'Are you volunteering to give us DNA samples now, then?'

'I have been as cooperative as I intend to be. I'm getting rather tired of this. My staff will be here soon and—'

'Then we'll get on with it. If you had no connection with this murder, how did you know how Sunita Akhtar was killed, Mr Edmonds?'

'I don't know what you're talking about. If you're trying to trump up some kind of case against me, you'd better—'

'Read it to him, DS Blake.' Peach was suddenly weary of his evasions.

Lucy Blake looked down at the page of her notebook she

had held open for several minutes and read the words she knew now by heart, 'Mr Edmonds said when interviewed on Sunday last: "I could no more strangle a helpless girl than fly to the moon".'

Peach studied his reaction for a moment before he said, 'How did you know how Sunita died, Mr Edmonds?'

David felt the blood draining from his face. He strove to keep the conviction in his tone as he said, 'I'd picked that up from the papers. The papers or the television. Or possibly the radio.' He could hear the desperation seeping into his voice as he ranged around the possibilities.

Peach shook his head with a grim smile. 'The method of Sunita's killing was not revealed in any of the early media bulletins. It was not even revealed that she was a young woman of Asian blood. We simply said that a female corpse had been found, that a woman had died in suspicious circumstances. In answer to questions, we said that a murder investigation was being mounted. The details of that murder had not been announced when I spoke to you on Sunday. They were revealed that evening, for publication in Monday's papers.'

'I must have assumed it then. I—'

'We shall be happy to let the lawyers investigate that one, if it's the only defence you can find. I think that they will find your assumption quite significant. It was the first of your mistakes.'

'And what do you think was . . .' David stopped, aghast at how he had been led on by Peach's assertion.

Peach's smile broadened a fraction, without losing any of its grimness. 'Why did you feel it was necessary to threaten Matthew Hayward, Mr Edmonds?'

'I really don't know what you're trying to—'

'We've talked to Dermot Stone. He's as good as admitted to threatening Matthew Hayward in a public house at Rufford on Monday, on your orders. I've no doubt that Mr Hayward will pick him out in an identity parade, if we decide it's necessary.'

'I don't know who this man is. You're barking up the wrong tree if you think that it was I who—'

'He's already said it was you who sent him after Mr Hayward. The mention of murder soon opens mouths, even in these violent times, I'm happy to say. You really shouldn't have employed the same muscle you've used from time to time in your business dealings. Too easy to trace back to you, you see.'

He was talking as if it was all over. And David was slowly realizing that it was. He tried to summon up more resistance, but found he was suddenly weary. He said, 'I thought you'd think it was Swift who'd threatened Hayward. It's more his style.'

'Maybe. But he'd have done it more effectively, more anonymously than you, I fancy.' Peach let his contempt shade the phrases. 'You might like to know that Matthew Hayward knew nothing which could incriminate you.'

Edmonds stared at him dully for a moment. 'I thought she'd have talked to him, told him that I'd threatened her. He was her boyfriend, wasn't he?'

'Not at the time of your association with Sunita, he wasn't. That was over.' Peach wasn't going to tell him that it was a Roman Catholic nun he should have been threatening. He was pretty certain that it would have been difficult to intimidate the sturdy Sister Josephine in her hospice.

'I thought he'd seen me coming out of that house in Sebastopol Terrace. He was just leaving the squat next door when . . .' Edmonds stopped, staring hopelessly from one to the other of the two attentive faces opposite him.

'When you'd killed Sunita Akhtar,' Peach quietly finished the sentence for him.

'I didn't mean to kill her.'

'But you did.'

'She'd agreed to work for me. Had started working, in fact. Then she was frightened off by Wally Swift. And she told him all about my plans, about the ring of dealers I was planning to set up. She shouldn't have done that.' His face set in a hard, obstinate frown. They saw him in that instant not as the prosperous property dealer he had become but as the

229

young and ruthless criminal he had been at the time of this death.

'So you killed her.'

'I told you, I didn't mean to kill her. I wanted to frighten her, make her see what she'd done to me. I had her by the throat, shutting her up, making her listen instead of shouting at me. She had a very thin neck.' He said it almost accusingly, as if it were her fault and not his that she had died.

'But you killed her.' Peach was implacable in the pursuit of his man.

'I found suddenly that she was limp, that I couldn't bring her round.'

Peach nodded. It was enough. The lawyers could argue it out, in due course. He'd no doubt that a clever defence counsel would go for a manslaughter verdict to avoid the life sentence, then plead that this family man had committed a youthful aberration which would never be repeated. You couldn't do anything about lawyers, but that was probably just as well.

'So you carefully hid the corpse behind the chimney breast and went on your way.' He'd get that into the statement in due course; it would show that this man had taken cool and careful steps to conceal his crime.

'I thought after all these years that it was done with. That she'd never be discovered.' Like one or two other murderers whom Peach had arrested, Edmonds sounded as if he thought that life was unfair.

He still had not used the name of his victim. Peach stood up and said, 'David Edmonds, I am arresting you for the murder of Sunita Akhtar. You do not have to say anything now, but if you conceal anything which you later wish to use in court, it may prejudice your defence.'

They handcuffed him to the uniformed constable to take him to the station. He gazed dully from the window of the police car, like one expecting to awaken from a nightmare. Their route took them past the new office development to the north of the town centre. Past the spot where, thirteen years earlier, Sunita Akhtar had died. Past the spot where, ten days earlier, that gaunt arm had been revealed so dramatically, reaching towards the heavens, as though beseeching justice.

The girl had her justice at last.